DROWNPROOFING

Karen Lea Armstrong

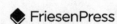 FriesenPress

One Printers Way
Altona, MB R0G 0B0
Canada www.friesenpress.com

Copyright © 2023 by Karen Lea Armstrong
First Edition — 2023

Author photo: Katelyn Malo (katelynmalo.com)

Cover art: Violeta at Prints Finds (www.etsy.com/ca/shop/PrintsFinds)

ISBN
978-1-03-918352-0 (Hardcover)
978-1-03-918351-3 (Paperback)
978-1-03-918353-7 (eBook)

1. FICTION, LITERARY

Distributed to the trade by The Ingram Book Company

To Northern Ontario health care workers:
such difficult work,
so few people understand.

Consider this (likely you haven't): What is your favourite part of a birth?

If you ask her (also unlikely), Bets will tell you hers.

How many births has Bets attended in her career, five hundred? Two thousand? Sometimes, she wished she had kept track. Like most people starting out, the idea of doing the same job for years, for decades, seemed impossible and perhaps undesirable. She never wrote down names, she never put tick marks in a book the way one colleague showed her; hundreds and hundreds of tick marks in little hand-drawn square boxes over the years, filling a notebook that no one else would ever understand.

Most of her nursing colleagues, if you asked them, had a favourite moment. The baby's first cry: a signal of success, confirmation of a new beginning. Placing the baby, wet, and writhing and still attached by the cord, on the new mother's chest: life to life, warmth to warmth.

For Bets, it was a single moment—perhaps a single second—when the baby's head truly began to emerge from the birth canal. Often, the crown of the head rocked in and out for a long time, especially in first-time deliveries: back and forth, excitement rising initially, then waning as time passed without change. Always, there was a moment when more and more and more of the head came through, when it reached the temples, the point of no return, and you knew it was happening, after minutes or hours of pushing, after hours or days of labour, you knew for sure, as surely as if the infant could say, *I'm coming, get ready.*

I'm coming.

CHAPTER ONE

I could be a hermit, thought Bets.

She sat looking out into the yard, watching the birds at the feeder competing for seeds, diving to retrieve them from the snow. The kitchen was tidy, the house was tidy, she was showered and dressed, the afternoon sat in front of her like a puppy cocking its head, *now what do we do*?

To become a hermit, were there criteria? Could she qualify as a hermit if there was occasional telephone contact? Could she work with the public and still be considered a hermit? Was an isolated cave or cabin required? Matted hair? Fingerless gloves?

She wasn't ready to withdraw from life completely, far from it; she loved her home, the view out the back window where birches and cedars extended towards the creek, her walks in the nearby coniferous woods. To be honest, she was happy to return to work, despite everyone telling her it was too soon. Too soon for what? What else did she have to do? Clean out Raz's closet? Sit and think about the strange empty vortex he had left swirling just behind her, threatening to pull her into a place of unimaginable darkness, from which she might never escape?

She put these thoughts into a box and closed the lid. She put the box away deep in the closet, in the basement, in the sub-basement of her mind. Just for now. Just while she processed. If that was even, was ever, possible.

Bets' coffee had gone cold. She had already reheated it several times, it would taste terrible, why was she still carrying it around? She continued to eat—why were people so obsessed with bringing food during grief— but she tasted little. She had no plan to wither away, but she didn't find food appealing, either. Shannon dropped off some bottles of liquid meal replacement, the kind they gave elderly people in the hospital, and she had a few of those, because they were easy and sweet. Maybe the reason elderly people needed supplements was exactly the same as hers: they just didn't care whether or not they ate. Why force them? Was it better to exist on strawberry-flavoured chemicals—did that actually fall into the category of nutrition?

Bets squinted at the future, yet again, and tried to make a plan. Work? Yes. Move towns? Where would she go? Start over, somewhere that she knew no one? Didn't see a familiar face around every corner, didn't know the doctors, the other nurses, had never met any of the pregnant women coming in, became a blank slate to be filled any way she liked? There was an appeal to anonymity, but also an intense inertia at the thought of the planning involved in making such changes. She might lose her seniority, her pension. Did that even matter? She wasn't planning to retire anytime soon, even though she qualified, even though people started asking, it seemed, the minute the first gray hair emerged. During high school people asked, what will you be? Not *who,* but *what,* as if your future had to be decided right then, that minute, at the age of seventeen, as if people wouldn't change their minds a hundred times. Then, about five years into a career, after all that buildup, after all that training, after finally achieving that thing you sought, the conversation switched into getting time off, retiring, living the life you *really* wanted.

We're doing everything backwards, Bets thought. If you were supposed to "follow your dreams" into a perfect career, shouldn't you love being there and want to do it forever? Ideally, you'd begin where she was, at thirty or forty years of experience. You'd say, here are the really awful things about this line of work. Here are the things that will thrill you. Consider what you can handle. Try a variety of options. But she remembered her seventeen-year-old self, just wanting to get started, wanting everyone to stop talking and let her do things. She wouldn't have listened.

What about being useful? What about work for the sake of *occupation?* As Bets' grandfather had aged, as his memory dimmed and he became wispy and bent, people opened doors for him, refused to let him help in the kitchen, told him to relax and enjoy himself. He didn't look like he was enjoying himself, sitting alone on the couch, with his glass of ginger ale, in his shirt and tie, always a shirt and tie. They thought they were helping him, protecting him; they took his travel bag the moment he arrived. But Bets also remembered him standing in the entryway, rail-thin, empty-handed, grumbling, "Why am I still here, if I can't even carry a goddamn suitcase?"

The doorbell was so unexpected it made Bets jump. Regular visitors, like Shannon, just knocked and came in. The doorbell now signified strangers, flower delivery, people who meant well but weren't really welcome. Sometimes, they were members of religious groups, and Bets felt slightly sorry for them when she said, *not today*. Not sorry enough to let them start speaking, but sorry enough that closing the door in their hopeful faces caused a twinge of guilt.

Bets set her mug on the hall table and observed the silhouette outside the front door, partially visible through the opaque glass. Maybe it was a good idea, today, to see how she could be saved.

She opened the door and found a teenage girl standing on the porch. She was wearing a bright red toque and large glasses, smiling at Bets through a mouthful of braces.

—Oh, you're home!

She clutched a spiral notebook to her chest, much as you might clasp a beloved pet. As she spoke, the cold air made a puff of vapour that swirled around the voluminous hair protruding under her toque.

—Do I know you?

—Um, no, said the girl, flushing slightly, but you're Bets, right? Bets Malcolm?

—Okay, and you are...

—Oh! Sorry! My name is Hannah.

—Of course it is. Bets gave a small laugh. How many Hannahs had she delivered over the years?

—Are you selling something, Hannah?

Hannah gave a little cough and straightened her shoulders under her parka.

—I left you a message last week? I've decided, I think I've decided, I want to be a nurse. My um, my guidance counsellor said you might be a good person to talk to? We have a project. For Careers class.

Hannah tapped her glasses up the bridge of her nose.

Bets thought about her phone, which she had stopped answering a few weeks back, stopped checking voicemail, unable to face the relentless slow trickle of condolences.

—How does your guidance counsellor know me?

—Oh! She said you delivered her baby because the doctor didn't make it in time! It sounded so exciting! She said you were a wonderful nurse and could tell me everything I needed to know.

Bets looked at Hannah for a moment: the toque, the glasses, the braces, the parka, the overwhelming hair, the earnest face. She held the door wider.

—I guess it depends what you need to know. Why don't you come in? They stood in the entryway, Hannah barely reaching Bets' shoulder.

—Here, give me your coat. How old are you, Hannah?

Hannah's glasses had completely fogged up when she entered the house, and she set down the notebook and began polishing the glasses on her shirt.

—Oh, I'm seventeen. I know I look younger.

Bets would have said thirteen, but with adolescents it was so difficult to tell. Hannah replaced the glasses, straightened her oversized shirt, tugged her leggings. Bets hung the coat on a peg and found herself smoothing her short gray hair, tucking her shirt into her too-loose jeans, doing a quick scan of her socks for holes.

—Age, said Bets, shrugging, it's just a number. Come into the kitchen. Do you drink coffee?

Hannah used one foot to pry her other boot off.

—No, thanks. Actually, okay.

Bets started the coffee, and they sat at the table. Hannah's long dark hair was wavy at the bottom but crushed flat by her hat on top. She fluffed it and tapped her glasses upwards again.

—So, um, is it okay if I make a few notes?

—All right, though I feel like I'm being interviewed for the paper.

Bets sat across from Hannah, who busied herself with the notebook, extracting a pen from the spiral binding.

—How much time are we giving to this project?

—Oh! I didn't even ask. Do you have time now?

Hannah stood, gathered her notebook, her hat, knocked her pen onto the floor.

—I could come back another time.

—Sit, sit, said Bets, amused at the chaos. We're having coffee, remember? We'll answer some questions and see where we are. I don't work until seven.

—Okay, thank you!

Bets organized two mugs of coffee, placed the milk carton and sugar bowl in front of Hannah, watched the girl struggle as Bets sipped her black coffee.

—If you haven't had coffee before, I'd suggest milk and sugar, prompted Bets. It's not an easy flavour.

Hannah added a spoonful of sugar and some milk to her coffee, stirred, tasted, made a face, added more sugar. Bets laughed.

—Don't drink it if you don't like it. It's a terrible habit, really. Let's get down to business.

Hannah pushed the mug aside and opened her notebook, where she had some questions written. She bent to retrieve her pen from under the table.

—What made you want to become a nurse? She asked, pen poised.

—Oh. I thought this was more about *being* a nurse.

—It is, agreed Hannah, but I want to know everything. I want to know how you started. I want to know everything.

Bets sat back in her chair, holding her mug with both hands. What made her want to become a nurse? It was like going through a series of old files, trying to decide which one was the first.

—I suppose, she said, it started with the grocery store.

Hannah, pen immobile on her page, looked confused.

—The grocery store?

***

Bets often accompanied her mother on grocery trips when she was young, and was good at finding things on sale, selecting ripe melons and smooth yellow bananas without spots, and she was in charge of the plastic clicker—one button for the dollars, one button for the cents—that kept track of their purchases to make sure they had enough cash for the bill. Her mother didn't like holding up the line to write a cheque.

Why were they even in the junk food aisle that day, that day when Bets was about eleven? Pop, chips, and candy were never on their list, yet there they were, and Bets remembers eyeing a large bottle of bright red cream soda, imagining other prettier, friendlier girls who likely sat drinking it for an afternoon snack, likely in a group, maybe listening to records in their rooms. She could picture these cream-soda girls, with their smooth shiny hair, their stylish clothes, their uninhibited laughter.

At that moment, in the middle of Bets' daydream, one of the large glass cola bottles further down the aisle suddenly exploded, with a sound like a child's pop gun. A man walking past shouted, and clutched his neck, as another swore and pulled a piece of glass from his arm. The man with the neck wound sank to the ground, blood dripping through his fingers, and a woman pointed and screamed. A middle-aged woman ran to the man, pulling off her T-shirt and placing it firmly over the bleeding wound.

—Get help, somebody get help! She looked around her, a crowd forming. She pointed to Bets' mother.

—You, she said, get someone to call an ambulance. It's urgent. Jugular vein. You, she pointed to Bets. Find some diapers for this wound, I need more pressure.

She cradled the man's large head in her lap, talking to him, pressing her T-shirt, now soaked with blood, into his neck. Many customers stood around looking stunned. Bets' mother hurried off as instructed, leaving Bets alone, clammy with indecision, wanting to follow her mother, but not wanting to fail at the job she had been given. Finally, she raced away, up and down the aisles looking for diapers. She grabbed the first pack she saw and ran back to the junk food aisle, where the woman, still only in her bra, was now draped in someone's coat, and the man, barely conscious, made incoherent noises as a pool of blood formed on the floor. People were hollering instructions, arguing, and the woman gestured for them to stop.

—I'm a nurse, she said. Please let me do my job.

While Bets was getting the diapers, a customer had fainted, and a short, sweating manager with a comb-over appeared in the aisle, barking orders at staff, who ran for mops and brooms to clean up the soda, the glass, and the blood. Under the nurse's direction, Bets ripped open the package of diapers, took out two, and the woman folded them over the wound. She gestured toward the open package.

—You're doing a great job, honey; here, put these under that poor man's head, the one that fainted. She looked back down at her patient.

—Stay awake! Ambulance is coming!

Bets looked at the expanding puddle of blood on the floor and thought, *this man is dying. He has to be.*

They all heard the sirens as Bets unfolded diapers and placed them under the head of the fainting man, who was now stirring. He touched the back of his head, where a lump the size of an apple was forming. A store worker rushed into the scene with a mop, saw the blood and vomited in the aisle, causing the manager to wince and smooth his sparse hair. Customers began to disperse as the sound of radio transmitters and heavy boots preceded the paramedics with their stretcher.

Once the patients were dispatched to hospital, the manager asked the nurse and Bets and her mother, as well as the man with the bleeding arm, to stay behind.

—I'll need to file an incident report and a complaint to the soda company, he said. His shirt was soaked with sweat. He turned to the nurse.

—You just saved that guy's life. He would have died in my store.

—I'm a nurse, she said. It was lucky timing. She looked over at Bets and her mother.

—And I had help from these fine women. She gestured toward them, having washed her hands and retrieved her own coat from her cart.

They went into the manager's dingy beige office, filled with stacked milk crates and old cardboard displays, and provided written statements, and he wrote out gift certificates for all of them. The nurse turned to Bets' mother.

—I'm Linda, she said, and you are...?

—Eve, said Bets' mother, and waved vaguely in Bets' direction. This is Betsy.

—Well Betsy, you did a great job keeping your head today, said Linda. Maybe we have a future nurse on our hands!

After handshakes all around, she touched Bets' face before leaving. Bets followed her mother out of the manager's office.

—Well, said her mother. Wasn't that something!

That was all her mother ever said about it, and Bets sometimes wondered if her mother forgot about the event. But how could she? Bets could clearly remember, even now—fifty years later—the explosion, the blood, the screaming; the fainting, the vomit, the sweat; her eleven-year-old self running panicked in the aisles, Linda in her black lacy bra—so different from Bets' mother's underwear—shouting "Get help!" and "I'm a nurse!" and the weight of Linda's hand on her cheek.

***

—Wow, said Hannah. Nothing exciting like that ever happens to me.

The light had changed, and the sun was lower. Bets got up to adjust the blind. Hannah closed her notebook, in which she had written only two words: Grocery store.

—I guess you need to get ready for work?

—I probably should.

—Can I come back and talk to you some more? I have a lot more questions.

—I'd like that, Hannah. I haven't thought about that story in a long time. Hannah smiled her metallic smile.

—How about next week? Thursday again? I'm off school at three! I could come right after!

Bets felt a small caffeine-jolt of energy, absorbing Hannah's enthusiasm.

—Okay. I'll see you then.

Hannah put on her outdoor clothing and extended her hand, shaking it vigorously when Bets clasped it.

—Thank you, Bets! May I call you Bets? Thank you so much!

Hannah left in a flurry of activity, catching the cuff of her coat on the door handle, smiling in apology, pulling the door closed behind her. Once she was gone, it was like the house had exhaled and all the air had been discharged along with Hannah. Bets sat on the stairs, chin in her hands.

—Well, Bets, she said out loud—her habit when she was alone—what has started here?

CHAPTER TWO

Walking to work, bundled against the cold, the evening was so still Bets' exhaled breath hovered and her boots crunched on the snow-covered sidewalk. Why *had* she become a nurse? The grocery store incident had definitely planted the seed, but had she really been so easily influenced by a complete stranger? There must have been more to it than that. Bets tried to imagine her teenage self, but it was like trying to view a film made with the camera going in and out of focus, and some pieces of the film missing completely.

What was so influential about that grocery store experience? Bets watched the tail end of a pickup truck slide sideways as it tried to gain traction on the icy road. Clearly, the influence had been Linda. Linda taking charge when everyone else just stood there. Or vomited. Or fainted. Linda doing what needed to be done to save the man's life. Linda shouting, telling people what had to happen. Linda knowing what to do. Bets stopped for a moment, breathing the frigid air, silence settling around her.

She had seen that deer-in-the-headlights look, like so many of the store patrons, on the faces of her parents, and her patients, many times. Bets herself spent much of her adolescence wondering, questioning, doubting. Of course, there was appeal to a job that meant knowing how to handle an emergency. Of course, she would like to know exactly what to do, rather than waiting for someone to tell her.

It wasn't the greatest reason, wanting to know what to do, Bets acknowledged, walking again. You were supposed to say you wanted to save lives, or heal people, or provide comfort.

On the other hand, it really helped to know what to do in all of those circumstances. Maybe it was a matter of semantics, rather than motivation.

Why not be a doctor then? Why a nurse? Colleagues, friends, patients had asked her over the years, especially once she began to take leadership roles. She had never yearned to be a doctor. Not early in her career, when they were all expected to scurry around doing the bidding of the doctors, who were usually men, and who usually talked about their lives and decisions with supreme confidence, even when they were clearly wrong. Not later in her career, when she valued the time she spent with her patients, and the care she could provide during their labour, while the doctors rushed in at the end. What was the pleasure in that?

But shift work, friends said, you must stop doing shift work. Previously, her answer had been simply, I don't mind shift work. People spent their careers complaining, but her partner was a miner; all the miners did shifts. She and Raz wove in and out of each other's weeks: time together, time apart, someone sleeping all day, someone sleeping all night. It just worked. It wasn't perfect, but it worked. Sometimes they had midweek days off together between shift changes; lingering over breakfast on a Wednesday felt like luxury.

They were always tired, it was true. The duration, the quality of sleep—they never seemed to catch up, doing the shifts. Sometimes, Bets wanted to lower herself into the waist-high snowbank during the walk to work, carving out a space for her body, staying there for the day, caressed by snowflakes. Sometimes, she and Raz had joked that their shifts would kill them. Not the best joke, perhaps.

Bets shook her head. She looked up at the hospital, now visible a few hundred metres ahead, the large blue sign with its white H lit up against the night sky. She watched an emergency vehicle, lights whirling, roar into the ambulance bay, watched a silhouette of a person limp slowly from their car toward the emergency entrance, watched the flashes of blue and pink and green scrubs pass the back-lit windows on the three floors. Her heart rate surged.

Why am I doing this?

Over the years, there were so many reasons that had kept her coming back and back and back for every shift. Right now, if Bets was honest, she was returning to work because of her house, large and empty without Raz. The impossible creaking quiet of it enveloped her when she walked through the door, grabbed her in its fist. She turned on the TV or the radio, but then grew irritated with the terrible music or endless ads. She felt a constant pull toward Raz's study, where she could stand for hours, motionless, trying to feel a breeze of him, a particle of scent, a molecule. Trying to feel and not feel at the same time. If only that were possible.

Reaching the hospital doors, Bets felt a wave of doubt, followed by one of exhaustion. No one would challenge her if she just turned and went back home, and yet, this return was her own choice. She wanted to work. Despite the impossibility, she wanted her life to return to the way it was before.

The other nurses greeted her with smiles, but also with caution, as if she might be contagious, or explosive. Bets opened her mouth to say *I was wrong, I can't do this,* closed it again, got changed.

She'd deliberately chosen this shift, knowing that Shannon would be there, and going to the desk to review the shift assignments with Shannon felt so familiar, she felt a small pulse of hope.

—Welcome back, said Shannon, smiling her uneven smile, the harsh overhead lights illuminating the grey streak that meandered down her river of black hair. She flipped her ponytail over her shoulder. Are you sure about this?

—No. Yes. I have to. Shannon squeezed Bets' arm.

—We had you on outpatients this evening, but there was a sick call so we're short on labour and delivery. I thought it might be good to be busy?

—In for a penny, in for a pound, said Bets, not letting herself think about it. Who's on call?

Dr. McIlroy was on call. He was renowned for going to his cottage, even in winter, a good thirty minutes away if he hit all the lights, forcing the nurses to anticipate every event, infeasible at the best of times. Labour and delivery meant approximations, guesses, and sudden dramatic events. How many times had Bets seen a woman, after struggling for hours, suddenly cry out and deliver in one push? How many times had she checked the patient and found her faint, gushing blood, or passing fluid thick with meconium, signaling a distressed baby?

Dr. McIlroy always scoffed and said if they needed him, he'd be there. Well. Easy for him to say from his cozy cottage, far from the intense action going on while everyone waited. Bets felt that nothing would change until something bad happened.

Please. Not today.

Her first couple, Jamie and Jackie, were calm, pleasant, appreciative. Jamie was contracting regularly, and Jackie coached Jamie through her contractions incredibly well, which meant a lot less work for Bets. She was thankful for the oasis of their room, compensating for the first-baby anxiety of Angelica, who had apparently come in three times already during the previous shift. Convinced she was in labour, even though her body showed no signs of it other than cramps, she was tearful, certain something was wrong despite all evidence to the contrary, and her husband kept referring to articles he had read online.

Dr. McIlroy, likely tired of the multiple calls, had asked them to admit Angelica and he'd reassess things in a few hours. Bets answered a seemingly endless stream of questions but, as sometimes happened, Angelica calmed a bit once in the hospital bed, and having been up the previous night "contracting" and worrying, settled to sleep, her husband curling into the recliner beside her bed. Bets dimmed the lights, checked that their call bell was within easy reach, and left them alone.

Jamie was contracting well, but the baby wasn't descending into the birth canal, which was unusual. She'd declined an epidural, but still tolerated Bets' deep internal probing.

Hmmmm. Bets checked Jamie's bulging belly from the outside again, trying to find baby parts. Bum at the top, head at the bottom…or was it? Sometimes it was difficult to tell. She called Dr. McIlroy.

—Jamie's six cm dilated, doing well, hasn't ruptured her membranes, but the presenting part is really high, and I'm starting to wonder about the baby's position; maybe you should do an ultrasound to confirm baby is head down?

Dr. McIlroy sighed.

—If she's still high, we have some time. See what happens once the presenting part is down nicely. Maybe it's much ado about nothing. How's our anxious Angelica?

—Sleeping.

—Lovely, he said, sounds like you have things well in hand. Now it was Bets' turn to sigh. She hung up.

The call bell summoned. Jamie appeared panicked and Jackie rubbed her shoulders.

—Pretty sure her water just broke, said Jackie, turning to look at Jamie, who had two large tears rolling down her smooth brown cheeks.

—There's a lot, there's so MUCH, cried Jamie. Oh God, here comes another contraction.

The blue birthing ball had a stream of water down the side, and a substantial puddle forming on the floor. Bets busied herself getting supplies, and once the contraction had finished—Jamie moaning quite a bit more than previously—she encouraged them over to the bed and cleaned Jamie up, noting the clear fluid still leaking out.

—After this contraction, said Bets, we'll check and see what Adelaide is up to in there.

She was usually carefully neutral about baby genders, but Jamie and Jackie apparently had ultrasound proof.

Adelaide. One of a slew of ancient granny names that were coming back into fashion: Ruby, Mabel, Lillian, Dorothy. *Could do worse*, thought Bets, *but some names should just stay in the past.*

Putting on her gloves, Bets reached inside Jamie, feeling the presenting part now well down in the vagina, and frowned. That was awfully soft to be a head. And that, that could only mean one thing. Jamie's contraction started, and when Bets removed her hand, she could see the labia beginning to separate. The baby was coming now, and fast.

—Okay, said Bets, casually pressing the bell on the wall for assistance, I have a couple of things to tell you. Jackie, why don't you sit down there beside Jamie? Perfect. Everything is okay. Your baby is coming now, and pretty quickly, you might need to push soon. The only thing is, the baby is bum-first. Breech.

Jamie gave a little shriek, then groaned as a contraction started. Jackie squeezed her hand, rubbed her back, breathed with her, spoke soothingly. The moment the pain crested, she looked up at Bets.

—Isn't that dangerous? Don't you do a C-section for that?

13

—For a first baby, usually we do, said Bets, but we aren't going to have time here, and it's coming down well. I think there will be lots of room.

Breanna appeared in response to the bell.

—Call Dr. McIlroy, and tell him to get in here, we have a surprise breech delivering. Breanna's eyes widened, and she immediately turned down the hallway.

—And call in pediatrics! Bets shouted after her. Pediatrics!

—What's happening? Jamie wailed. Is the baby okay? Oh God, they won't stop! They won't stop!

She cried through her contraction as Bets rolled in the table with equipment for delivery. Bets' entire body was pulsating, and when she arranged the instruments on the delivery table, her hands shook slightly.

Okay, Okay. This will be fine.

Bets felt a pressure in her chest, felt as if her lungs had lost all pliability, but then she heard singing in the hallway. As one, Jamie and Jackie stopped their rhythmic breathing and looked at her.

—Not to worry, said Bets, as her lungs regained function. I'll be right back.

Breanna was already in the hallway, standing beside a tiny elderly woman whose spine was so curved she could barely look in front of herself. Her pure white hair hung in a wispy braid down her back. She shuffled along using a wheeled walker, and wore a hospital gown that dwarfed her, nearly dragging on the floor. Over the gown, she wore a hand-knitted orange and brown afghan, torn and fraying in several places, with one large hole through which she had pushed her head, so that the afghan hung around her like a cape. She had thick glasses, she was toothless, and she was singing.

—I'll take the high road, and you take the low road, and I'll get to Scotland afore ye…

—What is your name? Asked Breanna, reaching out to touch the old woman's arm just as Bets shouted, don't! The woman snatched her arm away and struck ineffectively at Breanna.

—Back off, bitch! Don't touch me! Breanna jumped back as if burned.

—It's Daphne. Her name is Daphne, said Bets. She doesn't like to be touched. Hello Daphne, nice to see you again.

Daphne peered at Bets, her eyes enormous, magnified by her glasses.

—I don't know you, she said, and recommenced singing.

—I'll watch her, said Bets. You call Geriatrics and tell them Daphne's over here. She heard a long, low bellow from Jamie's room.

—Daphne, you've got quite the timing, said Bets. Come over here with me.

She could see Breanna at the desk, speaking into the phone, as she walked back toward her labouring patient. Daphne followed, switching to God Save the Queen as she inched her walker forward with each shuffling step, so agonizingly slowly that Bets wondered how she managed to slip out of the locked Alzheimer unit on a regular basis.

—Not exactly a speed demon, are you? Their snail's pace finally landed them at the entrance to Jamie's room.

—Daphne, why don't you sit on your walker, and take a little break? Bets patted the seat of the walker.

—Help! Shouted Jamie from inside the room.

—Help! Shouted Daphne in response.

—Oh, God, said Bets, abandoning Daphne in the doorway and rushing to Jamie's side. Jamie finished her contraction with a small straining grunt.

—I need to push, she screeched. I need to push!

—Okay, said Bets, listen, Jamie. You can't push yet. The doctor is on his way, but he won't be here for a few minutes (*try twenty*). I need you to breathe hard and relax and NOT push, even though your body is telling you to. Can you try to do that? We'll get the nitrous oxide gas, that might help.

Both women now looked terrified, clinging to each other as if going down on a sinking lifeboat. Bets adjusted her face into a smile, her voice into soothing tones, dulling the edge that had developed.

—Jamie, you're doing so beautifully. This baby is coming in no time, we just need to delay briefly, okay? And Jackie, you're doing an incredible job coaching. Keep it up and before too long you'll have Adelaide.

Oh shit.

Bets suddenly realized there was more to discuss, but Jamie's contraction had started, and she shrieked,

—I need to push; I need to push!

Jackie said, Jamie, look at me, breathe with me, blow it out hard, and they stared at each other and panted together and Jamie closed her eyes and grunted while Jackie said,

–Stop pushing! Open! Look! Breathe! And they got through it.

Bets marvelled at them as she set up the nitrous oxide and handed Jamie the mask.

—Try this next time, it might help you get your mind off the pain a bit. Jackie, you're an absolute pro at this.

Breanna reappeared, giving Daphne a wide berth.

—They're sending someone over to get Daphne. Also, Angelica just rang. She wants an epidural.

—An epidural!

Bets looked from Breanna to Daphne to Jamie. She pulled Breanna aside.

—I cannot deal with Angelica right now. Go and check her and tell her for the millionth time she is not in active labour and doesn't need an epidural yet. Try to encourage her to walk around if she doesn't want to sleep anymore.

Bets and Jackie focused all their attention on not allowing Jamie to push, but Daphne rolled her walker into the room, and began imitating Jamie's cries.

—Daphne, said Bets, you can't be in here, I'm sorry. How about you wait in the hallway, and I'll give you some towels to fold?

She blocked Daphne's entry, and without touching her, encouraged her back toward the door, much like a border collie herding sheep. With relief, she saw one of the Geriatric nurses coming down the hall for the escapee.

Bets checked the clock on the wall. Seventeen minutes since they placed the call. Jamie's grunts at the end of her contractions were getting longer. Baby's heartbeat was still fine. The floor had been cleaned and the set up was prepared. The pediatrician on call sat nearby at the desk. Breanna came in to advise Bets that Angelica was four centimetres dilated. Bets threw her hands in the air.

—She finally goes into active labour and she chooses now, of all times!

—I called for her epidural. I'm supposed to be covering the walk-ins, so Shannon is covering that right now.

—Good idea. Thanks, Bree.

They heard a prolonged, high-pitched scream from down the hall, and exchanged a look before Breanna jogged off. Jackie and Jamie met Bets' eyes, terrified.

—Don't worry, she'll be fine, she'll be fine. She's a very nervous patient, said Bets.

Jamie started her breathing, but let out a long, guttural noise and was obviously pushing.

Bets lifted the sheet to check, and saw tiny buttocks emerging from Jamie's vagina. They had run out of time.

—Okay Jamie, here we go, the baby is coming. Jamie started crying.

— I can't, it hurts too much. I can't! I can't! Get it out! Jackie touched Jamie's face and turned it to her.

—Jamie, it's almost here. Listen to Bets. Listen to her.

—I can't!

—You have to.

Bets had never, in her long career, delivered a breech baby on her own. They were less frequent these days, and of course the doctor was usually the one delivering, but because of her age, she had seen several of them. Seeing was not the same thing as doing, but she knew the problem was the head. The head, coming last, could get stuck. The position was important. What did you do, to keep it in position? She couldn't remember. She'd have to remember. She knew, from the sign-out list, that the midwife wasn't in town, the family physicians that did deliveries were off, or too new to be helpful to her. There was another high-pitched scream from Angelica's room, and Bets closed the door.

Bets moved the parts of the bed so Jamie was in birthing position, the baby's buttocks clearly visible between her legs, and Jackie gasped.

—She's right there, Jamie! She's right there!

Another contraction came, and Jamie yelled and pushed. More of the baby came out, back upward, and Bets supported it with her hands as it came. Jackie watched in awe as Jamie did her work.

Two more contractions and the baby's lower body, supported by Bets, was half out of Jamie, who was now surprisingly calm, panting with Jackie, who continued breathing with her, forcing her to focus. Jamie had just started another contraction when they heard pounding footsteps and Dr. McIlroy burst through the door, the pediatrician right behind him.

—Right, I'm here, I'm here, said Dr. McIlroy, breathless, wiry hair askew, shedding his coat, tying on the plastic apron Bets had laid out on the equipment table.

—Lovely, lovely, things are going wonderfully well here, well done everyone!

He put on gloves, flexed his fingers, took Bets' spot at the end of the bed, grasped the baby. The pediatrician bustled around the warmer, double-checking equipment in case the baby needed resuscitation. Within five minutes, the baby was out, and crying lustily.

—A lovely bouncing boy! announced Dr. McIlroy, holding the baby in his large hands, tipping the infant toward Jamie and Jackie on its way to the warmer.

Bets winced.

—Oh yes, I forgot to mention…

But Jamie and Jackie weren't listening. They were clutching each other, and crying, and laughing, all at the same time.

—A boy! We have a boy? Adelaide's a boy!

Soon, the pediatrician had given the all-clear, and he gave the baby to Jamie. Dr. McIlroy finished a couple of stitches.

—Well! he exclaimed. That's that! Another success story! He turned to Bets.

—I told you I'd always be here!

Bets forced a tight smile. Breanna appeared in the doorway.

—Dr. McIlroy, Angelica just got her epidural and now has the urge to push. Dr. McIlroy beamed.

—Perfect timing! Things are smooth as butter here today, aren't they? He winked at Bets before shaking Jamie's and Jackie's hands.

—Dr. McIlroy, we can't thank you enough, said Jackie.

—Yes, said Jamie, we could never have done this without you!

Sure, thought Bets. *Never.*

Bets could hardly believe it when 7 am arrived. What a night! Jamie, Jackie, Angelica and her husband, delivered and well, paperwork done, Daphne safely back to geriatrics, and a couple of women in early labour organized before she left. By the end of the shift, the awkwardness had dissolved, the easy rhythm of the nurses was back, and it was as if Bets had never left, as if nothing had changed.

Walking home with the hood of her parka shielding her face, sunrise hinting on the horizon, Bets felt like days had passed since the walk to work. On the way there, lingering thoughts of her conversation with Hannah, questioning her choice of nursing, thinking of the people who had said she was returning to work too soon, should not return at all, should not return to shifts, had done her time, deserved a break, recovery, retirement. On the way home, thinking about her night, but also thinking in scrapbook pieces about so many other shifts before this one.

Bets had seen them all over the years: the fainters, the weepers, the yellers. The praying types, the academics, the bored and disinterested, the social-media-obsessed. The videographers, the overly solicitous (forever fluffing pillows and applying lip balm). She'd seen full-on screaming matches between bouts of pushing. She'd seen one man tell his wife to stop whining and the cup of ginger ale she subsequently threw at his head. She'd seen gagging and vomiting by both members of a couple, sometimes simultaneously. She'd seen hippie types with incense and candles and foot rubs. She'd seen warring mothers-in-law fighting over "their" baby.

She'd seen women screaming bloody murder at the first hint of a contraction, and women who gave a grunt and announced the baby was out. She'd had women beg her for pain medication, and others beg not to have any. She'd seen women—mainly teenagers—push out a baby and ask for a smoke and a Big Mac five minutes later.

She'd had women offer to name their baby after her, thank her, scream at her, ignore her.

She'd had partners swear at her, cry on her shoulder, buy her a coffee, call her a cunt.

Weirdly, Bets realized, it all contributed to the appeal. In addition to the knowing, the ability to assess and step in, there were so many other factors. Not just the good, obviously not just the bad. The variety. The every-single-day-is-different variety.

She would have to tell Hannah.

CHAPTER THREE

Bets slept better than she had in weeks, a deep, black sleep without dreams or position changes or hot flashes. She woke feeling she had slept for years; would not have been surprised to see the house covered in vines, the interior coated in dust and cobwebs. The clock showed she had slept for nine hours.

She got back into the routine of her shifts very quickly, amazed at the hospital's consistency, while the rest of her life had been turned upside down. It felt good to be busy, distracted, to be good at something, to feel needed. It felt good, also, to come home, and not have to pretend to be happy, or confident, or energetic. She found her appetite improved, that working a twelve-hour shift made her hungry. She found she looked forward to Hannah's return.

Hannah arrived right on time on Thursday. Her long hair was wound up on top of her head like a ball of wool, and she wore an enormous scarf that dominated her tiny form.

—I have questions about your name.

—My name?

—Yes. As in, is Bets your real name, and if not, what is your real name? Hannah widened her eyes at Bets and tapped her glasses up on her nose.

—This is for Careers class?

—Yes. Well, not this part, I'm just getting, you know. Context.

—I'm not sure how it will help with your future planning, but I can tell you why I go by Bets, she said.

—Okay! Perfect! Hannah leaned forward, clasping her elbows as they rested on the table.

***

Bets had fought her name for years.

Elizabeth, overall, was not bad, but no one was willing to call her that. Her entire childhood, she had been Betsy, chosen by her parents, of course, and around age nine she decided she didn't care for Betsy, and became more aware that it was not her actual name. She asked her parents to call her Elizabeth.

—Oh, it's too long. It's too formal for a little girl, said her mother, as if she herself had not chosen it.

Her parents swore it had nothing to do with the Queen. They were Canadian, after all, not British; they couldn't really remember how they came up with Elizabeth, just said they liked the name.

So, I'm named after the Queen for sure, Bets had thought. Why else would they have even thought of it? No one in the family had the name Elizabeth.

It was a time when Betty was waning and Libby was gaining; there were some Lizas and Beths; Bets did not really like any of the diminutives available, so she struggled along for a while, until she was saved by her Uncle Bob.

Her mother's brother was large and loud, with a bushy beard and a hearty bellow that initially frightened Bets. He loved plays on words, in particular saying "Bob's your uncle," whooping and slapping his knee, "Get it? Get it? Bob's your uncle!" as if no one would possibly have figured it out otherwise. It made Bets smile every time, even as she watched others roll their eyes, or her mother's mouth get tight.

They played a game, the one time in Bets' young life she remembered doing so as a family. It was horseshoes. Not real horseshoes, of course, (I'm not *that* old, Bets told Hannah), but a pre-made game made of plastic, meant for playing in a yard or at the beach. The plastic horseshoes were not very heavy, making the tosses unpredictable and wind dependent. They were in teams: Uncle Bob and Aunt Mindy on Bets' team, and her mother and father and Roxie on the other team.

For some reason, Bets excelled at the game. The men continually cursed as their tosses caught in the wind, going too far or landing short, never hitting the stake, while Bets managed to hit the stake nearly every time, sometimes even curling the horseshoe around the stake so it spun, making Bob whoop and high-five all around.

—Yes! Another score for us! All bets are off with this one! Then, getting no response,

—Get it? Get it? All BETS are off! He'd yell, slapping his knee or pulling her into a hug and dancing her around. Uncle Bob called her Bets all day. He wanted her on his team for every subsequent game, counting on her reputation at horseshoes, which in no way represented her skill at games in general.

—I need our Bets on my team! All bets are off!

As with his other jokes, it soon got old and tired, although everyone called her Bets all day. Liking the name better than any other version available, she subsequently referred to herself as Bets, and that was that. Her name tag at work said Bets, her signature said Bets, and if someone wasn't sure about her name, at first introduction, she followed up with "Bets… as in, all bets are off."

She thought of Uncle Bob every time she gave the explanation, even after he separated from his wife, even after he moved away and they rarely saw him, even after he seemed tired and old and not much fun. She never thanked him for giving her a name she liked, so she tried to compensate, if anyone ever asked, by saying she was *not* named after the Queen, and that, in fact, her Uncle Bob had named her.

It was close enough to the truth, anyway.

***

—I wish I had a fun uncle, said Hannah. And who's Roxie?

—Roxie's my sister.

—Oh! You have a sister! I've always wanted a sister!

—Yes, a lot of people say that. Hannah's smile wilted.

—You don't like your sister?

Bets reached for a tea towel to wipe the small puddle of sparkling water that had appeared when Hannah knocked her glass.

—Hannah, that's a really long story. Let's maybe talk about nursing for a bit, since that's the goal. Why do you want to be a nurse?

Hannah tapped her pen.

—It sounds, I don't know. Exciting. Delivering babies, knowing things, explaining things. Managing emergencies. Helping people.

I want to help people. It was the reply of so many trainees Bets had guided, the refrain that led them into health care, in early innocence, before the messy reality of helping set in, before the waters became sticky and opaque.

—Well, Bets said, there are lots of days that aren't exciting. I'm usually more labour support, remember; I'm not really supposed to be the one delivering the baby! And there are lots of other types of nurses, don't forget that.

—Sure, sure. Okay.

Hannah ran her finger down the lines in her notebook, tapped on one.

—What was it like when you first started? What was your first assignment?

—Oh boy. Bets laughed a little. My first shift during training was a bit more eventful than most, so I feel like it's misleading.

—Tell me!

—I just want you to know it's not always like that. Not at all.

—I'll remember.

Bets paused before beginning, wondering, *is this the right way to share*? She remembered, back in class, her instructor saying, you will see things that are difficult. You will deal with things other people do not need to deal with. You will need to figure out how to cope with that, each one of you. She remembered looking at her fellow nursing students, all raising their eyebrows, thinking, what's up with her? This is so *heavy*.

She looked at Hannah again, eyes bright, expression eager.

—My first rotation was on a general medical floor.

—What does that mean?

—The patients who are in for non-surgical reasons. Heart attacks, strokes, pneumonia, dementia, cancer… that sort of thing.

***

There were many difficult scenarios when working at a hospital, but most were never discussed during the clinical preparation sessions in Bets' nursing course, which had focused a lot, at that time, on blood pressure measurement and cleaning bedpans and starting IV lines and tucking sheets with hospital corners.

There had been a lot less emphasis on things like safe positioning when moving patients, medication administration (the number of meds being much, much fewer), and hospital-acquired infection, and a lot more on clean white shoes, clean patients, and bowel movements. Bets, not generally prone to nostalgia, still shook her head, thinking about the former uniforms. White, of all things. White! In a hospital! Thank goodness all of that had gone out the window by the time she started working in maternity, where one physician wore rubber boots, so prone was the job to splashing fluids and bloodstains.

She recalled quaking in her white shoes, could still picture her charge nurse, who seemed seven feet tall despite likely being average-sized, her gray hair pulled back severely, peering at the students over her dark-rimmed glasses, her mouth a firm flat line all the time, even when saying things to patients that were supportive or caring.

The charge nurse's name was Mary, but the junior nurses called her Scary. According to the more experienced nurses, she'd been called Scary for years; even when someone slipped up and used the name in her presence, she didn't really seem to mind, and had never formally reprimanded anyone for it.

Scary gave Bets three patients to wash, assess, and assist, and a strict timeline to report back for inspection of her work.

—Careful with Mr. Brody in Room 11, Scary said, towering. He has been confused and tried to climb out of bed. They had to put him in a restraint belt. You need to be firm, and calm.

—Firm, and calm, Bets repeated.

She turned and went to get her supplies.

Firm, and calm. Her first elderly patient was quite deaf, her hair completely flattened at the back and standing up at the top from lying in bed, her breakfast liberally spread onto the front of her nightgown. The woman completely ignored whatever Bets said.

—Eh? Did you say something? I'm deaf, you know! I can't hear a thing!

She cackled as though she had just told a wonderful joke, and talked loudly about her travels to Japan, Sweden, and Spain. At least five times during their short interaction, Bets heard about the travels to Japan, Sweden, and Spain. Firm, and calm. Japan, Sweden, and Spain. She assisted her patient out of her soiled nightgown and gave her a sponge bath, careful to get her cloth into creases, as she had been taught; the soggy crust of toast she removed from beneath the lady's right breast did more to reinforce the instruction than any lecture possibly could. How long had that crust been there? She attempted to comb out the wiry hair, fluff it at the back, calm down the top, but it remained resolutely Statue of Liberty. She placed the basin on the rolling table and gestured with a toothbrush, jumping slightly when the woman popped out her dentures and offered them to Bets for cleaning. Firm, and calm. When her patient was clean, her sheets tucked nicely, Bets gathered her things and waved good-bye, feeling triumphant.

She knew she was lucky. The woman was small, she could move herself, she was continent (Bets had already heard a colleague weeping in the supply closet after facing a bed full of diarrhea). Even so, everything had its challenges. Firm, and calm. Japan, Sweden, and Spain. Which would she prefer? At the time—not very aware of the world, sushi or minimalism or bullfighting—she chose Spain, mainly because she felt she could learn Spanish. Was it not close to French, which she heard all the time in her Northern Ontario community? She wondered if the patient, when she could hear, had been good at languages. Such was Bets' frame of mind when she strode, more confidently, into her second room, armed with a new load of supplies.

The gentleman had been extremely confused the previous night, she'd been told. He had continually shouted "Help!" or "Nurse!" He tried to climb out of bed, pulled out his IV, and kept the other patients awake. They had moved him into a private room where, finally, early in the morning, he had settled. No one had gone in after that, fearful of disturbing him and starting the whole performance again.

When Bets pushed open the door, which had been left partially closed to reduce the noise, she stopped so suddenly, she dropped her armload of supplies, including the metal bedpan, which made a terrible clanging noise, followed by wow-wow-wow as it rotated a few times before settling itself.

The shades were lowered, but the shafts of sunlight sneaking around the sides of the window gave enough light to see quite clearly. Mr. Brody, it seemed, had tried to climb out of bed again. He'd managed to get his arms under the restraint belt, then appeared to have slid partially off the bed. The belt, too tight to slip over his head, had caught him by the neck on his way down. His face was purple, his eyes open and bulging, his denture partially out of his mouth, and he was clearly dead. Bets flicked the light switch and illuminated the tableau further; she walked closer. She reached a tentative finger to touch his grayish hand: cold, waxy.

To this day, Bets can't really explain why she didn't scream, or panic; perhaps it was the charge nurse (*firm, and calm*). She left the room and walked briskly to find Scary Mary, whispered urgently to her, and the two of them speed-walked (*never run*) down the hallway, other staff stopping to stare as they zoomed past.

Scary stood in the doorway and looked at Mr. Brody, at his awkward, ghoulish pose. She approached him and placed two fingers on his neck for a pulse. She shone a light in his eyes, listened to his chest, tried to move his fingers, which were stiff.

—Time of pronouncement 0810. Document that in his chart.

—Should we put him into bed? asked Bets. Scary shook her head.

—No, this will be a coroner's case. We have to leave him. I'll notify the staff so that no one comes in.

She sighed, removing her glasses and placing fingers and thumb on the bridge of her nose for a moment.

—This is on me, Elizabeth. This is not your fault, it is mine, and you were right to come to me immediately.

Bets, who had never even considered that it might be her fault, having never set eyes on the man in her life, floundered for a response and settled on, "Thank you." Was Scary crying? Impossible! No, she settled her glasses back on her nose and touched Bets' shoulder.

—You did a fine job with Mrs. Perreault. You're off to a good, if difficult, start here. Carry on.

She didn't ask Bets if she was all right, or if she had seen a dead person before, or if she had questions, or if she needed a bit of time to herself. Instead, she squared her large shoulders, thrust forward her equally impressive bosom, and walked out, holding the door for Bets to pass, then closing it firmly, and going to the nursing desk to telephone the family and advise the staff. She was the first person that Bets encountered who put emotions into a box, and Bets tried to do the same, for the rest of that shift.

She learned later that there was a formal investigation and Scary got into a lot of trouble for not moving Mr. Brody closer to the nursing station or keeping the door wide open so he could be observed more closely. Scary didn't lose her job, but it had been a possibility. In the end, she chose to retire a few months later. Bets learned that Scary had protected her, telling the investigation that she took all responsibility for care of the patient, and Bets was not to be involved in any questioning whatsoever, or any court proceedings. Maybe that was as it should be, but Bets thought about Scary often, whenever she had students, whenever there were confused or combative patients, whenever things went wrong and people blamed each other and argued over what must be done.

***

Hannah's pen was frozen in mid-air as if she had rusted into position. There was a clunk, and the heat vent in the floor began blowing.

—I can't believe you saw a dead body, Hannah finally said. On your first day.

—I know. It was bad luck. We had new protocols for confused patients after that.

—But how could you keep working? After that?

—I'm not sure. I guess I just put it away for a while. Until I had time to deal with it.

—What if somebody can't put it away?

Hannah pulled her scarf up higher, over her chin.

—I feel like I've scared you. Remember, that was a really weird thing to happen on a first day. Really unusual.

She watched Hannah withdraw into her scarf like a tortoise.

***

About a year ago, Bets had overheard a group of young nurses.

—I need more time, said one. I work, like, all the time. And I can't get anything done, because when I'm not working, all I want to do is sleep.

—I know, said another. It's the shift work. It's killer. I want to switch to a clinic.

—We should ask for shorter shifts. Like eights instead of twelves.

—But then we'd have to do more of them.

—But maybe the extra could be on call in case it's busy; sometimes we're just sitting here with hardly any patients.

—We should ask.

—Who's charge today? Bets?

—Yeah.

—Well, don't ask her. She'll say no.

—Yeah, she seems kind of… angry.

—Not with patients, though, just with us! Like we can't do anything right! We're supposed to be perfect all the time!

Bets had moved away from the conversation without letting the younger women see her. There were no women in labour, so she went to the nursery, her favourite place to think.

At night when the lights were low, and the frantic ins and outs stopped for the day, she sat with the babies, the ones too sick to room in with their mothers. The tiny premature infants tucked inside their incubators, sometimes on respirators, their bodies completely dwarfed by snaking tubes and huge back-lit faces of the screens, humming and whirring, that recorded every breath, every heartbeat.

Some were under phototherapy lights to help with jaundice, and these wore little eye masks, like napping divas. Some were placed on their fronts, and curled themselves back into fetal position, tiny diapered bottoms up in the air.

There were also babies whose mothers had diabetes, improbably large newborns who emerged initially unable to control their blood sugars. Bloated from extra insulin, they appeared gigantic beside the frail prems, nearly too big for their bassinets, bulging out of the newborn sleepers.

Bets sat in the rocker when the work was done, listening for mewing cries, and imagined lives for the babies. That one, with the nasal tube and scalp IV, legs splayed, eyelids thin as a baby bird's, will that one live? Will that be the coddled child with asthma and daily fear, or will that be the one that grows to be six feet tall, and everyone howls when they bring out the tiny onesie and say, "You used to fit into this!" Or, will the enormous baby be large all her life? Will this one constantly fight weight gain, unfairly judged and ridiculed for her size, dissatisfied and unhappy, or will she rise above and embrace it (how did some people accomplish that feat so much better than others?) Or will this one be the lanky adolescent shown their baby photos amid choruses of "Look at that! Where did those arm rolls go?" Sometimes she worried about the babies, even at home, well after her shift; sometimes Raz looked at her far-off gaze and said, Let the babies sleep, Bets.

Bets imagined lives for the babies and occasionally found out the truth; she ran into people who remembered her and introduced the now-grown child. The way the child "turned out" often surprised her. She witnessed that children, bearing no early resemblance to their parents, became eerie replicas of them during adolescence. Or, that the very early, very sick babies sometimes never progressed, even at two, or five, or sixteen, and she wanted to say, this must have been a very hard parenting road. But she did not.

After overhearing the younger nurses, Bets had checked the nursery board, found a preemie due for a feeding, heated a bottle of donated breast milk, and sat in the rocking chair with the baby held against her, his mouth groping through the air like the tiniest chick, finally finding the bottle's nipple, suckling, immediately choking.

—Good Lord, said Bets, setting down the bottle, flipping the baby and tapping his back, like tapping a deck of cards. The baby settled down and they began the process again.

Sitting with the baby, rocking, feeding, Bets couldn't deny the truth of the junior nurses' words. If they'd come to her requesting shorter shifts, more time off, she knew she would have mentally rolled her eyes. *Of course, you want to work less.* You'd work the minimum amount to get by, given the option. You'd work less and less, yet want a raise, or extra benefits. You don't understand how to work hard.

Why? Why be so negative toward those in the exact position she had once been in: new, anxious, innocent, fearful, fatigued?

The young nurses sometimes saluted when she turned, called her Sergeant Major. Bets pretended not to see or hear. Nurses scattered when they saw her approaching, got to work when she was charge nurse. She saw them testing the suction, the oxygen bag, refilling the supplies, and tried to catch them doing these good things, and praise them. But they were right, she frequently felt angry that people were sloppy, didn't double-check, weren't prepared.

It wasn't really anger at them, or was it? Bets sat the baby up, leaned him over her hand, tapped his back to encourage a burp; instead, the baby looked up at Bets with a concerned expression, then grimaced and filled his diaper beneath her hand.

Now, a year later, sitting at home, thinking about her start in nursing, Bets considered her shifts with Scary Mary. Someone needs to keep things in line, she thought, and make sure things happen that need to happen. In my case, someone needs to make sure the babies get saved, the moms get supported.

Someone needs to know what to do.

I can be Sergeant Major, thought Bets. If it helps them in the end: the nurses, the mothers, the babies. *Save the babies!* A slogan for a television campaign; ridiculous. Bets shook her head at herself.

That day in the nursery, once she had sausage-rolled the baby back into his blanket, after she finished feeding and changing and thinking and her frustration dissipated in the soft light, the baby looked up at her, even though his eyes couldn't focus yet. Of course, it was just a reflex, but she felt like he smiled.

CHAPTER FOUR

Hannah did not show up on Bets' doorstep every week, for which Bets was grateful. While enjoying Hannah's questions and scattered energy, she sometimes needed some recovery time afterwards. She talked to Hannah about classes during nursing school—the entire process would have changed by now, of course, but Hannah wanted to hear it anyway—and about the stress, the huge errors, and the camaraderie of her nursing class. They discussed different types of nursing and the pros and cons Bets knew about each: surgical, medical, maternity, emergency, community, public health, mental health, and subspecialized areas like neonatal intensive care, dialysis, oncology. So many options.

Hannah asked more questions as they went along, sometimes interrupting, which Bets tried to quash early on, but it was difficult to stop the energetic barrage of curiosity, and Bets soon gave up trying to change Hannah's style. It seemed like a lot of information for a project, but she admired the commitment.

Hannah had midterms, so it had been a few days longer than usual when she called and asked if she could come over. Walking down the hallway, Hannah stopped before the framed photographs on the wall.

—I've always wanted to check these out in more detail.

Bets thought about hurrying her along but paused. Hannah, perhaps sensing the tension, did not ask about every photo. She pointed at one, a favourite of Bets', featuring Bets and Raz, leaning into each other, with their foreheads nearly touching.

—Is that your husband?

—Yes. Raz.

—Raz?

—It's a nickname.

—Where is he?

—He died. A few months ago.

Hannah covered her mouth with her hand. Spoke through her fingers, muffled.

—Oh, Bets. I'm sorry. My mom says I ask too many questions.

Bets pulled Hannah's hand away.

—If I didn't like questions, I wouldn't have let you in that very first day, or since.

—True.

Hannah gave a small, relieved smile. They went into the living room this time, Bets tucking herself into a corner of the couch while Hannah rummaged and dropped things. Once settled in, Hannah opened her notebook and smoothed the page with her hand.

—Bets? Can I ask you about Raz? How did you meet him?

Bets hesitated a beat, two.

—I'm sorry, said Hannah quickly. It's none of my business. My mother said that I'm bothering you too much.

Hannah made such statements frequently, and each time Bets waited for her to explain further, but she never did. Clearly, her mother was aware of the visits, and seemed disapproving; did she know the assignment? The goal? Did she know how often they diverged from the topic of nursing?

—It's okay, said Bets, I can tell you how we met. If you really want.

***

She'd agreed to a beach holiday—her first—with her friend Katie, Katie's husband Carter, and their young son Sam, who had just discovered his own will and the complete chaos he could generate by exerting it.

—Come with us! Katie begged, as Sam dangled screaming from her arm, protesting whatever small task had been requested: shoes, coat, nose wipe. It will help to prevent us from killing him. We'll all be on our best behaviour because of you.

Bets, needing a holiday, did not love the idea of spending her time at the beach entertaining a three-year-old, but admittedly there was a part of her that felt, *bring it on, Sam. I can handle the likes of you.* She was childless but, at least in her own mind, enlightened; she knew better than to expect perfect behaviour in small children and believed in the concept of temperament. Didn't she see, every day, the same thing in the newborns in the nursery? Babies who, from the first moment of existence, arched and screamed and refused the very breast that would nourish them, while others lay placid and blinking, as if astonished by life, but willing to participate.

She went on the trip with eyes wide open and little toys and puzzles in her bag. She had enough sunscreen for a small town, and still burned in the sun with her fair hair, her freckles.

The beach in the Mayan Riviera was exquisite, just as it appeared in the brochures. The perfect white sand was dotted with colourful umbrellas and minimally covered sunbathers, and the blue, impossibly clear water reminded Bets of Aqua-Velva, and burned her eyes and nose when she swam underwater. Feet scorching on the sand, she and Sam ran screaming from the towel to the water's edge, continuing this tradition even after they had learned to keep their sandals on until the last possible moment. Bets ignored the irritated looks of people dozing in the sun and kept her full focus on Sam and his enjoyment, knowing that he was fast and distractible. Katie and Carter protested when she took him, they took no advantage— "we'll go in shifts"— and she agreed, but she could read a magazine without interruption at home, or enjoy a drink, whereas at their stage of life, such things were transient luxuries.

Also, as she had expected, Sam showed less resistance with her. They all enjoyed the ensuing peace, however temporary. Bets learned quickly to identify fatigue, to offer snacks early, to slow things down when he was getting worked up, to let him be in charge whenever she could. It was easier to anticipate, to be fun and creative, when it was not a 24-hour-per-day job. Plus, there were no deadlines, and she could wait him out whenever she needed to.

—I *won't* go back to my towel, Sam announced, planting his feet, glaring at her with chin thrust out, arms folded, so that Bets had to suck in her cheeks to avoid laughing out loud.

—Well, Bud, we need to get out of the sun for a while, and we have snacks and drinks there, and we can show your mom and dad the shells we found, but whatever. We can stay here instead.

She leaned back on her elbows, pretending to settle in. Sam dug into the sand with his feet, appreciating his victory, glanced up at the shady area, and inevitably wanted to return to the towel within moments. Bets acted astonished at his fantastic idea, and back they went.

Katie watched it all from a distance, amazed.

—You're a natural, Bets. How do you do it? I wish we could keep you with us all the time! I'd have ten kids!

Bets just laughed and handed Sam over for a while so that she could get a mojito or join the beach volleyball game. Katie had agreed long ago not to set Bets up or make a big deal about her single status, but sometimes she talked a bit too much about how great Bets was with children. It could get into Bets' head if she let it. She knew, without being reminded, that the clock was ticking.

The day they lost Sam, Carter was in charge. Katie had already commented a few times on his inability to multitask.

—Carter, she said, in much the same tone she used for Sam, you have to watch him every minute. You can't be distracted by the Frisbee, or the bikini boobs. You have to *watch* him.

Carter never protested or puffed out his chest, only nodded mutely. He really was a good guy, Bets reflected during the holiday, watching him accept criticism, watching him toss his son in the waves, create miniature running races with him on the beach, or let him bury his legs in sand over and over and over again. He was a well-built, muscular man, and Bets watched him sometimes before catching herself and thinking, *you are not here to admire Katie's husband, Bets.*

The day they lost Sam, Carter had started a little impromptu soccer game on the beach with some other small kids, a few parents, and some random add-ins. Bets and Katie were on beach chairs well back from the water, talking and resting. Bets was quite certain she remembered saying,

—I feel so relaxed right now. Let's just stay here forever!

Immediately, as if invoked by her words: commotion.

They couldn't see anything with all the people wandering around looking for a spot to sit, but they heard Carter's voice.

—Sam! Has anyone seen Sam? Sam! Sam!

Katie was instantly alert and upright, scanning the beach. She stood up. Bets touched her arm.

—I'm sure he's right there. He's right there.

There was a second of silence and just as they were about to relax, the calls resumed, now with several male voices and a couple of females, and they could see people fanning out, pushing through crowds, jogging along the water's edge.

It seemed to Bets that Katie's feet did not even touch the sand, so quickly was she facing Carter, tall and easily located, his eyes wide and panicked.

—He was *here*. He was right here. He was playing with us. And then he wasn't. He was just gone.

Later, Bets found out that some girls had joined the soccer game; that one had sweetly asked Carter for pointers. They had stepped outside the game for a moment, just for a moment, but in that moment, for whatever reason, Sam had gone.

Three years old. This high. Brown hair. What was he wearing? Carter looked crazily at Katie and Bets.

—Green bathing suit with T-Rexes on it, Bets supplied.

They hailed a lifeguard, who gestured at the crowds of people and tried ineffectively to clear the water using his whistle. There was a lot of Spanish. Carter, Bets, and Katie each chose a direction, a meeting spot, kept moving, eyes scanning continuously. Carter told Bets later that as he ran, all he could think was, he's gone, and my marriage is over. He's gone, and my marriage is over. I will always be the one who lost our son. Katie was blinded by tears, gasping, pushing people aside, running along the sand, occasionally choking out Sam's name. Bets knew enough Spanish to manage boy, three years, green clothes, sometimes unleashing a torrent of incomprehensible words in response, a few people pointing down the beach saying "*Perro*," which made no sense but encouraged her to keep going. *Sam, don't be drowned. Don't be taken. Be okay Sam. Be okay Sam.* Bets could barely breathe, yet called his name over and over, hoarse. She was so busy scanning at three-year-old level she nearly ran straight into a man, and had she only looked up, she would have seen Sam much sooner, perched as he was on the guy's broad shoulders. Sam was crying loudly; he held out his arms and fell upon Bets.

—Sam!

Bets felt her legs go weak, and lowered herself to the sand, holding Sam. She squeezed his body to her, let him drip his eyes and nose all over her back and shoulder, kissed his gooey face, then stood up and gestured toward the man.

—We should put you back up there, Sam. We want your Mum and Dad to be able to spot you quickly.

—No! I want Bets! I want Mom!

Sam lost all muscle tone and dangled from Bets' arm. Bets glanced at Sam's rescuer, who seemed amused.

—Sorry, I'm sure you might have things to do other than carry a toddler around. Thank you so much for helping. I need to get to his parents.

—He was following a big dog and then didn't know how to get back, I think. He did this… floppy thing when I first tried to carry him.

—Yes, kind of his specialty, admitted Bets.

They watched him writhing on the sand for a moment, then the man, without preamble, scooped up Sam, flung him into the air twice as if he weighed no more than a sofa cushion, and settled him, magically acquiescent now, back on his tanned shoulders. They started back toward the meeting point, which was the tall lifeguard chair. Bets scanned for Katie and Carter.

—Do you speak Spanish? Bets detected an accent.

—None. I'm French, from Québec.

—Oh! We're from Ontario, Northern Ontario! I'm Bets—pointing to herself as they speed walked—and he's Sam. My friend's son.

—Raz, he said.

—Raz?

—It's a nickname.

They shook hands while still moving, and Sam shouted "Mom! Mom!" and then Katie was there, folding him to her, weeping, and then Carter was there too, and the crowd sensed the relief, and the joy, and some people even applauded.

It had made Bets think about loss. About how loss was someone's fault, sometimes. Even if we try to convince someone otherwise, someone who is already hurting, perhaps paying for their carelessness in the most terrible way, we know, deep down, that it might not have happened if only. If only! Relationships could sever, could drown, could turn to poison because of that simple phrase. If only.

If only you'd locked the door, if only you'd done what I asked, if only you'd remembered, if only you would listen, if only you hadn't, if only you had.

Here was Sam, well, cherished, and none the worse for wear, and here was Katie, and Carter, and everything would return to normal. Or would it? Would Carter ever move beyond the husband who lost his son while teaching soccer moves on the beach? Surely it was only a moment. Surely every parent experienced the panic of losing a child, even briefly, and then became hypervigilant for a short—or long—period afterward, but eventually, went back to usual life and began, again, to sigh and cajole and reprimand.

Even Bets, who had seen Sam at his worst, who knew how tired Katie and Carter were, as parents raising their son while working and maintaining their relationship with each other, who knew Carter to be caring, and considerate, and intelligent; even Bets had a fleeting moment of wanting to push against Carter with all her might, yank his hair, kick his shins, shout, You idiot! You stupid fool! Look what you risked, look what you might have lost, you stupid, stupid man! Realizing, of course, that it could have been her. Thinking it, although it was unthinkable. She knew—as Katie did, surely—that it could have been any of them, that he could have been lured, or snatched, or drowned. That was just the risk, and it was out there, and you had to live with that possibility, you had to keep going and pretend you could control it by being careful. What, thought Bets, does being careful even mean when it comes to strong-willed, pigheaded three- year-olds?

Predictably, Katie and Carter kept Sam very close after that, and were constantly asking each other: You've got Sam? Ok, you're good with Sam for a bit? I'll take Sam to the pool? You've got Sam while I get drinks?

Bets, denied her role temporarily, felt very much on the outside, as if the family unit had closed the gates, hauled up the drawbridge. It stung, but she understood. Relieved of her Sam- related duties, Bets was restless. She woke up early despite not needing to work, and although she was free to relax and enjoy the resort, she could not. She went to the little café that opened at six am, the one that offered every fancy caffeinated beverage you could imagine, and ordered a black coffee, to the amusement of Miguel who worked there. After that, he had her coffee ready for her every morning. Once up, she couldn't read, couldn't lie in the sun, couldn't relax in the hot tub (especially at a family resort with small children—she just knew there were things happening in the hot tub day to day that didn't bear thinking about). Finally, she threw herself into activities; she played tennis, beach volleyball, beach soccer, even the ridiculous-looking Aquafit class which, when she let go of judgement, was quite fun.

She was also, despite herself, keeping an eye out for Raz—who had melted back into the crowd at the beach—hoping to run into him again. He differed from the men she knew, with his easy manner, his accent, his calm with children mid-meltdown. Not to mention his tan, the crinkles at the sides of his eyes when he smiled, and the easy way he'd tossed Sam, showing his strength. She knew nothing about him, of course, but felt herself wanting to know more. And, if the whole thing was a bust, what better place than a resort she'd never return to, among a crowd of people, most of whom she'd never see again? Raz, however, proved maddeningly elusive. Perhaps he'd already gone home; Bets felt foolish even looking.

One evening, Katie and Carter decided to have supper early with Sam, and then go to the kids' movie and straight to bed.

—You're welcome to come to dinner, of course, said Katie, but I'm thinking that pizza at five pm and a child's cartoon might not be your idea of a resort vacation.

Bets joined them for pizza, greatly enjoying the time with Sam. When she said she wasn't coming to the movie, however, Sam threw a tantrum and Bets realized, frustrated, that she'd triggered behaviour easily avoided if she'd left the little family to themselves.

She went to one of the outdoor bars, done up tiki-style with a thatched roof, and surrounded by palm trees. The resort was all-inclusive, so many people started the day with a margarita and continued from there. Bets drank little in general, and she'd had Sam to consider.

That night, she drank her first margarita quickly and ordered another. She considered striking up a conversation with someone, but the women beside her were deep in conversation, the man on the other side was so drunk he could barely speak (were there different rules on resorts about not serving alcohol to visibly drunk people?), and the bartenders were all shouting and edging past each other to get bottles and ice and limes. Ironic, thought Bets, that the one time she was considering branching out and talking to strangers, there were none available.

She listened to the beat of the music, the buzz of conversations around her, and people calling out drink orders in English and Spanish. Feeling the warm breeze on her shoulders, watching the softening light as the sun began lowering into the ocean, she wiped the salt from the rim of her glass with her finger, placing it onto her tongue. She was leaning across the polished bar to get the attention of the server when she heard a familiar voice behind her.

—Should I drop to the ground and scream to get your attention?

As if she'd conjured him by the sheer power of her isolation.

***

—Well, I'm never having kids, said Hannah. That sounds so stressful. Also exhausting.

Bets laughed.

—Well, you don't need to decide right this minute. But yes, it's not an easy job, being a parent. No one's there to teach you what to do.

—You sound like you were good at it!

—Maybe, said Bets. Maybe I was just lucky, at that time.

Much later, on her way to bed, Bets noticed the photo tilted slightly on the wall, and straightened it, fingers lingering briefly on the frame. She could see Raz in her mind so clearly, with his clean white shirt that set off his dark hair and tanned olive skin, his jeans and sandals, could see herself gesturing—slightly wobbly on the spinning barstool—to the stool beside her, abandoned by the very drunk man.

—I'd be happy if you joined me.

She couldn't figure out her best position, crossed and then uncrossed her legs. He settled in, ordered a gin and tonic.

—Where is your sidekick? Gone to bed?

—Probably, by now. They've closed ranks on me, since... well... you know. Who are you here with? She was suddenly bold.

—I'm here alone. I was supposed to be here with someone, but we, uh, broke up just beforehand.

His drink had not arrived, and he searched for the bartender with his eyes.

—Shit, said Bets, surprising herself. Sorry about that.

His eyes returned to hers.

—Well, he said, there are worse ways to grieve, gesturing around him. His drink arrived, and he took the glass from the bartender, swirled the ice.

—That's why you are here this evening? To listen to tragic tales?

She shrugged, a gesture she normally detested.

—I'm here to meet interesting people, since up to this point, my date has been a three- year-old.

—Well, he chuckled, I'm not sure I qualify.

—Oh, you qualify, Mr. Oddly-named French-Canadian with a past.

She held out her glass, and they clinked and drank, and Raz began to talk.

Raz told stories of his family, his work, so bilingual that he slipped French phrases in and out of his speech without even noticing, like a satin ribbon woven through the fabric of the story. At times, he gestured wildly with his hands, at others, he threw back his head and laughed. They left the bar after a while and walked on the beach, although Bets was a bit off-balance. Raz grabbed her arm to steady her, and she was very conscious of the place his hand had touched.

Bets found herself thinking in ways she'd never thought before, considering things she'd normally dismiss immediately. *I'm drunk*, she thought, but it was more than that. It was the drama with Sam. It was the beach, and the sound of waves, and the lack of responsibility, and it was Raz, now sitting beside her on the beach, scooping sand into a pile as he told her about the girlfriend who had left him for his friend. He wasn't self-centred, he offered her openings, he asked her questions, but all she wanted was to watch him, to listen to his voice, his laughter, to feel the barest outline of his body beside her.

—I'm talking so much, he said, after a period of silence. You keep throwing the conversation back to me. I see what you're doing!

He smoothed out the pile of sand he'd created, turned back to her.

—So tell me now, who is Bets? What does she want?

It was the opening she didn't know she was waiting for, and against every rational fibre she possessed, she leaned forward and kissed him. He made a small, surprised sound, but responded immediately. They broke apart, and he touched her face.

—Quiet, but expressive.

He kissed her this time, wrapped her in his arms, rolled onto his back so she lay on top of him.

—Get a room! Called a man walking past on the beach, followed by catcalls from a group of boys going in the opposite direction.

—Looking good, buddy! One shouted, the others hooting.

Raz and Bets broke apart. She rolled off him, and they lay side by side in the sand.

—That was an unexpected pleasure, said Raz. Thank you.

Bets propped herself on an elbow so she could look at him. She touched a button on his shirt.

—I'm not great at talking, she said, especially to someone I don't really know. Although I feel like I know you much better now.

They both laughed.

—You should know, she continued, I'm never like this. I'm not impulsive, I'm not spontaneous, I don't usually drink. I overthink things. I'm not really fun.

Raz propped himself on an elbow, too.

—Bets. Why are you saying these things?

—Because, said Bets, pausing, breathing, because I want you to take me back to your room. If you want.

Raz reached out, traced her eyebrow, her cheekbone. *Oh God*, she thought, *he thinks I'm an idiot.*

—That, said Raz, would be the most beautiful thing I could imagine.

—But?

—But…I'm a bit drunk, and you're a bit drunk, and I think, I'm thinking, we should spend the day together tomorrow. And see what happens. I don't want you to have regrets. *Ça serait terrible.*

He lifted her hand to his lips, and her tears spilled over, but they weren't embarrassed tears anymore, and where his thumbs wiped them away, her skin buzzed and remembered.

They had two days together at the resort. After the first, Bets felt light and fluttery and smiled much more than usual as she beat back the hope that raised its head and cheered. Obviously, this situation was completely out of character and going nowhere. Obviously, vacation romances were just for pleasure and should not have any expectation or strings attached. Bets, usually very good at eliminating frivolity, felt a bit like she was driving a car without brakes. She'd had dreams like that a few times—careening around corners, becoming airborne over bumps in the road—waking up sweating and terrified, relieved it had not been real. Now, she didn't so much feel out of control as dependent on fate. She'd never believed in a higher power, but someone, or something, was going to determine whether this fling was going anywhere, and it couldn't possibly be her.

She still saw Katie and Carter, and offered to take Sam, but they remained inside the family fortress.

—Come with us! Said Katie, you're not just a nanny, you can still do things with us!

—Of course, I know that, said Bets, but then Raz found her, and kissed her right in front of them, and she couldn't speak.

Raz extended his hand to Katie, saving Bets.

—I'm Raz. We met, but it was a very stressful time.

Katie looked at Carter, confused, but Carter jumped up and pumped Raz's hand and slapped him on the back.

—You found Sam, you found our son. We owe you everything.

Carter's voice cracked on the last word, and they all looked elsewhere, except for Raz.

—You owe me nothing, he said. He found me, and I just picked him up. With a bit of convincing.

He turned to Sam, ruffled his hair.

—Hi Sam, how are the waffles?

Sam, deconstructing his Belgian waffle piled high with whipped cream, looked at Raz and did not reply. Katie recovered and stood to hug Raz.

—Thank you, she said. Did you say Raz?

—It's a nickname.

—Breakfast on me! announced Carter, the standard joke at an all-inclusive resort.

Raz pulled up a chair and joined them. Comfortable, it seemed, among people he'd never met, his sentences sprinkled with occasional French words, his laughter frequent and natural. Bets could barely speak or eat, watching him.

—You talk funny, said Sam, finished mangling his waffle.

—Sam! Katie admonished. Raz smiled at him.

—It's okay, he said, it's true, Sam, I don't speak like you. That's because when I learned to talk, it was in French.

—Like at daycare, said Sam, and Katie nodded.

—Yes, just like at your daycare! People around here speak Spanish, have you noticed?

Sam looked around, then slowly nodded, picked up his cup of juice, took a drink, and spilled the rest down his front.

—Language lesson over, said Katie, diving for napkins.

It turned out that Raz, a miner with a lot of experience, was highly sought in Northern Ontario, for example in Bets' community. It turned out that he was perhaps looking for a change in location. It turned out that being bilingual was an asset, and his wage would increase if he moved.

—I can't afford not to, he said to Bets during one of their many post-resort phone calls. The calls sometimes lasted hours, in which Bets spoke about things she hadn't thought about in years, spun out tales, added little jokes, wondered if the problem, all along, was not that she didn't speak well, but that no one listened properly. Until now.

He was careful, he didn't pressure her. He created time and space around her, let her schedule the next phone call, waited for her to suggest a visit. He made it impossible for her to tell him all the things her brain was screaming at her like the frustrated parent of a teenager: it was too soon, they had only seen each other a few times,. She smiled for no apparent reason, she gazed lovingly at the phone. She helped him with forms, applying for a health card, a driver's license, things that were different in Ontario than Québec, even though they lived side by side in the same country. *This is insane,* she thought. *This can't possibly be happening.*

He didn't ask to live with her, just asked if she could find leads for him toward getting a place. She looked at newspapers for about five minutes before crumpling them up, but she waited five days, just to be sure.

—I've been thinking, she said during their next phone call, and I know this might seem weird, or too soon, but it doesn't really make sense for us to pay for two places when we could get one, nicer, place—together.

Raz didn't answer right away, and Bets briefly wondered if her heart could actually stop.

—What are you thinking? She whispered.

Raz cleared his throat. Started to speak, cleared his throat again.

—I was just thinking, I was hoping you would say something like that. I was really hoping.

Bets sat, absurdly smiling into the telephone, and then she suddenly burst into tears.

—Bets? Bets? What's wrong?

—Don't worry, don't worry. I do this sometimes. Occasionally. I'm just happy.

—Come soon, she croaked eventually, come as soon as you can.

***

He was still on her mind as she walked to work that night, noticing that the snow squeaked less, that the wind had less of a raw edge, that the peak of winter had maybe passed. She walked past simple two-story homes, some with large-screen TVs easily visible through large front windows, portable silver-tarp-covered structures housing garage overflow items: trucks, snowmobiles, all-terrain vehicles, boats. Some driveways showed black tarmac instead of full snow coverage. A blue spruce dropped snow from its branches as she walked by, seemed to stand up straighter after shedding. She felt lighter, and more hopeful than she had since she lost Raz.

She worked the first half of her shift with this new sense of lightness. *I don't know what people were talking about. Returning to work is the best possible thing for me.* She worked in the nursery, murmuring to the infants, checking monitors, feeding, turning, documenting, and settled into a chair for a feeding, a little preemie blinking up at her from the blanket. Shannon came in, leaning against the doorway. For a moment Bets just smiled at her, rocking with her miniature bottle and miniature baby, her smile slowly fading as she noticed Shannon's face.

—What's wrong?

Shannon didn't answer right away, took a deep breath.

—It's a stillbirth, said Shannon. You don't need to come if you don't want to.

But Bets always did the stillbirths if she was on shift.

—I'll come.

CHAPTER FIVE

What does it mean, exactly, to be good at stillbirths?

The young nurses, often, were too upset, too undone by the bare, raw grief that permeated the corridors and spilled through doorways. Bets should really have been most affected of them all, for many reasons, but she dealt with things anyway.

Bets asked the young mothers, crying with their own mothers or husbands or partners, if they wanted to hold the baby right away, or after Bets made the baby nice for them. Often, they chose the latter, but sometimes they just wanted the baby in their arms, to hold it, touch it, make it real, just for a short time.

Sometimes, the medical team tried to save the baby if there had been a heartbeat during delivery. The parents, worn out from labour, endured the sight of tubes being inserted, oxygen bags pumping, chest compressions done with two fingers because the chests were so tiny. It was different from an adult resuscitation, which always seemed to involve a lot of people and equipment and noise: Bets vividly recalled adult resuscitations in the past, hearing the doctor shout "Give epi! Give epi!" and the nurse shouting back "1 amp of epi in," while the respiratory therapist yelled for the ambu-bag, or another nurse called for the IV line, while someone shouted "Stop compressions!" or "Clear for shock!"

In the nursery they huddled around the baby warmer, and there was only room for three or four people, and the parents were there, so they all spoke softly and communicated with their eyes, trying not to let parents hear things like "I'm not getting a pulse" or "Oxygen saturation 50%."

At some point, someone had to decide to stop trying. Usually it was the pediatrician, and often multiple people were crying by the time they reached that point. The worst moment for Bets, perhaps for everyone, was detaching the bag from the breathing tube, turning off the oxygen, turning off the suction, turning off the heart monitor, which kept alarming otherwise, all of which left the room in a sudden desperate silence, other than the grieving noises of the parents. Sometimes they were supposed to leave the body until the coroner was called and Bets remembered a nurse timidly telling the pediatrician so on one past occasion. The pediatrician, who was at least sixty and had seen his share of unhappy circumstances, stared down the nurse and said in a deadly calm, slow voice,

—Take out the tubes. Give. This mother. Her baby.

And then,

—Please.

They did just that, and the parents took the baby into the bed with them, the father climbing in as well, and the three of them lay like that for a long time, for hours. Bets left the call button within easy reach and said, "Call when you need us." The nurses, the pediatrician, the anesthesiologist, the respiratory therapist, all filed out into the impossibly bright lights of the hallway and went back to work, praying that no one would complain they had been kept waiting, praying that things would be smooth for the remainder of the shift so they would not lose control, so they would not have to scream at the top of their lungs, "A baby just *died* in there, *I might need a moment.*" Staff were allowed to leave, if it wasn't too busy, but usually no one did. Maybe it was easier not to think about it too much.

If the parents wanted Bets to make the baby look nice first, she wrapped the little body and took it to the nursery, her sanctuary of quiet as long as it wasn't busy, which it never seemed to be when these things happened. It was as if the entire cosmos took a deep breath and held it for a short time, just to acknowledge the immensity of a new, innocent, and unfulfilled life.

Bets bathed the baby, made sure the water was warm, gently slid the soft facecloth into infant corners and creases. She sprinkled powder. She placed a fresh diaper, she dressed each baby in the softest, best-fitting sleeper she could find in the stacks of donated items. Sometimes there were deformities, and she covered them as much as she could. She was artful with hats.

She took clippings of hair, she combed, she did hand and footprints, and finally she swaddled them tightly into their blankets.

Sometimes she hummed a soft tune, but she never sang. If she sang, she learned early on, her voice cracked and she broke down. And once you broke through that wall, once the levee was breached, there was no turning back.

She returned the babies to their parents, and entering the room was like going out on a too-humid day; like walking into a thick, heavy wall of pain. She offered to take pictures, which were often initially refused but later cherished. She was calm and respectful, and stayed off to the side until she saw she was needed.

It was a skill, Bets knew, to take grief and put it into a box and deal with it later. Some could do it, like herself, and others could not, and she didn't blame them for that.

Bets knew that her problem was not storing emotions, it was forgetting (or avoiding) taking the contents out and facing them. Eventually, that had to happen, or else grief crept out in bits and pieces, showing up in unexpected places: next thing you knew you broke down completely because your suitcase warranty ran out just before the handle pulled off, or the server at the coffee shop used soy milk instead of cream. If not managed, grief could make her the person who fell apart over nothing, and Bets did not have time for that.

If Bets knew she was building an unhealthy box load (snappish, impatient, impossible expectations, poor sleep) she rented a "chick flick" —a term she hated, so condescending— where she could count on a death, breakup, or family separation. At some point the floodgates opened, sometimes by obvious cinematic emotional manipulation, which Bets recognized and resented, despite achieving great personal improvement from the subsequent cleansing weep.

When she was with Raz, she chose times when he was away, or on night shift, so he would not witness this ritual, even though he knew about it.

—You're not a robot, he would say, you have to feel something, sometime, you shouldn't be so ashamed of it. *C'est complètement normal.*

Without Raz, there were times when she wished she had someone, again, to lean on, cry on, complain to, laugh with, share with, coexist with. She worked hard not to fall into bottomless pits like nostalgia or regret, but they beckoned at times. She wrapped herself in work like a suit of protective armour, and if she ventured out into the dangerous world without her armour, the navigation would be tricky at best, likely impossible. Admittedly, work had its own minefields, but ones she was willing, had always been willing, to risk.

CHAPTER SIX

Hannah, despite her continuous fluster, was quite dependable. She showed up most Thursdays on Bets' doorstep, between 3:15 and 3:30 pm, full of braces and windblown hair and breathless energy. Bets alternated between annoyance at the weekly intrusion, anticipation of the conversation, and appreciation of the reliability, in this day and age when it seemed that teenagers—and young nurses, for that matter—cared for no one other than themselves. Some days, however, Bets just could not face the prospect of Hannah. The week of the stillbirth, she told Hannah it wasn't a good time to talk. She felt guilty and nearly changed her mind, then reminded herself of Raz's advice: Just say no. Then stop talking.

The next Thursday, after watching *Steel Magnolias* with predictable results, after a few good sleeps and a few uneventful shifts, she felt better.

Settling themselves at the table, Hannah removed her snow-sodden toque and shook her hair out like a dog, spraying the kitchen.

—Are you all right, Bets? Were you sick?

Her concern, unexpected, flooded Bets with warmth, and she came dangerously close to tears.

—No, no, I wasn't sick. She busied herself finding Hannah a towel. I had a difficult shift. I needed a bit of recovery time.

—There must be so many hard things in your job! People in pain, and people who have sick babies, and complications.

—How do you know about complications?

—Well, we're supposed to find out everything we can about our chosen profession. After we talked, I started looking up, you know, the different kinds of nurses, and I did some reading about maternity nurses. I hope you don't mind.

Bets handed over the towel, the scent of fabric softener clouding around them.

—Mind? Why would I mind?

—Well, you know, said Hannah, wrapping the towel around her hair like a turban, I'm supposed to be getting all of this information from you, with our talks. But I want to hear about other things, too. Like Raz, and you, and the other people on your wall. And my mom says I talk too much and I shouldn't be bothering you all the time. So I just thought I'd do extra reading.

—Hannah, I'll let you know if you're bothering me. I'm not known for putting up with things I don't like. You can tell your mom.

—Okay. Thanks.

—Let me ask you something, said Bets. How long is this project you're doing? Not that I mind, but—the entire semester? I can't picture all the students spending this much time.

—Well, actually, it was just supposed to be one or two interviews. Hannah steadied her towel-turban. But I don't know, I just wanted to keep coming. If that's okay.

—Sure, said Bets after a pause. Is everything all right at home?

Hannah picked at a thumbnail.

—Yeah, it's just nice to come here, and not have to think about school, or the store.

—The store?

—My parents have a deli. Downtown? I usually work there after school.

Bets waited for more information, but none was forthcoming. Hannah checked her notebook.

—I have a lot of questions about Raz after our last visit.

—Hannah, I can't do Raz today. I'm sorry.

Bets used her gentlest voice, but still prompted more thumb picking and glasses tapping.

—Sure. Sure. Okay, what about an example? Like we're talking about? A difficult situation at work?

It was right there: the opportunity to talk about the stillbirth, to share it instead of holding it deep inside her, yet Bets could not do it. The young woman sitting before her deserved to ease into the world of health care, and Bets had already bowled her over with tales of the first day and the dead body. She'd tried to keep things light for a while after that: fainting husbands, tangled IV lines, male babies peeing on people. Perhaps Hannah was ready for some heavier stories, but not stillbirth. Not yet.

—I'll tell you about something that often gets overlooked, she said finally. But every nurse, not just maternity nurse, needs to know about it, and look for it, and have a plan.

***

Bets, overall, felt that she helped people, although cringed at the phrase itself, with its sanctimonious overtones. She tried to treat everyone the same, and if a woman or her partner seemed a bit more down and out than usual, she might provide extra diapers to them before they left the hospital, or allow them to keep the donated onesies and sleepers the hospital provided.

There were times, however, when she wasn't sure if she, or other health care providers, had helped at all. Or if they had even caused harm.

They were trained to ask all the women if there were problems at home and if they felt safe. Bets agreed with the policy but found the results frustrating: women with black eyes or missing teeth had many excuses—clumsiness, falls down stairs, running into doors—or if they disclosed the truth, rushed into an explanation: he didn't mean to, he'd been drinking, he's changed, he loves me, he's so excited about the baby. Bets, possibly showing plain doubt, outlined options for these women, including safety plans, counsellors, resources, and signed them up to see the social worker, but they mostly declined. Unfortunately, no one ever knew the long-term outcomes, and Bets scoured the obituaries at times, just in case.

Child protection was part of the problem. The women knew that disclosure could mean losing their babies to a system designed to protect them. Trying to juggle a woman's safety versus her right to choose was difficult and heartbreaking enough, but trying to figure out whether a baby was better off with its own parents or some other temporary ones, was nearly impossible. There were rules, and you could get into big trouble not following the rules, but rules in the hospital, like everywhere in the world, didn't always work.

Violet came in full of confidence, thrilled about her baby, flashing her large diamond ring, bragging about her husband's money and all the new things she'd been able to buy for the nursery. She had an enormous cascade of dyed black curls, and false eyelashes thick as an old-fashioned doll. She had long shiny fingernails, the fourth fingers on each hand sporting little jewels at the tip of the nails. Another enormous diamond nestled on a chain between her ample breasts, which she assured Bets were real.

—These are my girls, my sugar babies, she said, lifting a breast in each hand, laughing. They just sit there making me money, all the time.

Bets found herself smiling, despite the caricature of the woman; admiring her unapologetic self.

When Bets helped Violet with her hospital gown, she saw the marks on Violet's back and wrists, but the worst was after removal of the small scarf around her neck.

—Violet, said Bets in her best neutral tone, did someone try to strangle you? Violet's face shifted momentarily before she returned to her sunny self.

—Oh, Freddie, haha, he doesn't know his own strength. We were just playing around a little bit, you know.

She lowered her voice and tipped her head toward Bets.

—In the *bedroom*.

Bets pretended being strangled during sex was a perfectly common expression of love.

—What did he hit you with, on your back?

—Oh, you're getting the wrong idea, protested Violet, he loves me, he does! He gets carried away sometimes is all. He buys me something really nice after, because he's so sorry. He even cries because he feels so bad.

Bets sat beside Violet on the bed, touched her arm.

—Violet, she said, your husband is hurting you on purpose. What if he hurts your baby?

Violet humphed.

—He'd have to get through me first.

—I don't doubt that, but what if he does? He hurt you while you were pregnant—what if he hurts you so much you can't protect your baby?

Bets let the question hang in the air for a moment before adding, in the softest butterfly- wing voice she could manage,

—Violet, I need to call child protection services.

Violet yanked her arm away from Bets.

—You can't call child protection! They'll take away the baby!

—That's not what this is about. They just need to know about your situation, so we can make sure the baby will be safe. The social worker can help you, give you options.

—They'll take my baby! I know they will! I should never have told you anything! Why didn't you mind your own business?

—Violet, I'm trying to help you. You're getting hurt.

—That's *my* business and I will deal with it. Now get out of here! I want another nurse!

—Violet…

—GET OUT!

Violet struck at her. Bets withdrew immediately, left the room, and called Shannon over.

—I need to call social work, she's being abused. She's kicked me out, can you cover labour and I'll take the next one?

—You think things will be different with me?

—I don't know, said Bets. But she won't let me back in. Just blame everything on me, and probably she'll be fine with you.

The labour proceeded as expected, and there were no issues with Shannon. Violet's partner, Freddie, showed up part way through the active labour.

—He wasn't what I expected at all, whispered Shannon to Bets when she came to the med room for supplies, he was all, "If you don't mind" and "Thanks so much" and holding her hand and stroking her forehead.

—Well, said Bets, it's not like they come in with a neon sign flashing "ABUSIVE."

Things changed when the social worker went in for her assessment. She brought the security guard as a precaution, and asked Freddie to leave, whereupon he discarded his smooth deferential demeanour.

—What's the meaning of this? Who called you? How dare you ask to speak to my wife without me present?

—It was her. It was that bitchy nurse. The skinny one, Violet told him.

—Where is she? I want to speak to her.

Murmurs from within the room. The deep voice of the security guard.

—I'm leaving, I *said* I was leaving, let go of my arm. Don't touch me!

Freddie walked out in front of James, the thick-necked security guard, whose arms swung widely at his sides due to his overdeveloped biceps. Bets deliberately remained at the desk. As they walked by, Freddie, clean shaven and black-haired, dressed in jeans and a beautifully pressed dress shirt, stopped to meet Bets' eyes.

—Are you the one who called the social worker?

—I am, said Bets.

James moved a step closer, even though the high counter separated Bets and Freddie quite effectively.

—Where the *fuck* do you think you get off, nosing in our business? He leaned forward into her face.

—Sir, said James, step back now.

Bets looked into the angry green eyes inches from her own and, without thinking, said,

—What happened to you that made you like this?

Freddie tried to jump at her across the counter, and in two swift moves, James had Freddie's arm up behind his back and his cheek against the countertop.

Bets stepped back, breath raspy, and raced down the hall, leaving James to his job.

—Call police, she said as she passed the registration desk, going straight to the staff washroom, locking herself in, and sinking to the floor, back against the door. The look in Freddie's eyes had been unlike anything she had ever experienced, a wild creature intent on its prey. The interaction had been over in seconds, yet she felt like she had sprinted a mile.

All she could think about was Violet and a tiny helpless newborn. Violet's candy-coated finish had cracked quickly enough, but she was clearly no match for Freddie. Bets pictured the baby crying, a background of shouting, screaming, crashing crockery, broken glass. She finished her shift, and Violet had not yet delivered her baby, but the police had come, and they had removed Freddie from the hospital.

All night, and in the shower the next morning, Bets wondered whether the baby had a chance. The best place for a child was with its mother, but what if the mother came with a monster? What if she herself was a monster? Foster homes were variable and temporary; children shuffled from home to home to home, during years when attachments were critical to their development. What was the right thing to do? What was a good outcome for Violet and her baby? Violet, so proud of her diamonds and her riches, who could clearly provide everything she wanted for her child... if she stayed with Freddie.

Bets didn't work the day they discharged Violet from hospital, the day the child was apprehended by Children's Services. It was Shannon who filled Bets in on the details during their next shift, in a rare lull where no one was in labour, no one needed support or medication, all babies were with their mothers, and there were no walk-ins. They went to the nursery to sort and fold the newly donated baby clothes.

—Bets, it was unbelievable, Shannon said in low tones, as if Violet herself would jump out from behind the baby warmer, hurling accusations. The social worker went in with two other workers and a security guard. They told Violet they were apprehending the child, and she just went crazy. Screaming, pushing people, trying to get out of the room, Shouting don't take my baby! Don't take my baby! Over and over. The whole floor could hear her. It was terrible.

Bets closed her eyes for a moment. The protective maternal instinct was so deep.

—Then, continued Shannon, pausing for effect, Freddie showed up. She raised her eyebrow, waiting for reaction, which she received.

—What? I thought he was taken out by police; he was forbidden on hospital property!

—Well, apparently, he didn't care about that. He showed up yelling, and Violet kept on screaming, and there was Jules the security guard.

—All five feet of her. Surely there should be a height requirement for security?

—You should have seen her, Bets! She stood in front of Freddie with her arms crossed and said sir, you are not allowed to be here. He actually stopped! He stood there looking at her and said, what are *you* planning on doing about it?

Bets stood clutching a onesie, all pretense of folding abandoned. Shannon adopted the pose and voice of Jules.

—She said, "Police are on their way. They were called the minute you stepped into this building. I suggest you leave right now before they get here and arrest you again, which will not help you two get your baby back."

—And then?

—And then, he swore a few times, and he yelled, "Violet! I'll be back for you!" Shannon used her best Rocky Balboa voice to imitate Freddie.

—And he *left*?

—And he left.

—And had anyone called the police? Was that true?

—No idea. But maybe being arrested the first time at least made him realize what he was getting himself into.

—And Violet?

—Kept screaming. Bets, you would not believe the words coming out of that girl's mouth, but now it was all focused on Freddie, calling him a coward, a fraud, a cocksucker, and worse, and then Jules did exactly the same thing with her.

Shannon folded a couple of sleepers, tossed her long ponytail behind her, not looking at Bets, clearly enjoying her performance.

—Meaning?

—She stood in front of Violet and said, "Listen. You're not helping yourself here. You think a screaming tantrum is going to get your baby back?" Because of course they had left with the child by then.

—And what did Violet say?

—Violet just stopped screaming and started crying.

—And what did Jules say?

—She said, "What you need to do is go back in your room, pack your things, and figure out whether being with that man is worth losing your child."

They had emptied one box of clothes. Bets carried the folded items and put them into the cupboards above the sink. She hauled a fresh box onto the table between them.

—Wow. Jules.

—I know. She's also a black belt.

—*Jules?*

Bets sat down for a moment, and Shannon stretched and arched her back.

—So Violet packed up and left?

—Yes.

—To go back to him?

—I'm not sure. I don't think she told anyone. She just left. They'd given her all the information, the shelters, the safety checklist, all that, but you know what she was like. I don't know if she even took the pamphlets with her.

—And where's the baby? Foster care? Grandparent?

—I don't know. The social worker is very particular about confidentiality.

—As she should be.

—I guess.

But deep down, they both felt as if they had a stake in the situation, and a right to know.

***

—So, did you ever find out? What happened? Hannah asked.

—Not for that one. I'd love to know. Hannah slumped back in her chair.

—I can't believe she stayed with him. If she did.

—I know. But it's what happens. I mean, he was providing for her, and who knows, maybe she really loved him. Love makes you do unexpected things sometimes. The point is, you need to look for these things, because women try to hide them. You need to know what options exist for them.

—But the story feels incomplete.

—I agree. But it's just being nosy once she's not under our care anymore. That's a good lesson, too.

Bets pointed at Hannah with her glass.

—Write that one down: confidentiality. You have to be able to keep a secret. You have to be able to come home and not tell your parents, or your partner, or anyone, any revealing details about the person.

—That sounds impossible!

—Sometimes it can be really hard.

Hannah paused, looking at her notes.

—So, was Violet her real name?

—Good question! And no, it wasn't. I don't use real names.

—But is your husband's name Raz?

—Yes, laughed Bets, I'm not bound by confidentiality with him!

Hannah started gathering her things, then sat back down.

—How do you know if someone will be like that?

—Great question. I wish I knew the answer. I think you need to look for signs, and get out as soon as you see them. Trust your gut.

Hannah swung her pack, knocked over her glass of water, and said goodbye. She didn't notice the water, which Bets watched as it puddled on the table, dripping slowly onto the floor.

CHAPTER SEVEN

S orry I'm late, puffed Hannah, it was the smokers.

—The smokers? Asked Bets, sweeping the napkin she'd been shredding into the garbage.

—Yes, the smokers. They always hang out in the alleyway beside the school, and I have to pass through to get home.

—And the smokers delayed you?

Hannah climbed into her chair, clawing hair away from her face.

—They always make a big thing about me stopping to have a smoke with them. They just want attention. Today my friend was there, so it was worse.

—Your friend smokes?

Hannah rolled her eyes.

—She's just doing it to be popular. It's so stupid. But of course, I couldn't say that with them all standing there.

—True.

Sometimes at work, even as a non-smoker, Bets felt that moments required a cigarette. Especially when recovering from something particularly stressful, especially when standing with someone for whom there were no useful words. The act of offering, lighting, sharing, seemed to say what a person could not. What else was possible? A stick of gum? In British novels and movies, people frequently offered cups of tea in difficult situations, but it was too involved. Waiting for water to boil, fussing with milk and sugar. She sometimes wondered, does anyone ever just sit and share now... without a screen of some kind, without a cigarette, without a drink? What do people do?

—Do you have any Coke? Asked Hannah.

Bets blinked, brought herself back to the present.

—Do you need caffeine?

—Sort of, said Hannah. But coffee was awful. No offense.

—None taken. What about tea?

—I'll try it.

Bets got out the electric kettle, noting the irony.

Hannah settled herself at the table, where a large wooden box sat in front of her.

—What's this? Can I look?

—It's silverware. I think I'm going to sell it, but it needs polishing. I thought we could do it while we talk.

Bets brought over a basin of water, the silver polish, some soft rags, and showed Hannah the basics.

—Do you smoke? Hannah asked Bets, fumbling with a fork.

—No. But my sister did. It always makes me think of her.

—I've been wanting to hear about your sister! Sisters are the best. Roxie, right?

—Roxie.

—As in Roxanne?

—Yes, but no one ever called her that. Except teachers. And my parents. You have brothers, then?

—I have neither. It's just me. And my parents. And the store.

—The downtown deli. Bets started on the knives.

—Yes, said Hannah. It runs my life.

—How does it run your life?

—Everything is about the store! Opening the store, closing the store, what happened to the order, the cash didn't balance, the shelves aren't tidy.

Hannah shook her head, finished her fork, grabbed another.

—That's why I like coming here. You don't tell me what to do every minute of the day.

—Do they know you come here to talk about being a nurse?

—Yes.

—So, no pressure to take over the store after you graduate?

Hannah gave an exhalation somewhere between laughter and frustration.

—Oh, there's pressure. We fight about it all the time.

Bets left a space, waiting for Hannah to fill it, wondering. They each developed a rhythm in their work, Hannah moving more slowly, sometimes dropping her rag on the floor.

—Maybe a sister or brother would make them see what I want, said Hannah finally. They don't listen to me.

—Maybe. Or maybe they'd be completely different from you. It can go both directions.

***

As children, left largely to their own devices, Roxie and Betsy spent a great deal of time together. Bets remembers feeling responsibility for her sister, for training and guiding her, even when she was only five or six years old. Bets could tell, even then, that her parents were not up to the task.

When Roxie was young, she talked all the time, chattering away to Bets, to her toys, to their parents, to complete strangers: one of the precocious toddlers that make people look and laugh and marvel. At home, Bets generally enjoyed the stream of consciousness, but she lived in fear when they were out.

—Look at that man! He has braids! Roxie shouted in the supermarket. Or, why do you only have one arm? Why is that man so fat? Why do you ride in one of those? (Pointing to the supermarket's motorized scooter). What's your baby's name?

People often stopped to talk to her, which horrified Bets. Despite herself, however, she learned about people. The man explained his braids and how important they were to his culture. The woman with one arm explained her work accident. Even the overweight man, surprising Bets, said, "Too many Twinkies, my dear," in a tone more amused than upset. It was like little Roxie was a walking confessional, and rarely did anyone say something angry to her.

Bets tried to picture her mother in these scenarios, but could not. When had she started using the clicker? Where was Roxie on the day of the pop bottle explosion? Her memory failed her, and the more she strained it, the less it gave her, crossing its arms and refusing to go further.

They usually stuck close to their mother in the supermarket, but sometimes went off on their own to look at things more interesting than chicken thighs and broccoli. They were sent, Bets recalled, to find cereal, and they could choose any cereal they wanted. Roxie chose her sugary cereal in two seconds flat, while Bets stood agonizing in the aisle, wanting to make sure she knew all the options, fearing the wrong choice.

—Betsy, just *choose*, said Roxie, pulling at Bets' sleeve. Bets shook her off.

—I want to make sure I'm getting what I want.

—But you don't even *know* what you want, said Roxie, sitting down on the floor and dancing her cereal box up and down. Bets ignored her and continued her assessment of each cereal. She finally chose some Shreddies.

—Okay fine, I'm done, she said, but when she turned, Roxie was gone.

Music played over the loudspeakers; people walked placidly with their carts of groceries, apparently unaware that the entire world had just turned sideways.

Bets was eight, but her thought was not to find her mother, only to find Roxie. She ran, looking down each side aisle as she went. She looked in the cashier lines, where gum and candy tempted right at child level. Scanning the glass front doors leading to the parking lot, she glimpsed a small blonde head. She ran out the front doors of the store, and there was Roxie, holding her cereal box, talking to a man who was old and had scruffy hair, and a beard, and a knitted hat even though it was spring, and whose coat looked ancient and tattered, and who, as Bets approached, smelled like the dirty laundry hamper at home.

—Roxie! She walked up and yanked Roxie's arm despite an intense wave of relief.

—What's wrong? I'm talking to Jimmy. He's down on his luck.

Jimmy smiled at Roxie, revealing a large space where his upper teeth should have been.

Bets recoiled slightly and focused on Roxie.

—Roxie, you can't just leave me like that, leave the store, that's very dangerous! Never do things like that!

—Don't worry, little lady, said Jimmy unexpectedly. I was about to send her back in. I'da made sure she didn't go out in the parking lot.

Roxie beamed at him and pulled her arm away from Bets.

—See, Betsy? Jimmy's nice. He's my friend.

Bets looked at the man, who looked like many other people she'd seen, when they were at the bank with their mother, or when they went downtown—rarely—to get ice cream. She remembered what her mother had said as she hurried them past.

—Are you... homeless? asked Bets, despite her inclination to march Roxie back into the store immediately.

Jimmy looked at the ground and scratched his head under his hat.

—Well, right now I stay at the shelter, so that's okay. I'm gonna figure things out. Roxie smiled up at him and held out her cereal box.

—Here, Jimmy, do you want this? Are you hungry?

Jimmy smiled back and took the cereal.

—Well thanks, there, Honey, I sure am hungry sometimes.

Jimmy and Roxie turned to look at Bets. She looked down at her cereal, chosen with such care, and took a moment before holding it out to Jimmy.

—Here, she said. You can have mine, too. We have to go. She took Roxie's hand and steered her back into the store.

—Have a nice day, ladies! Jimmy called.

—Why did you go out there in the first place? hissed Bets as she pulled Roxie along, scanning for their mother.

—I was following a lady. She had a red coat; it was so pretty.

Bets stopped and faced Roxie, hands on her shoulders.

—Never do that again. You have to always stay with me. Or Mom, she allowed. Until you're bigger. People could take you away!

—What people?

—Just, I don't know. People.

—And anyway, I'm already bigger, said Roxie, putting her hands on her hips. At that moment, their mother appeared with her cart.

—I was wondering where you two had gone! It's time to leave.

—We got cereal! shouted Roxie, jumping up and down, we gave it to Jimmy! He's down on his luck!

She skipped beside the grocery cart, one hand gripping the side.

—Okay, Roxie, said their mother, distracted, steering the cart around an elderly man wobbling on two canes. As they went into the parking lot—both girls now holding the cart, as was the rule—Roxie waved at Jimmy, who waved back. The boxes of cereal lay at his feet, and as they watched, a patron coming out of the supermarket took a jar of peanut butter out of a bag and set it down beside the cereal. Jimmy thanked the person and, seeing the girls watching, gave them a thumbs-up. As they helped their mother unload the shopping cart into the car, it dawned on Bets that Jimmy was begging outside the store.

And they had just stolen cereal and given it to a homeless man.

***

—She sounds fun! Said Hannah. I like her!

—Everyone liked her, said Bets, taking Hannah's mug and refilling it with tea. Everywhere we went.

—Was it hard, being her sister?

Bets paused with her mug halfway to her mouth.

—Yes, sometimes it was very hard being her sister. Very hard. We were very different.

—You were more practical.

—Yes, and she was more, I don't know.

—Carefree?

—Yes. Carefree. She was carefree, I think. For a while.

***

Roxie, perpetually happy and full of energy, complied initially. Like many younger siblings, she just wanted to be with Bets and do whatever Bets did. She did everything with more noise, more exuberance; she sang, she coloured outside the lines, she made up alternate endings for Bets' beloved books even as they sat reading them together. Bets could tell that she would not be able to contain Roxie for long; she remembers the alternate endings with a sense of awe, but also remembers telling Roxie to stop. That's not how it goes. You can't just change it when it's already written. You *can't*. And yet, she waited for the ideas she herself had never even considered: Sleeping beauty wakes up, smacks the prince for taking so long, and tells him to clean up the messy castle overrun with weeds. Cinderella tells her stepmother and stepsisters she's going to the ball, but instead she locks everyone out of the house and kidnaps the fairy godmother so she can have whatever she wants. They were hilarious and freeing, but they bothered Bets for reasons she couldn't explain. Some days, she just shut the book with a snap, and Roxie screeched, "Betsy is the evil stepmother! Betsy is the evil stepmother!" falling on the couch giggling.

Their favourite game, for a while, was the mirror game: they took their mother's old- fashioned silver-edged hand mirror and held it in front of them, reflecting the ceiling, if inside, or the sky, if outside, and pretended the world was upside down. They imagined walking along the ceiling, jumping over the chandelier, or they created adventures that centred around the brown water stain in the bedroom, the ceiling fan, the bed that might shift and fall onto their heads. Outside, the mirror showed sky, clouds, tree-tops, and that was where they lived in their game, mostly jumping cloud to cloud, or chasing birds out of trees so they could live there.

Roxie's friend, what was her name? Bets closed her eyes. Georgina. Her friend came over and the two sisters were playing their mirror game and Bets still remembers Georgina's nasal voice sneering, this game is *stupid.* It's *boring.* Let's do something else! She remembers Roxie standing back, looking from Bets to Georgina, like she had never considered that the game might not be desirable. After an endless moment, she handed the mirror back to Bets, not meeting her eyes, and took Georgina's hand, and they ran together, toward the big sugar maple in the yard, the one Roxie always wanted to climb, and Bets refused because it seemed dangerous. Your sister's no fun, she heard Georgina say as they ran off.

After that, Roxie spent less time at home and more with her friends. Or, if she had a friend over, they did their own thing, and Bets was not involved. Bets convinced herself that she didn't want to be down at the creek digging up dragonfly nymphs, she didn't want to build a ragtag treehouse, she didn't want to ride a bicycle around town, ringing doorbells and running away. As if she would ever do that! There weren't many children her age in the area, and she felt overwhelmed at the idea of joining a softball game or other activity already in progress, while Roxie just walked up, caught the ball in the outfield and threw it to first base as if already part of the team. She came home filthy, her hair everywhere, her shoes missing, her feet black from the street or the woods, always ravenous, always laughing and with some story to tell. Betsy loved hearing the stories but also felt like her insides were being gradually scooped out of her, cupful by cupful, story by story. Her parents smiled at Roxie, and nodded, and made little noises of either approval or apprehension. Her mother often told Roxie to comb her hair, while her father sometimes launched into a story of his own childhood; he had about five and cycled through them in rotation.

Roxie did well in school, despite her endless socializing. She rarely studied anything, she rarely got into trouble, and if the teacher called on her as a surprise because she was chattering with a friend, she often knew the answer. She was athletic, artistic; she had flocks of students of both genders around her all the time, wanting to be a part of her inner circle, wanting a piece of the phenomenon that was Roxie: a break from the tedium of times tables and phonics and rules.

—*That's* your sister? People said to Bets admiringly, and Bets felt herself slide up a notch in their esteem.

—*That's* your sister? People said to Roxie, looking Bets up and down, shrugging with indifference. Roxie always smiled, she grabbed Bets, she showed her off, she hugged her in public, she never passed her without saying hello. Bets, after a while, just waved, and kept on walking.

—Why didn't you stop to talk at school today? Roxie asked her one day, falling into step as they walked home.

Bets was in grade six, the top grade at the school, a coveted position.

—You looked busy with your friends.

—Just because my friends are there doesn't mean you can't be there.

—I know.

—Do you? Asked Roxie, stopping. Bets stopped as well.

—What's that supposed to mean?

—I feel like you're mad whenever I'm with my friends.

—I'm not mad.

—Okay.

—I said I'm not mad!

—Ooookay.

Roxie had a gaze that went right through Bets sometimes. Bets wanted to grab Roxie in the tightest hug she could manage, wanted to tell her she missed her and wanted to be friends again, wanted to tell her to be careful, to look out for people, not to be taken in by their adoration, that they could never love her like Bets. Instead, she said,

—I have to get going.

She walked away from Roxie, just as a cluster of younger girls flocked past her, squealing to find Roxie alone.

***

Hannah, finished with the silver, was balancing her pen on her upper lip like a moustache. She let it fall onto the table.

—I still wish that I had a sister. Even if she was different from me. At least it wouldn't just be me.

—I think I'd feel that way in your position, said Bets.

***

Roxie had what Bets would call a "natural high:" happy, full of energy, full of ideas. Why, thought Bets for the millionth time, would Roxie need drugs or alcohol?

Bets could have used some euphoria at times. It's hard to beat a feeling of confidence, of peace, a feeling that all will be well… rather than her constant foreboding sense of it all going terribly wrong.

Bets didn't drink very often, but she saw the appeal. It was, she had to admit, easier to blend into a group with one or two glasses of wine on board, it was easier to find words, easier to enjoy others' company, easier to get outside her own head and silence the judgements that surfaced. But the falling-down-drunk, slurring, staggering, making ridiculous expressions of love, or questionable, dangerous choices—what was the point of that? She tried to ask Roxie once, as she sat up with her yet again, as Roxie vomited into the toilet, and then lay murmuring softly with her cheek against the cold tile floor.

She knew she didn't have to stay up with her. Roxie always told her not to, but she did it anyway. Who else would look out for Roxie? And if not for Bets, who would make sure the bathroom the girls shared looked and smelled clean by morning?

Maybe I should have left it, thought Bets. Maybe if forced to face the evidence, my parents would have done something. But surely, they had known. What could they do? Ground her, lock her in her room? You might as well try to catch wind in a basket, hold waves in your fingers. Roxie was an uncontainable force.

Roxie said she got drunk because it was fun. Sometimes she said it right before vomiting, and found the irony hilarious, and clutched the toilet bowl, shaking with laughter.

—Why, doesn't it look fun? she'd slur, then heave again.

—You should try it sometime, Bets, she whispered later, when she was lying on the floor, and Bets was applying toilet bowl cleaner.

—You just don't care; you just do what's most in your heart. You're strong, and you can believe in things. In yourself.

She was difficult to understand and kept pausing. Bets stopped scrubbing and looked at her sister, toilet brush in hand.

—But why go to such extremes? You're always strong. You can believe in things without booze on board. Or other, you know. Substances.

The response was a gentle snore. Bets finished with the toilet and sat down heavily on the floor, back against the wall.

—I'm worried about you, she said to Roxie's snoring form. I'm worried you're not in control of this, it's happening so often. I'm worried no one will watch out for you when I go to university. I'm worried you're going to get into an accident, or that you'll damage your brain and you won't be Roxie anymore.

Bets peeled away her rubber gloves and cleared her throat in response to the tremor in her voice.

—You don't need this stuff. You are so full of life. You don't need this stuff. And I need, *I* need you to be okay. You're my only sister.

Roxie was fast asleep, or passed out, what was the difference anyway? Bets sat with her for a while longer before waking her up and helping her stagger into bed, making sure she lay on her side. Bets climbed in the other side and lay listening to Roxie breathing until she, too, fell asleep.

The next day, close to noon, Bets asked her again. Roxie was grayish and had large circles under her eyes. She drank coffee and smoked a cigarette beside the open window, blowing the smoke outside. Bets got a large glass, filled it with ice and water, and set it on the counter beside Roxie.

—Do you have to make so much noise with the ice? Roxie winced.

—Do you have to go out and get ridiculously drunk all the time and vomit all over our bathroom? Bets instantly regretted her words.

—I can do what I want. You're not my mother.

Roxie drank some of the water, then returned to the coffee. She tapped her cigarette outside the window. Their mother had gone to visit a friend and seemed completely unaware that anything had occurred in the middle of the night.

—No, said Bets. So why am I always looking after you?

Roxie left her cigarette butt in her coffee cup. Bets fished it out, threw it outside, and rinsed the mug. *The question is,* she thought as she dried the mug, *which one of us is making me angrier?*

CHAPTER EIGHT

In life, Bets felt, there were many acquaintances, but few friends. Even the so-called popular people, the extroverts, continually surrounded, how many could they truly count as intimate friends? As people who understood, who were unconditional, who said I accept you for you? Not many, she suspected. Maybe not any. Imagine discovering, one day, that your coterie of admirers was nothing more than illusion; that all could change in a moment, alliances shifting, loyalties vanishing like smoke. Bets knew a lot of people but had few friends. Those she had, she knew were true.

At various times, despite years, even decades, Bets had looked at Raz with a twinge of guilt, or amazement. How had this relationship happened? He came, he stayed. Having him was like having a glass sphere that surrounded and protected her, that was fragile, that could break at any time, having been conjured from thin air.

She'd had Katie for nearly the first half of her life. Things between them had never recovered from their trip, although they tried for a while. When Bets questioned the awkwardness, Katie admitted seeing Raz reminded her of losing Sam and the intense stress that had provoked. Shortly thereafter, Carter transferred to Ottawa for work and the family moved away. Bets planned to visit. Each year when she got their family Christmas photo, she planned to visit, seeing Sam with missing teeth, and then bad haircuts and acne, and suddenly the square jaw and prominent brows of a man. Somehow the visit never happened, and when Sam's university graduation photo arrived in the mail, signed by Katie, Bets thought, *he doesn't even know who I am.*

Now, she had Shannon. Months after Raz was gone, Shannon still appeared intermittently with muffins, or bread, or eggs. Sometimes a plant, along with instructions for maintenance and pleas not to kill it. Sometimes she stayed for a few minutes, or a half hour, sometimes she just dropped off and left. Shannon, with her aura of peace, her gentle understanding, her tidbits of gossip, could mean the difference between a day in pyjamas and a day of doing something productive. Thank God for Shannon, thought Bets, or who knows where I'd be. Still in bed under the covers, likely. Soiled and emaciated.

After dropping off a salad one day, Shannon stayed just long enough to hint that the latest locum's gum-chewing habit might be hiding an alcohol problem. She turned and nearly ran into Hannah, who was jumping up the steps two at a time without looking ahead of herself.

—Whoa! shouted Shannon, turning to the side as Hannah barrelled past.

—Sorry! Sorry, I wasn't looking! Hannah paused.

—Are you a friend of Bets'?

—I'm Shannon. She held out her hand. You must be Hannah.

—Yes. She shook Shannon's hand firmly.

—Are you a nurse? Bets is teaching me about nursing.

—Yes, said Shannon. Bets teaches me about nursing, too.

She looked sideways at Bets, tucking a strand of hair behind her ear, a corner of her mouth curling up.

—Don't listen to her, said Bets from the top of the stairs. She teaches me, not the other way around.

—Hannah smiled, looking back and forth between them, bouncing on the balls of her feet.

—Well, you have enough energy for both of us, laughed Shannon. Go give some to Bets.

She waved and continued down to her car. Hannah finished leaping up the steps, pausing when a book flew out of her bag onto the steps. Bending to retrieve it, she dropped her gloves.

—Good lord, Hannah. I've never seen someone so prone to dropping things.

—I know, said Hannah cheerfully, it's true. I don't know why I'm like that. Have you and Shannon been friends for a long time?

—A really long time, said Bets. Longer than you've been alive.

—Do you have a friend group? She asked, as Hannah flopped onto the couch, fished for her notebook.

—Honestly? I'm not sure. There were three of us, since elementary school, but now things are, I don't know. Different.

—Different?

—I just feel like we're maybe going in different directions.

Hannah flipped through her notebook.

—Kayla's smoking, and it's just to be cool, she doesn't even like it. She's trying to impress the popular girls, and they don't care about her, but she won't listen to me. And Zoey used to be really supportive, but now she says nursing is stupid because I'll never be in charge. She says I should run the store.

Bets considered the weight that teenagers gave to the opinions of other, equally inexperienced teenagers.

—What do you think?

—I think nursing sounds great, said Hannah, and I think the store is stupid. And I know sometimes you're in charge, right?

—Sometimes, said Bets. You could be a doctor, if you want.

Hannah snorted.

—No, I couldn't. My grades aren't high enough. Plus, it's, I don't know. Pretentious. It's what all the overachievers want.

—Well, sometimes it's nice to *not* be the person responsible for everything, too.

—Yeah, like my parents, stressing all the time!

Hannah made a frustrated noise.

—Anyway. My friends and I still text and everything. I'm just sort of taking a break.

—A break can help a lot, sometimes, agreed Bets.

—Shannon seems nice, Hannah said, changing her tone. Is there, did something happen to her face?

—She had a Bell's palsy a long time ago. It causes muscle paralysis on one side of your face, and she didn't fully recover. That's a good nursing observation, Hannah.

—Is she your closest friend?

—Shannon has saved me many times.

***

They were friends during nursing training, often on the same clinical rotation, and developed a rhythm in their work. It was Shannon, months after that memorable first shift, who had told Bets about the disciplinary meeting and its outcome for nurse Scary.

—How did you know about that? Bets asked her.

—I listen. Shannon tapped her ear. People in health care talk and don't even realize they're talking, let alone that someone might be listening.

Bets had noticed Shannon initially because, despite a large Indigenous population in the community, it was still unusual to see someone in a professional role, at that time. She noticed Shannon's height, her long, silky black hair, and also the slight asymmetry of her face, the way the left eye, cheek, side of her mouth never quite moved as much as the right.

But as they worked, what she noticed was Shannon's quiet manner, her gentle way with patients, her thoughtfulness. Bets noticed and tried to emulate her. During every interaction, Shannon straightened the bedclothes, asked about pain, ensured the water glass was filled and cold, explained who she was, and why she was there. Most of the nursing students were in a constant state of overwhelm, and sometimes forgot to even say what they were doing before doing it. Patients, understandably, lost patience when they were suddenly moved without warning, or their covers were pulled away without explanation. Older, confused patients in particular, had to be approached quietly, with lots of preparation, or they might punch or yell. Sometimes Bets heard a great bellow, followed by a young colleague skittering out of a room to collect herself in the hallway, trembling.

Such events were rare with Shannon, who knew just how to approach, talking calmly even if they were hard of hearing, listening to their confused conversation. Some insisted they had to get to work, had to catch a bus, when in fact they'd been in hospital for months.

—Where do you work? She'd ask, instead of saying don't be ridiculous, of course you don't need to go to work, you're in the hospital. They'd often tell her while she spooned in some breakfast, or handed them a tiny cup with their pills.

—Which bus do you take? She'd ask, as she set up the basin at the bedside —Let's sit you up— as she listened, helping them prepare for a morning wash.

Shannon was good with her hands. She could insert intravenous lines into the most difficult veins; the ones that were tiny and impossible to see, and the ones that appeared large as hoses yet rolled away the moment the needle approached, as if in fear. More than once, early on, Bets struggled with her intravenous lines and just as the patient balked and asked for a proper nurse, Shannon appeared and spoke in her kind tones, and asked the person's veins why they were not cooperating with Bets this morning, as if the veins themselves were at fault. Even if unsuccessful, she made the patient feel they were a special case, a difficult puzzle, rather than the subject of clinical inexperience.

As students, they had individual assignments, but more and more they worked together, getting their work done more quickly as a team than either of them could alone. With four hands, they could shift heavy patients, change gowns and bedding, do dressings and catheters with great efficiency, all the while having conversations with the patients, being careful not to just speak to each other. Bets, after a time, tried to suggest that the nurses work in team assignments all the time, but experienced her first taste of a system digging in its heels, saying this is the way we do it. Who are you to change things?

When no one was around, Shannon could do dead-on impressions of other nurses, doctors, patients. She loved to whisper-drop tiny explosions of gossip when Bets least expected them:

—Guess who's taking over as manager? Guess who's sleeping with the medical resident that started last week? Guess who was caught stealing from the narcotics cart?

Boom.

—How do you always know these things? Bets asked, shaking her head, or laughing. Shannon just tapped her ear.

Early on, Bets had noticed things but didn't always process them. Some patients pulled away when Shannon touched them, but didn't with Bets. Some were more direct:

—Your kind aren't clean. I prefer my own people looking after me.

In those cases, Shannon said, All right, I'll leave you with Bets then. She'll do a wonderful job with your care.

Sometimes she even smiled at them before leaving, and Bets felt she needed to say something, or do something, but what?

It wasn't just the patients. Bets heard other nurses talking about drunken Indians in the ER, about "those Natives with all their kids," speaking about laziness, lack of jobs, the free ride they had, their horrible living conditions, as if they chose to live eight to a crumbling home, or on the street in winter. Bets had once heard a physician say, "Well, I'll treat him, and then he'll go into withdrawal, and he'll leave, and get drunk, and we'll find him in a snowbank again tomorrow. That's the way it is with these people. They can't help it, it's the way they're made."

As a student, Bets had observed these things, absorbed them, felt within herself a nodule of anger forming, firmly attached like a weed, one you try to pull from the lawn but cannot, and which, if you ever succeed in its removal, comes all at once with an enormous root, leaving behind an unexpected and significant hole.

Shannon, like Bets, listened to the flurry of conversation around her but rarely contributed. She had a great sense of humour and could burst out laughing, sometimes when the other nurses (or patients) were deliberately being funny, and occasionally when they weren't.

She and Bets often exchanged amused glances as conversations went on around them. They liked their rhythm, knew when to help and when to stay back, were good at keeping an eye out for each other during a shift. Over the years, they both gravitated to the maternity floor, and remained there.

Early on, Bets was at the desk charting when a patient's husband asked her to come in to his wife's room.

—The squaw there, she wants you to come, he said, with a slight smirk.

—You mean your nurse? *Shannon*?

Bets injected as much cold as she could into each word. After the baby came, when they were back at the desk and alone, she finally spoke.

—Was that man as rude to you in there as he was out here?

—What'd he say?

—He called you a squaw.

Shannon's mouth tightened, barely perceptible.

—He wasn't that blatant, but he questioned everything I did. Asked if I spoke English when we first met, told me he didn't want the placenta for any weird rituals like "my folk."

—How do you stand it? Don't you get angry?

—You get used to it.

—That wasn't the question.

Shannon stopped fiddling with forms.

—I get angry. But what's the point? People like that don't deserve much thought. Or much time. At some point, anger will consume you.

—And yet you looked after his wife's birth.

—*She* didn't say anything. And if she had— Shannon thought for a moment—I guess I just block my feelings out of it, just think, this is a lady in pain, so she wants me to hurt, too. Usually, they're not like that.

—Well, I wanted to punch him in the face.

—Which would cause you to lose your job. And then where would I be? Shannon gestured around her.

—Here, all by myself! Without my fierce protector!

She touched Bets' arm and went back into the delivery room.

In general, Bets felt the other nurses respected Shannon. She hadn't heard comments from them, but it was not the first time with a disrespectful patient. On the other hand, comments weren't always race-based, they could be gender-based, too. All the nurses experienced it, from a leering "How about a sponge bath?" to grabs at body parts, to being treated like the help in someone's home. Maybe, thought Bets, that's actually why I ended up in maternity, to avoid the ogling and the comments. But for Shannon, there's no escape. What do I do about it? The question lingered in her mind, unanswered.

Shannon and Bets were both new to the maternity unit when there was a bad outcome, as sometimes happened. A terrible hemorrhage, where the baby had to be transferred out, and the mother ended up in intensive care. Hierarchies were still clearly delineated then and, at such times, provided the only path for frustration and anger. The physician yelled at the senior nurse, who listened wordlessly, then turned on Shannon, blaming her for things no junior nurse could possibly have known or controlled. Bets heard about it from her peers and searched the floor until she found Shannon hiding in the equipment supply room. Her eyes were red, but dry.

Bets sat on the floor beside Shannon, sharing the silence, passing it back and forth. The hallway noises were barely audible as they sat surrounded by boxes and boxes of pads and dressings and sterile-wrapped forceps and clamps and scissors. Shannon shifted her weight, and a stack of metal K-basins shifted with a clang, causing Bets to jump.

—I think I'm done with this, Shannon said finally.

—With what?

—With nursing. I'm not cut out for it.

—What are you talking about? You're a wonderful nurse, you know everything! Bad stuff happens, Shannon, you know that. It's not your fault.

—Geneviève was pretty sure it was my fault.

—Right, and the doctor was pretty sure it was Geneviève's fault. Shannon was quiet.

—I've heard, said Bets, in some places they have a meeting after something like this. To figure out what went wrong and make things better. Like the way there was no O-negative blood on site—things like that. They make sure everyone is okay. Instead of blaming each other.

She touched Shannon's arm. Shannon sniffed.

—Well, we don't have that here. And they're already looking for reasons for me to fail.

—What do you mean?

Shannon gestured to her own hair and body.

—You mean because you're… Bets trailed off.

—Yes, because I'm Cree, because all they see is an Indian!

Bets started to protest, but in a flash could hear physicians speaking sharply to Shannon, senior nurses berating her, patients speaking rudely. She had seen it, but never addressed it.

—God, Shannon, I'm a terrible friend. I forget about it, sometimes, because I don't have to live it. And I never know what to do. I'm sorry.

—No, said Shannon, leaning her head back against the shelves. You're not a terrible friend. You're the only person who doesn't notice I'm different.

After a time—miraculously, no one came in for supplies—Bets cleared her throat.

—Well, she said, if you're done, you're done. But if you go, then I'm going, too.

—What? What are you talking about?

—I'll go, too. We'll go and work someplace else. I can't be here without you; it would be terrible. Who'd I hang around with, Geneviève?

Shannon let out a little squeak of laughter, covered her mouth. She took Bets' hand, squeezed, released. They shared the silence again.

—Okay, Shannon said finally, here's what we'll do. We'll keep going, and we'll watch for a sign. Something that tells us what to do.

—Are you religious? Asked Bets, surprised.

—Not really. But the world knows what we need, that's what I think.

—What kind of sign will you look for?

Bets pictured spotlights, angels, artifacts.

—I don't know. But when it happens, I think we'll know whether to stay or go.

Bets found the plan a bit irrational, but Shannon sounded like she was possibly staying, and that was enough for her. They left the supply room, and no one said a word, or had even noticed they were gone, which in itself was a sign for Bets, so unusual was it to escape constant supervision.

A few weeks later, Annie came, already in active labour. She was a young woman from far up the James Bay coast, who had transferred at thirty-six weeks, as many people did, to wait for delivery in a city with anesthetists and obstetricians, rather than the local nursing station. Bets was on labour and delivery, and she and her senior nurse, Max, saw the immediate problem when Annie spoke to them.

—We don't speak Cree, said Max. Do you speak English? Annie grimaced with a contraction, gripped the sides of the bed.

—They usually come with a translator, muttered Max, as if inability to speak English was quite inconsiderate.

—Sister, said Annie. My sister.

—Is she coming? Max asked. Annie shook her head, curled into a ball on the bed, let out a wail.

—Well, this is a problem, said Max to Bets. She's really active, and the sheet says this is baby number three.

—I'll get Shannon. Maybe she can help.

—Why would she be able to help?

—I think she speaks Cree.

When Bets found Shannon in the nursery, her friend was doubtful.

—I haven't spoken Cree in years. I don't know.

—Shannon, the woman's going to deliver having no idea what any of us are saying. Come on!

Bets grabbed Shannon's hand and pulled. After some initial resistance, Shannon followed.

In the labour room, Annie cried out loudly just as they entered.

—She won't let me check her, said Max, who was setting up the delivery table. I can't explain to her.

—Annie, said Bets, once the contraction had passed, this is Shannon. Shannon stepped forward, eyes anxious.

—*Wâciye, Annie.*

The transformation was immediate. Hearing her own language, however imperfect, Annie's demeanour changed. She reached for Shannon, chattering away to her. Shannon made a few responses, and Annie slowed herself down. Shannon listened, nodded, frowned in concentration, said a few words more. She gestured to Max. Annie nodded just as another contraction started. Shannon talked her through it, then turned to the other two nurses.

—I can't understand everything. Her Cree is a bit different from what I'm used to, but there's a problem with her sister who was supposed to come with her. Her husband has their other kids, he's still up North. She's asking us to call her cousin—or it might be her aunt, I can't remember the words—and she doesn't want pain meds. She just wants the cousin. Or aunt.

Shannon gestured to Max again.

—I told her you need to see if she is ready to deliver and then we can figure out calling the family member.

Annie whimpered, followed by a long, low grunt.

—Maybe we don't need to check, observed Bets. She's pushing.

Shannon spoke to Annie, who was crying and starting to get wide eyes and thrash on the bed. She spoke in low tones, and Annie's breathing slowed, and Bets and Max swooped into action, getting the bed ready, removing the blankets, getting the baby warmer and equipment.

With the next contraction, under Shannon's guidance, Annie pushed, and they could all see thick dark hair emerging. Annie shouted, panted, and with coaxing, reached down to touch the baby's emerging head. Her face broke into a smile, the first they'd seen since she arrived.

Bets heard a noise behind her, and the doctor was there, but making no move to the bedside. Normally, the doctors rushed in and the nurse's role changed immediately to that of assistant. This time, they all watched as Shannon talked Annie through her delivery, a three-push affair with immediate crying from the baby as Shannon placed him on his mother's chest. She looked up for the first time, saw Bets and the doctor, moved aside immediately to stand beside Annie, who was murmuring to her new baby, marvelling at his thick black hair, which was standing straight up.

—Sorry, doctor, said Shannon, but he shook his head.

—I didn't want to disturb such a smooth delivery, he said.

After the placenta, he did a quick check on Annie and stood up briskly.

—Nothing for me to do here. He removed his gloves, shook Annie's hand, then turned and shook Shannon's as well.

Bets checked and weighed the baby, rolled him into his blanket, gave him back to Annie, who expertly put him to breast for a first feeding. Max left for another delivery, and Bets cleaned up the floor and delivery table.

—I should get back to the nursery. I'll call her aunt/cousin. She had this in her pocket.

Shannon held up a piece of paper with a telephone number on it.

When the department had settled down, Bets found Shannon cleaning out cots in the nursery.

—That was a great delivery.

—Gotta love multips, said Shannon, wiping the plastic sides of a cot. Too bad you can't have your third baby first, much easier.

—You know what I mean.

Bets stood beside her, bumped her with her hip.

—What did Annie say to you when you were leaving?

—She thanked me. Shannon stopping her cleaning. She said I made her calm, and then she said she's never had a nurse who spoke her language at a birth, and so this was her very best one. She said I saved her life by being there.

Shannon glanced at Bets, half-smiled.

—Or something like that, anyway.

They didn't really talk about it. They didn't really need to.

CHAPTER NINE

Please don't take this the wrong way, said Hannah.

—Uh oh, said Bets, setting Hannah's tea mug down on the table.

—I just… do you ever wonder what it would be like to be beautiful? Like, really beautiful?

Hannah looked at Bets from beneath her froth of hair, glasses sliding down her nose.

—Define beautiful.

Bets kept her face neutral, trying not to be insulted even as she fully understood the question.

—You know, Hannah waved her hands. Beautiful! Gorgeous. Perfect.

—Different for everyone. Bets crossed her arms, stretched out her legs. There's no single, definite beautiful. Internal. External.

—Do NOT talk about having a good personality. You know what I mean!

—I do. I do know what you mean. I'm just trying to challenge your meaning, Hannah. As you get older, your feelings about beauty change.

Hannah spun her mug slowly for a moment, watching it.

—Do you think I can ever be beautiful?

Bets felt the question deep inside her, a squeeze somewhere, recognizing, remembering. She didn't pause, it was critical not to.

—I do, Hannah. I definitely do. There are so many beautiful things about you right now, and you're right, sometimes we kind of, I don't know. Grow into beauty. And, in the end, it might not be quite what you think.

Hannah looked slightly puzzled at this response, but her face brightened a bit.

***

In adolescence, Bets had gone through the usual stages: unbecoming haircuts, braces to close the gap between her front teeth, a bout of acne that made her cringe to leave the house. She felt like turning herself inside out, keeping her outer self hidden until maturity, as if skinless glistening muscles and undulating intestines would distract from the harsh reality of her outer appearance. If she could have built a cocoon for a couple of years, she would have; she envied butterflies their ability to transform fully before revealing themselves to the world. She wore oversized shirts, baggy jeans. She ducked her head, avoided eye contact. More than once, well-meaning teachers asked if everything was all right at home. She looked at them in bewilderment: what, at home, could be worse than the self she was projecting onto the world?

Later, Bets felt warmth spread over her as she thought of those brave teachers, bothering to notice her, bothering to care that instead of herself, perhaps she was trying to hide from alcoholism, or divorce, or abuse. Maybe an eating disorder. She told them she was fine, and other than her appearance she was, but of course, at that time, appearance was everything.

Roxie, at the same time, developed from a beautiful child to a stunning young adult. Her hair was thick and shiny, and every haircut looked just right, provoking a slew of imitators at the school, but no one pulled it off like Roxie did. Her eyelashes were long and dark without mascara, her eyes were large, her laugh infectious. Her legs grew long and well defined, her breasts became round and full, seemingly overnight. Bets saw people turn to watch Roxie walk by; she looked at Roxie, and looked at people looking at Roxie, and thought, what's the point? She could get her braces off and get a good haircut and wear different clothes, and it wouldn't change a thing. There would still be the endless refrain of people saying, that's your *sister*?

Bets understood the universal attraction to Roxie, but took a while to comprehend the extent of this attraction. She began to hear comments like, I'm meeting Roxie after school, if you know what I'm saying. Or, Hey, have you spent time with Roxie behind the stadium? Always boys, who guffawed and shook each other's shoulders, or punched each other lightly. They never noticed that she was nearby.

She wandered out to the sports field one day, when there was track practice going on, but no one else around. She walked slowly behind the stadium bleachers, unsure of her motivation, unable to deny her curiosity. Halfway around, largely but incompletely hidden by the bleachers, was Roxie, or at least Roxie's hair, spread on the ground, and Roxie's long legs, wrapped around a boy who was lying on top of her, pants around his knees.

Bets turned abruptly and started to leave, and then didn't. Instead, she sat on the ground a few sections down, her back against a pillar, and waited. A few minutes later, the boy walked past her briskly, straightening his shirt, not even seeing her. After a while, Roxie also ambled out, saw Bets immediately, and sat down, crossing her legs in front of her, smoothing her skirt over her thighs, a gesture that Bets found ironic under the circumstances.

—Hiya Betsy, whatcha doing?

Roxie lit a cigarette and took a deep inhale.

—Don't call me that.

—Okay… want a smoke?

—No, thank you.

—Okay.

—What the hell are you doing, Roxie?

Roxie blew smoke away from Bets.

—I'm having a cigarette behind the bleachers.

—You know what I mean.

—I'm having a bit of a fuck behind the bleachers.

—Yes, I got that part. Why, though?

Roxie laughed softly.

—Do you really have to ask?

—That's not what I mean. You've been doing half the senior class, if the rumours are true.

—Is that the rumour? Roxie leaned back and smiled. You can't even say the word, can you?

—Do you really want to be the school slut?

—Might as well be known for something, said Roxie pointedly. Bets fell silent, then spoke again.

—What if you get pregnant?

—I won't.

—Said every girl in high school who ever got pregnant.

—I'm not stupid, Bets. Roxie waved her cigarette. I just enjoy sex, okay, and I enjoy attention. You know this. And I always use, you know, protection.

Roxie blew smoke while Bets picked at the grass for a moment.

—You know it's not true, the douching with Coke, right?

—Oh my GOD, Bets, laughed Roxie, you're such an old woman! No, I'm not douching with fucking Coca-Cola. Jesus.

—What about, you know. Bets paused. Diseases?

—Did I not just say I was using protection? Answered Roxie. Anyway, what's it to you? Wouldn't you love to see me get pregnant? Or get a disease?

—What are you talking about?

—Oh, I don't know, the *looks* you give me. And the homeless person getup—gesturing at Bets' outfit—is making me think you might have some weird psychotic thing going on.

—What? Bets rearranged her shirt, played with a button. I just don't want to show my body right now, all right?

—Why not?

Bets glared at Roxie, who seemed genuinely perplexed.

—Because I'm not you, Roxie, some of us have weird proportions, and hair that isn't perfect, and pimples and braces, and look terrible instead of having every boy we see want to take us for a fuck behind the stadium!

Roxie ground out her cigarette. She stood up.

—You're right, she said, you're not me. Believe me, you don't want to be me. But no one thinks you're ugly except you, Bets.

Roxie bent, grabbed Bets' chin in her hand.

—You're the one who has decided to be invisible. Roxie kissed Bets' lips, then pushed Bets' face away.

—And that's definitely not me!

She threw her arms in the air and did a spin, shouting Meeeeeeee! She flipped her hair from her face, saluted Bets.

—See you later, Betsy.

Strode off, leaving Bets alone under the stadium.

A short while later, a gangly looking boy appeared, hands in pockets, shoulders hunched, hair falling into his face. After looking around for a few moments, his gaze fell on Bets.

—Are you Roxie?

Bets gave a snort.

—No, I am definitely not Roxie.

—Oh. They said I could meet up with her here.

—Nope. She left.

The boy's prominent Adam's apple bobbed as he thought. He looked back at Bets.

—What about you? Do you want to...

Instantly, Bets was on her feet.

—Oh my God. No! No! I'm not, I was just leaving. No.

—Oh. Okay.

The boy scuffed the ground with his foot and slouched away, hands still in pockets. Bets, incredulous, watched him until he disappeared from view. Laughing at the absurdity of the moment, she shook her head and removed her oversized shirt, stuffing it into her school bag, wearing just her long sleeved T shirt. She ran a hand over her hair, wavy and unmanageable. She tried to spin and shout like Roxie but stopped as soon as she started. *Nope, not me.*

Definitely not me.

***

—People must always want their babies to be beautiful, right? Hannah asked.

—What is this obsession with beauty? But yes, in general.

—And do you think all babies are beautiful?

Bets laughed.

—Definitely not! Newborns are often quite odd looking. They get better a week or two later. Have you seen one?

Hannah shook her head.

—They can be wrinkly and sort of squashed looking. Sometimes the parents are a bit unsettled when they first see the baby, if they aren't used to it.

—What do they do? Asked Hannah, reaching for her notebook, sloshing her tea. Bets got her a paper towel.

— Well, that depends on the person, I guess. People have different ways of coping, different expectations.

***

As with most enduring memories, the births Bets remembered most vividly were fraught with emotion. Either the parents, or the staff; either the circumstances of the delivery or the personalities of the people involved.

Sarah had been labouring for hours, and finally started pushing two hours ago. Bets was worrying, and Dr. Jenna was more insistent with her coaching.

Bets placed the Doppler on Sarah's abdomen, then double-checked Sarah's pulse to make sure she was getting baby's heart rate and not mother's.

—Heart rate 85, she said softly to Dr. Jenna.

Too slow.

Sarah slept between contractions, endorphins offering a welcome rescue from the pain and pressure. The pushing was wearing her out. The head was showing during pushes now, then sliding back in. Bets rechecked the heart rate. Still 85.

—Connect the vacuum extractor please, said Dr. Jenna. Sarah, Sarah? Can you hear me? Can you open your eyes?

Sarah opened, eyes rolling around for a second before focusing on the doctor sitting at the end of the bed.

—Your baby is getting tired in there. I'm going to give you a little help with the vacuum.

Bets tested the vacuum suction, passed the equipment to Dr. Jenna, who sat forward to place it but was suddenly blocked by Sarah's husband. Was it Dean? Shane? Bets absolutely could not remember, and the chart was on the other side of the room. Sarah, during labour, had been unhelpfully calling him Babe. Right now, Babe stood facing the doctor, gesturing at the vacuum.

—No suction cup! He said this forcefully, blocking the view of his wife's splayed legs. Bets recognized his type immediately: The Husband Who Thinks He Is in Charge.

Usually they were in two subgroups: the ones used to actually being in charge (police officers, firefighters, bank managers); Bets understood, when they began to bluster and demand, that they were doing what they were used to doing, trying to corral the one wild thing that was entirely, completely out of their control. The second subgroup was more difficult: the ones who never had control of anything in their lives, so they tried to advance the theory that they must be important. They wanted control, but no one was buying in. It was questionable whether they themselves believed in their power.

Dr. Jenna glanced at Bets, then back at Babe.

—Well, the baby's heart rate is low. That's a sign that the baby might not have enough oxygen. Sarah's doing a great job, this will just give the little extra help she needs.

—No suction cup! We agreed to do this naturally! It will harm the baby!

He stood, paunchy, eyebrows ferocious, chin receding, turning his ball cap front to back as if sending a message.

—Babe, said Sarah weakly, reaching for him. Let the doctor do her job.

—Her *job* is to deliver this baby safely, properly! Not using some primitive medical machinery! On our baby!

He batted his wife's hand away.

—Baby's heart rate is low. If you want a healthy baby, you need to let me help her get it out. Dr. Jenna's voice had developed an edge.

Abruptly, still standing at the end of the bed, he turned to his wife, red-faced, pointing.

—Push it out! You need to push it out now! They will hurt the baby! DO IT! Sarah's face sagged, a deflated balloon.

—I'm trying, she gulped, I'm trying so hard!

Bets grasped Sarah's hand.

—We all know how hard you're trying, Sarah.

Sarah gasped through a contraction, no pushing. Wasted. Bets released Sarah, put the Doppler back on, moved it around.

Nothing.

Bets and Dr. Jenna's eyes met.

—OK, it's time to step aside now… *sir*.

Bets realized Dr. Jenna had forgotten the father's name as well.

—If you want me to deliver a living baby, you need to get out of my way *right now*.

He visibly faltered, but didn't move immediately, his face frozen in an expression halfway between anger and fear. Bets stepped forward, grabbed his arm, and pulled him toward her.

—See to your wife. She needs you.

She somehow passed back the vacuum, wedged herself between Babe and Dr. Jenna, and reached for the call button, all at the same time.

—I need to push, shouted Sarah, I need to push!

In a millisecond, Dr. Jenna placed the cup on the baby's head, nodded to Bets to pump up the suction.

With Sarah pushing and the doctor pulling, five, six, seven centimetres of scalp were showing… and the cup popped off, nearly knocking Dr. Jenna off her stool. She swore quietly, reapplied the cup.

—Push, Sarah, push!

Two more nurses arrived, responding to the call button; they hurried into the corner with the baby warmer, unfolded blankets, unwrapped the oxygen bag. Babe yelled throughout: Why are all of these people here? I said no suction cup, why is no one listening to me? Get the baby out! Get the baby out!

Bets stood her ground, not letting him past her, giving Dr. Jenna the space to do her work. *How can she focus, with all this noise?*

Sarah pushed, and eyes, ears, chin appeared—suction cup removed, quick delivery of the shoulders, the body sliding out immediately afterwards, Sarah screaming with delivery of the infant and then slumping in exhaustion.

The baby was deep purple, eyes closed, limp and hanging in the doctor's hands.

—It's dead! Babe's eyes were wild. It's dead! You killed our baby!

He lunged, and Bets somehow blocked him, a defensive player in the middle of the delivery room. Sarah opened her eyes and began crying again. No, no, no! Cord clamped and cut, baby rushed to the warmer, dry blanket, stimulate hands and feet.

Nothing.

—Heart rate thirty, said one nurse at the warmer, quietly.

—Start compressions, ventilation, help her out! Dr. Jenna gestured to Bets to take over at the foot of the bed and joined the cluster around the warmer.

One nurse started pumping the ventilation bag over the baby's face, another used two fingers to do CPR.

—What the fuck! Babe hollered, you fucking killed our baby! Our baby is dead! What are they doing to it?

This time, Bets did not wait for Dr. Jenna's cue.

—Sir, you need to calm down. They're not killing your baby; they're trying to save her. You need to let them work. Right now, they are... launching into an explanation of oxygen, of blood circulation, was anyone listening? At least he quieted for a moment, and stayed in place, as the placenta slid glistening into Bets' hands.

Bets saw the baby's colour improving as she glanced back and forth, and she kept a steady stream of useless information as she cleaned Sarah and applied a pad. She heard the murmur to stop compressions. Saw the tiny legs flex, a miniature hand come into the air.

Finally, after what seemed an eternity, but was likely about two minutes, the sound of a muffled cry inside the plastic mask. Sarah shrieked, and Bets had tears in her eyes, watching the nursery nurse and the doctor touch their gloved fingers together in relief and support.

—Heart rate one-twenty, the nurse announced loudly, and Bets tapped Babe's hand.

—She's okay now. She's going to be okay.

—She? It's a girl?

Sarah pulled her husband down into an embrace, both crying.

The nursery nurse, once the baby had a couple of minutes of lusty crying without assistance, wrapped her in a blanket and presented her to the overwhelmed parents like a baby burrito.

Sarah ran a finger across the forehead, down the nubbin nose. She removed the tiny knitted hat to see the matted hair. Her husband, gazing lovingly at her side, stepped back.

—What the hell is that?

Bets peered around him at the bump on the baby's head.

—Oh, that's just a little hematoma from the vacuum. It will be gone in a couple of days.

—I knew it! He roared. I knew you were hurting our baby! I should have never let you near her with that thing. Look what you've done to her. Look what you've done!

—Babe, said Sarah, they had to. She nearly didn't make it! You saw her!

—She is *deformed*. Our baby is deformed, and it's all these people's fault! He looked around, swept his arm to indicate communal guilt.

They stayed in hospital less than forty-eight hours. They named the baby Gretchen, and they went home and no one on staff ever saw them again. Babe never said thank you.

The nurses did what they always did in such circumstances: joked about it. Bets whispered, "NO suction cup!" every time Dr. Jenna asked for it over the next few weeks, or the nurses announced, "It's deformed!" with every hematoma or temporarily misshapen head, snorting with inappropriate laughter, hoping that no patients were around to overhear.

Bets, after the commotion of Gretchen's birth, had laid her hand on Dr. Jenna's arm.

—Don't let him get in your head. You guys saved that baby. You saved her life.

Which should have felt really good, but somehow did not.

Definitely, everyone wanted a perfect baby. People recognized they were being shallow. They said they just wanted the baby to be healthy, and didn't care about anything else, but they didn't mean it. Babe was just an example.

But if that was the case, what about Mei?

It was Mei's first delivery, but she progressed well, and her partner Shawn was very supportive.

The delivery was more difficult, because the baby was born face up, instead of the usual face down, but Mei surprised them all and pushed the baby out anyway. They reached the point of no return, the baby's head emerged, and both Bets, at Mei's side, and Dr. Jenna, doing the birth, abruptly stopped their coaching and cheering. A sudden silence fell.

It was less common, nowadays, to have surprises. In the past, many birth defects were not known until delivery, and sometimes there was even an unexpected twin that showed up. With routine ultrasounds, such events were rare. Not only did the scans see the babies, the growth, the fluid, but even details like spinal cord defects, or heart abnormalities, some of which were corrected surgically with the fetus still in the uterus. It was an incredible thing, to Bets.

With new technology, birth defects were usually easy for the ultrasonographers and radiologists to see, but they did miss things. Mei and Shawn's baby, born "sunny side up" as the nurses liked to joke, gave Bets and Dr. Jenna a full view of the worst cleft palate either of them had ever seen. Not only was the top lip divided, but widely divided, almost certainly involving the roof of the mouth as well and extending into the left side of the nose. It looked like someone had roughly torn open the baby's face. The baby, meanwhile, had started a mewing newborn cry.

Mei lay back in relief, her pain resolved, and Shawn held her hand at her side.

—Listen! Said Shawn. Listen to our baby! He looked from Bets to Dr. Jenna and immediately said, What's wrong?

Dr. Jenna clamped and cut the cord and took a moment. Bets could see her mentally sifting for the proper words, like selecting buttons from a box.

—It's a boy! She said first, you can hear he's doing well!

—But? Asked Shawn, and Mei opened her eyes, and both were fixed on Dr. Jenna's face.

—You'll see that his mouth and palate didn't form properly. It's not your fault, you didn't cause this. It happens sometimes. Usually we know from the ultrasound, but for some reason they didn't see it.

—May we see him? Asked Mei, her voice cracking slightly.

—Of course! Here he comes!

Dr. Jenna lifted the baby onto Mei's chest, where Bets had helped her to loosen her gown. Once they were skin to skin, Bets draped a blanket over top. There was another silence as the couple turned the baby's face towards them.

Bets' lungs felt like cement. She pictured feeding difficulties, out-of-town specialists, surgeries, speech problems. Bullying.

Mei gazed at the baby, tracing the fleshy opening above his mouth, touching his hand, which reflexively gripped her finger. Mei, with her smooth black hair, her flawless skin, Shawn with his chiselled cheekbones and flat-top afro, a beautiful couple expecting a beautiful baby.

Part of Bets expected the parents to gasp in horror, cover mouths with hands, push the baby away. Instead, their heads came together over their newborn.

—Hello, you, said Mei.

—Our son! Said Shawn.

—You're gorgeous, don't you worry, Mei whispered, bending to kiss the baby's nose.

***

Hannah played with her pen for a moment, then said,

—I hope I can be a mother like Mei.

—I thought you weren't having kids, Bets teased.

—Well, it's not *for sure,* Hannah sounded exasperated. It just seems very difficult. Plus, I don't want to be a father like Babe.

They both laughed.

—Babe, well, I don't know. Wanted to help, I guess. Thought he was advocating.

—Or he was an asshole.

—Yes.

—You didn't get super angry?

—Firm, and calm, Bets said. It all goes back to Scary Mary. Write that down! Hannah dutifully wrote.

—But did you ever really lose it, really yell and scream?

—You can't. You just can't. Not with people you are looking after. You win by staying calm.

—Firm, and calm, said Hannah, smiling, underlining. Just like dealing with customers at the store.

—Yes. Exactly. Also, beauty is in the eye of the beholder. There's no one true definition. Mei and Shawn showed that.

—I guess.

—Why the sudden concern about beauty?

—I don't want to care. But people share photos, people rate them. I don't want to care, but I do. It just doesn't feel fair that some people are perfect.

—No, said Bets quietly. It doesn't feel fair.

CHAPTER TEN

Finally, finally, spring seemed possible. March, as usual, brought teasing warmth, followed by several snowstorms that challenged even the strongest psyche. Just as she thought about putting away the shovel, Bets woke to snow-covered tree branches and everything blanketed in white again; beautiful in November and December, but by April, enough to send her back to bed.

Winter here never changes, thought Bets, *why do we never adapt?*

But now, it was May. Although April showers were meant to bring May flowers, the rhyme never applied in Bets' town. Rather than the fulsome spring of Southern Ontario with the tulips and crocuses and buds and green, Northern May was more of a bedraggled, staggering spring, possibly with post-traumatic stress, with brown lawns and leftover dead leaves that hadn't been raked in the fall, an accumulation of snowplow-shifted gravel on the streets, and runny dog turds along the trails and sidewalks, buried in snow for months. Other small discoveries made when the snow finally melted: the rake! It was out here all along! Or, I remember searching for that key. I dug in the snow for an hour!

May brought other signs, too: people were resilient, and as soon as the sidewalks were clear of ice, the bikes came out, children and adults alike, even though they still needed mittens. The die-hard cyclists wore hats under their helmets, layered Gore-tex over their spandex.

Portable basketball nets appeared, seemingly overnight, standing like bodyguards over driveways. People began clearing the winter debris, neighbours who hadn't seen each other in months met on porches or talked across fences. Bets particularly enjoyed watching her neighbour Nick drag his shop-vac out of the garage and vacuum the peripheral strip of lawn slowly emerging from the snow, to remove the winter gravel kicked up from the street. She saw a crocus, fully blooming, on another brown patch of lawn, the only area of the yard without a foot of snow. *Good for you. At least you're trying.*

The sun felt like it was actually giving off warmth, and the more optimistic people laundered and put away the scarves and hats, the warm winter boots, but then were blamed when the inevitable May blizzard arrived. (You caused this to happen! Never put away mittens before June!) The nurseries opened, which was a bit of a joke, since everyone knew you couldn't plant for at least a month without risk of frost.

Hannah's visits continued, although somewhat sporadically. School was more intense, another week her parents needed her for inventory at the store. Sometimes Bets just received a text, *I can't come this week. Are you okay for next week?* Although Bets was grateful for the downtime, she now looked forward to their visits, and missed the mini hurricane that was Hannah whirling through her home, talking, laughing, dropping things. Hannah, for her part, had unflagging interest in Bets' nursing information and her notebook was always full of new questions and scrawled notes. Bets, who had expected interest in the nursing project to drop off months ago, couldn't help being flattered at the ongoing attention, but sometimes wondered about the appeal.

Hannah asked a lot of questions about Bets herself, which Bets sometimes answered and sometimes did not. She wondered how much to share; Hannah was just starting out. Should she know about negative things? How much personal information was too much? It was easier to stick to the facts: these are the types of nurses. This is what an operating room nurse does. This is what sterile technique means. Hannah loved stories of the maternity unit, but Bets didn't want her to feel pushed into any one type of nursing.

On Thursday, Hannah showed up in a bulky sweater instead of her parka, her hair in an enormous ponytail right on top of her head, as if balancing a houseplant. She looked different, and it took a moment for Bets to realize why, as Hannah jumped into the house, grasping Bets' arm.

—It's *beautiful* outside, Bets! I feel like my petals are opening! You have to come out here!

She dragged Bets onto the porch, and they sat on the steps with the sun in their faces; warmth at long last. Hannah even removed her scarf.

—Can we talk out here? Asked Hannah, I'm so happy about the weather! She smiled broadly, and Bets realized what had changed.

—You got your braces off!

Hannah smiled even wider.

—I know! Finally!

She ran her tongue over her teeth.

— They feel so slippery.

—They look lovely.

Bets smiled at Hannah, marvelling at the houseplant hair.

Bets was particular about teeth. She did not, overall, consider herself prone to whims of fashion (tattoos, piercings, spiked and/or asymmetric haircuts, thumb rings), but teeth were different, for reasons she couldn't explain. The even white teeth of many of her friends and colleagues over the years generated envy in her unlike anything else. She especially loved the way shiny white teeth appeared in darker faces, such as Shannon's. Her own teeth were long and horse-like, a nod to her distant British background, and not especially white, even though against her better judgement she'd given in and used bleaching agents on them—she, who invariably disclaimed bleached blonde hair, plumped up lips, facelifts, any type of implant or cosmetic surgery unless the person was a burn victim.

Surely everyone has their one area of weakness, thought Bets, *we can't be perfect.* Even bleached, her teeth weren't perfect, but they were passable.

Raz had lovely straight, white teeth, beautifully contrasting his olive skin, but the front four were a removable plate, due to a hockey injury in high school (why would men never wear protective face masks when they played hockey?) Seeing him without the plate always made her laugh– he had a freakish face he called the "lisping Frenchman" along with a ribald song in both languages– but it still took her aback because of the immense change in his appearance.

It was Roxie, of course, who had the most perfect teeth Bets had ever seen, effortlessly shiny no matter how many wild blueberries she consumed after an afternoon of picking in the dense bush behind their home.

Her teeth were evenly-spaced, evenly-sized perfection, bringing to mind smooth river rocks, white squares of gum, glistening ivory.

Complete strangers commented to her, or to Bets, or to their mother, on the exquisite beauty of Roxie's teeth. Bets never knew what to say, fully agreeing with the compliment, but also recognizing the small slight against her own imperfect mouth. Her mother usually said something like, "Yes, well."

—It's not like they're complimenting me, her mother said, afterwards. What do I have to do with Roxie's teeth? I made her, that's all. She grew her teeth herself. People are so strange.

Bets, however, understood perfectly, and took an odd pride in Roxie's appearance.

—How's the store? Bets asked. You don't talk about it much.

—There isn't anything to talk about, said Hannah, shrugging. It's a deli... so, meat. Cheese. Hairnets. Rude people who want samples of everything and then don't buy anything.

—What do you do when you work there? The cash? Slicing meat?

—I do whatever Mom and Dad tell me. Unload boxes, stock shelves, spoon out salads, work cash, wash floors, whatever. It's a nightmare.

—Why?

—Have you been there? Third Avenue.

Bets had gone to visit the deli shortly after meeting Hannah, unable to deny her curiosity.

The shop was in the small mesh of streets that made up the once-bustling downtown, now struggling since the advent of malls and online shopping. Where there had once been clothing stores, flower shops and restaurants, empty storefronts now loomed, with cracked windows covered in cardboard, behind which lurked naked mannequins, filing cabinets, empty shelving. Some buildings were repurposed for jiu-jitsu and yoga, and there remained some tired-looking pubs and marijuana shops. Despite efforts to spruce up the buildings, offer free parking, better lighting, little festivals to lure people downtown, despite the banks and the bus station, the area felt like a hollowed-out shell. The deli was one of the updated storefronts, with a modern sign, attractive window displays, and a few people wandering in and out. Bets watched through the window, but didn't go in. Beyond the display of artisan cheeses and jars of antipasto and olives, Bets didn't see

Hannah's mother at all. She saw a gentle-looking man with a receding hairline and dark-framed glasses, smiling at a customer as he rang up a sale.

—I've been there, said Bets, but I'm interested in your take on it.

—Well. It smells like cheese. It's small, so it's always hot in there. People come in and all they say is how grown up I am and ask when I'll be taking over the store. My parents are always getting angry about something and then turning to smile at customers like everything is great.

Hannah expelled all the breath in her lungs and wiped the air as if erasing a chalkboard.

—I don't want to talk about the store anymore, if that's okay. I feel like it's in my head all day, every day. It's like that, plus school, takes up my entire brain.

Let the babies sleep, Bets.

—It's okay, said Bets. I just wondered. I know what you mean about it being in your head.

They sat for a few minutes, listening to the chickadees and the exclamations of children down the street playing basketball.

—I think we were discussing psychiatric nursing last time, said Bets finally.

—Can we talk about you today?

—What did you have in mind?

—Well, said Hannah, tapping her notebook with her pen, you've never mentioned any children. Did you and Raz have children? Are they grown now?

Bets paused, looked at the tiny, hopeful buds forming on her crab apple tree.

—We didn't have any children, Hannah. We wanted them, but it didn't work out.

Hannah looked down at her notebook.

—I'm sorry, Bets. I ask too many questions.

—It's good to ask questions, Hannah. You just have to be ready for the answers. Write that down.

Bets indicated the notebook with her chin.

—Whatever questions you ask, be ready for the answers. Sometimes they aren't what you expected.

She waited for Hannah to write.

—Anyway, I'll tell you about it if you want. It's not a secret.

***

It happened, more than once, that other nurses accused Bets of not understanding. They felt she was too dictatorial, too cynical. If you had children, they said, if you had been pregnant, you would understand. You would be different. And inside Bets, anger gathered like darkening clouds, building to a vengeful peak that could burst out at any moment into torrential rains and thunder. Bets became proficient in closing her eyes, blocking the storm before it truly wakened. Sometimes she said nothing, or Hmmmm. Sometimes, if she felt up to it, she said simply, I've been pregnant. In a way that closed the door firmly behind the words.

She remembered, very well, the feeling of being pregnant. The pleasure/anxiety of missing her cycle, but even before that, the sore breasts, the sense of fullness in her pelvis, the knowledge that something different was happening in her body. She remembered, vividly, the intense nausea that struck her in waves, made her run to the toilet to retch even if there was nothing left to come up. She remembered she could not go an hour without a snack and then got into trouble for eating between breaks. It felt like maternity floor staff should understand pregnancy best of all, but in fact they could be brutal, almost accusatory, no one wanting the extra shifts and increased workload that were inevitable when someone went on maternity leave.

Bets told very few people the first time, and lasted nine weeks before the cramps, the blood, the disbelief. It happened on a day off and the next day she got up, weak, pale, puffy- faced, spent, and went in for her shift even as Raz asked her—begged her—to call in sick.

—I can't just sit and think about this, she said.

She was irritable with the other nurses, with the new mothers complaining that breastfeeding was hurting their nipples. She was patient with the pregnant women who came in bleeding and terrified.

She wasn't sure she should name the fetus she had lost—who knew, in that clotted mass, if it was a boy or a girl—but she did anyway. She named the first one Robin, covering both bases just in case. She found hidden rooms in remote areas of the hospital to cry during her breaks, but only allowed herself five minutes before she washed her face and carried on. We'll try again, she and Raz said to each other. Next time it will work. They had, when she first became pregnant, bought little hopeful gifts, a cardboard book, a onesie—tiny enough for a doll—a pair of sweet little socks. *We'll still use them.*

Pregnancy #2: 11 weeks. Riley.
Pregnancy #3: 6 weeks. Mitch.

Each time, it took months to get pregnant, sometimes over a year. Each time, fear of the outcome tempered the elation more and more. The fourth time the cramps and bleeding started, Bets was at work. A woman was in labour and Bets used the woman's painful contractions, when no one was paying attention to Bets, to grimace and emit small noises herself. When she couldn't stand it anymore, she sought the nurse manager, finding her reprimanding another nurse for leaving the med room door unlocked.

The charge nurse, Connie, turned and saw Bets. She waved the other nurse away.

—What are you doing here?

—I need to leave.

—What? What are you talking about? You're in the middle of a delivery!

And Bets, who had never said the words out loud to anyone but Raz or Shannon, said, I'm having a miscarriage. I'm twelve weeks.

She expected… what? An eye roll, a terse dismissal, a sigh? What she did not expect was to be pulled into the woman's arms and clasped against her.

—Oh no, Bets. I'm so sorry. Not again.

Not again?

Bets pulled back, and Connie's eyes, normally shrewd, were soft with understanding.

—I've worked in maternity nursing for thirty years, Connie said. Do you really think I don't notice when someone is vomiting ten times a shift one day and none the next? You poor dear child.

That act, those simple words, were finally too much for Bets' fortified wall. It crumbled in a moment, and she wept and wept while Connie guided her to a private area, sat her down, waited. When her crying slowed, Connie gave her a cluster of tissues. How many times had Bets performed the same gesture with her patients?

—How many is this?

—Four.

—And what are you thinking?

—That I can't do this anymore.

Connie put her hand on Bets' shoulder.

—Do you want a referral to gynecology? They'll see you right away, do tests...

Bets took a quivering breath.

—I think... I think I'm done. I just. Can't.

Connie nodded and released her from duty.

Pregnancy #4: twelve weeks. Cory.

For a few years, Bets pictured the children they would have been, if all had lived: Robin, the eldest, bossy, manipulative. Riley mischievous, playing pranks. Mitch a daydreamer, needing constant cueing and forever getting lost. Cory the baby, spoiled, comical, tough, as needed to survive three siblings. She enjoyed this fantasy for a while until she realized how much of her time was spent on this imaginary family. Gradually, in her mind, she aged them; she sent them away to school; she made them leave.

Connie retired two years later. Bets wrote her a letter, expressing the support she had felt in a time of great need, and how she hoped to pass that along many times, to colleagues or patients, during her career. Looking back, Bets thought, *I have done that. I have really done it.* Given support, given privacy, given space. In fact, if she was completely honest, she often gave more support to the ones who experienced loss than the ones who gave birth.

She hated the expression, "Everything happens for a reason," and never used it. Things happened; terrible things happened. Things much worse than serial miscarriages happened, for no good or apparent reason. Bets would not take that away from others, or from herself. But sometimes, in a place that was supposed to be happy and a beginning, you needed someone who understood ending and desolation. Bets, unintentionally, was that person, even if her colleagues thought her tough and unfeeling. Even then.

She could have switched, of course; there were other opportunities in the hospital, in the community, even in a physician's office. Everyone seemed to need a nurse. She could have left the maternity floor and then she wouldn't have been reminded every day of her loss, of the things she couldn't have.

She considered hospice nursing at one point; it involved a lot of hands-on skills combined with a sense of when to talk and when to keep quiet. By then, she felt her edge was too sharp. Hospice nurses could not be nicknamed Sergeant Major. Hospice nurses, really, should be named Honey, or Serena; they needed to be people with no sharp corners; they needed to be able to repeat themselves many times, to many people; they needed to hug a lot. Bets was not a hugger.

Why am I like this? thought Bets, many times, reflecting on her intolerance of errors, her need for order and for quiet. Her impatience with whining. Her lack of spontaneity. Her infrequent laughter.

She had asked Raz, which was risky, given his tendency to speak his mind.

—Do you think it's because of my mother?

He'd looked her straight in the eyes, unblinking, like an owl.

—Did she abuse you?

Bets, taken aback, scoffed slightly.

—No! Then thought, *did she*?

Certainly, her mother had never put her down, called her stupid, or worthless. She had just been… disinterested. That wasn't abuse. Was it?

Bets had grown up watching other mothers and wondering about her own. Why were the other mothers always cheerful? Why did they seem to enjoy children so much more than her own parents? Why did they make lunches, bake, sew, plan elaborate birthday parties, buy expensive Halloween costumes? (Bets and Roxie made their own, from whatever they could find around the house). Why did other parents come to the school assemblies, where the children sang in raggedy choirs or performed badly acted plays?

Maybe these were the wrong questions. Maybe she should have been asking her parents, why not?

—Why did you ask that? She had asked Raz.

He pushed his chair back, hands behind his head: pontification mode.

—Well, a child, it's like a plant.

—Like a plant, repeated Bets, skeptical.

—Yes, like a plant. You give it food, you give it sunlight, water, the things it needs, you don't abuse or neglect it, and it grows.

He sat forward and placed his hands together, then separated them to indicate the growing.

—How does that explain why I'm like this?

Raz gestured toward Bets.

—You, you are the plant you were meant to be. Your parents planted a Bets seed, and it grew into a Bets. He gestured toward the door. They planted a Roxie seed, and it grew into a Roxie.

Raz stood up and took Bets' hand and kissed her cheek.

—You're who you are meant to be. That's why you're like this. I love you like this. Most of the time.

He snickered at his own joke. Bets pictured herself as a plant, something with a tough woody stem, a few thorns, maybe some flowers, or some berries. *Healing, or poisonous?*

Maybe a bit of both.

***

Of course, Bets didn't tell Hannah all of that. She told her about the miscarriages, and the kindness of her charge nurse, and they talked about the women, the senior nurses, who had affected Bets, each in their own way.

Hannah asked few questions. They sat side by side on the steps, and watched an elderly man walking his dog, a large man who walked with his shoulders well back, leading with his large belly, swinging his arms behind him, while his incongruously small dog trotted before him, confident to the point of arrogance.

—You're very quiet, said Bets, still watching the man. Hannah pulled her sweater around herself.

—It's so sad. It's so sad that you had to go through that, that you didn't have any children. You and Raz would have been great. Look how well you did with Sam.

—We only had Sam for short periods of time; Raz barely had him at all. Having a child all day, every day, is a whole other thing. But we were willing to take a chance.

They listened to the sounds of distant traffic, a lone crow making some sort of announcement from a nearby tree, and dogs barking, possibly at the one that had just strutted past.

The basketball escaped from the game down the street and bounced toward them, followed by a couple of children. A car turned the corner, and Hannah was down the steps in a flash, running to intercept the ball and block its pursuers. The car honked angrily, and Hannah waved at it with a big smile, extending her arm in front of the children. After sending the kids back to their game, Hannah returned, out of breath. She sat back down on the step.

—Some people are such idiots! I feel like that driver would not have stopped.

—Nice job, said Bets. Quick reflexes! I'd never have made it in time. *Hannah, you're full of surprises.*

Hannah checked her phone and jumped in alarm.

—I need to go!

—I'll walk you, said Bets, a habit they had developed intermittently.

—What about Roxie? asked Hannah, after they had walked silently for about a block.

—What about Roxie?

—Did she have children? Do you have nieces and nephews?

Bets walked on, listening to their feet, the two of them walking in rhythm. She tried and discarded a few responses.

—Roxie's life went in a different direction.

Hannah's house was not far. Set back from the road, a well-kept bungalow with a huge blue spruce in the front yard, which was east-facing and still well covered with snow. Both neighbouring homes had front doors without steps or porches, opening into thin air, a local quirk that apparently saved on taxes. The homes always had a side or back door, but Bets could never pass by without picturing someone exiting the front door and landing face first on the lawn.

Hannah's house had a flagstone walkway with matching steps and a wooden railing.

—See you next Thursday?

—Thursday.

Bets kept walking, not wanting to waste such a lovely afternoon.

She used to think about miscarriage daily. At some point, she had stopped thinking about it all the time; it was still there, but deeper. Now, it needed to be dug up, rather than sitting raw at the surface demanding attention.

It wasn't just miscarriages that they saw at work; there were terminations, too, despite it all being very hush-hush. Over the course of her career, abortion had gone from a taboo, to a secret, to a moderately acceptable situation. Nowadays, they offered termination services and there weren't any protesters, there were no bricks through the window, there weren't people getting shot, as in the past. Where did those people on the religious right disappear to? Did they change their minds? Did they realize it made no sense to kill someone for terminating an unwanted pregnancy? Were they all older, were they dying off themselves? Bets was unsure, but the change in the hospital was clear. In the past, women came, but were labelled "fetal demise" as if they had a miscarriage that was incomplete. They were booked for a "D&C," for "bleeding," despite everyone knowing what was really going on. Now, the operating room list simply read "pregnancy termination," and no one really thought much of it, at least as far as Bets knew.

It was frustrating that there were women trying so hard for a pregnancy— herself included—who could not succeed, while other women had unwanted pregnancies, and seemed to get pregnant every time they had sex, even if they were using contraception (if you believed them, which Bets usually didn't), even if they had just terminated a couple of months prior, even if they had just completed their menstrual cycle. It felt unfair, but Bets tried not to dwell on it. She believed women should have control of their bodies, and that was that.

She had been on pre-op duties one day, years ago, when the ward clerk announced a new arrival. The woman was here for an abortion. She was homeless, and the ward clerk mouthed "drug user," pantomiming injecting a needle into her arm.

A person was a person was a person. How many times had she heard that over the years, how many senior nurses tried to drill into them that they should not judge? That their duty was to care, regardless of context? And yet, she shared a bit of the ward clerk's bias, she had to admit.

She had a hard time thinking, *It's a disease, not a choice.* She had a hard time thinking about selling sex for a high. Ignoring the name label, she gave herself a pep talk as she headed into the room with her clipboard of pre-op questions. *This is a person, someone with an illness, someone who deserves to have control over her body.*

The woman in the room was lying on her side, facing the window. Her matted hair spread across the pillow. Her tattered jacket lay over her like a blanket. She had removed the worn boots with the split toes, now inert at the side of the bed, and lay in her socks, one with a large hole in the heel.

There was a sour, unwashed smell.

Bets, despite her best intentions, thought, *who had sex with this person?*

The woman, sensing her in the doorway, rolled over to face her, and there was a silence, finally broken by the woman on the bed.

—Hiya, Bets, said Roxie.

CHAPTER ELEVEN

As she noticed the changes signalling spring, Bets also noticed small changes in Hannah. She still came regularly, but sometimes seemed distracted, staring off into space with a small smile, twirling a curl around her finger in a very un-Hannah-like way. Bets started some spring cleaning, and they were reorganizing kitchen drawers and cupboards together while they talked. Hannah's notebook lay open on the counter, with few notes taken, as she now took more and more interest in Bets' background with Raz.

—Tell me about moving in together, she said. Tell me about your wedding!

She removed plates, wiped out a cupboard. Bets watched with amusement, suspecting, knowing.

***

Once Raz was present and working, Bets and Raz had limited time together. Both on shifts, but different shift cycles, they either both got home exhausted after twelve hours, or they missed each other entirely, one walking in as the other walked out.

They learned to have breakfast dates instead of dinner; they learned to match their days off whenever possible. They learned to fit in quick sexual encounters in the two hours between one getting home and the other leaving, sometimes grabbing at each other the moment they walked in the door, or else holding a hand straight out like a police officer directing traffic: don't even think about it.

Some weeks the system worked perfectly and there was supper waiting at the end of a shift, something Bets had not experienced in years, and superb red wine to go with it. Sometimes Raz gave a victory cry when he opened a drawer and found a neat pile of freshly laundered, folded white shirts.

—I hate laundry! he said, shaking out a shirt, inhaling, I've had stinky wrinkled shirts for years! *Quelle belle surprise.*

Sometimes they both came home tired and irritable and the house was a disaster and there was nothing in the refrigerator and each blamed the other: I had those meetings! I took the car in! Well, I had that appointment! I always do the groceries! Both wanting to say, I do everything around here. Everything! Raz swearing his litany of French curses that made him sound harsh and cold to Bets, even though the words did not offend her, having very little meaning in her world.

At their first fight, Bets was shocked at the level of anger rising in her, the instinct toward self-preservation. *I'm supposed to love this person, I've told him I love him, why do I hate him so much right now?* Not to mention that Raz, under pressure, reverted back to his first language, and Bets' basic French was not enough to follow along.

—Fight in English! She yelled one day, as the phrases flew past her, only a few understandable (unfortunately "*impossible*" and "*aucune idée*" and "*jamais*"—impossible, no idea, and never).

They fought well, Raz said afterward, which gave Bets a ridiculous sense of pride. They negotiated, they were honest, they compromised, they did little things for each other once the fight was over, to fill the relationship cracks that needed time to heal.

—We didn't get married, is what Bets said to Hannah, although after a time everyone referred to Raz as her husband. It just didn't seem important, for either of them, to take that step. Bets had never dreamed about a wedding the way some girls did; she found the whole ceremony perplexing, especially when the extravagance of weddings seemed inversely proportional to the duration of the marriages.

They attended weddings, some of which were great fun, and others that were stilted and formal. They invariably came home congratulating each other on their impeccable choice of partner and their decision to not have a wedding.

Although unmarried, they both wanted their commitment to be clear. Raz couldn't wear jewelry at work, and the hospital discouraged rings with stones and elaborate settings that could attract germs. They settled on plain wooden rings, crafted by a friend of Raz's who did woodworking in his spare time. The originals were maple, smooth and pale, and Bets loved hers until it succumbed to too much handwashing. Raz's lasted longer, living in his locker during his shifts, but eventually cracked when he was lifting furniture. They had replacements made, and after the third set of rings, Raz's friend said, you guys need titanium.

The new rings were darker than they were used to, and Bets missed the smooth wood that she often rubbed with her finger when thinking, but the titanium was undeniably perfect for them: attractive, yet indestructible. Bets was used to fielding questions about her ring and found it amusing that her wooden and metal rings seemed to attract much more attention than the glittering diamonds set in white and yellow gold that each bride felt was completely unique, and yet which all looked the same in the end.

It was a game between them, the non-wedding planning.

—Look, there's your wedding dress, Raz would say, tipping his head toward someone in a particularly garish cocktail dress, or passing a shop window with some gauzy confection replete with satin and tulle.

—He's wearing your wedding suit! Bets would hiss, poking Raz, if a man wore mustard yellow leather pants, or a frilly vintage tux. Your wedding shoes, your wedding hat. An endless game; they never tired of it. *We're that irritating couple*, thought Bets, *with the inside jokes that no one else finds funny.*

They went on with their together life, which involved mostly jeans, scrubs (Bets), or coveralls (Raz), and thanked Providence that they had found someone who appreciated comfort. Sometimes, they dressed up for a party (or a wedding) and appreciated each other in their finery, then felt the immense relief of kicking off dress shoes, sloughing constricting fabrics, moving back into their comfortable zone. Sometimes after such events, Raz—usually "three shits to the wind," as he called it—took off his suit, stretched, and walked around completely naked to enjoy the newfound freedom, sucking in his tummy and flexing his biceps just to see Bets roll her eyes.

***

—Oooookay, said Hannah, waving her hand as if fending off an odour. I did NOT need to know all of that!

—Maybe a bit too much information, agreed Bets, laughing. Sorry. I got carried away.

Hannah tsked, I can't believe you didn't have any type of wedding at all! She replaced mugs on a newly wiped shelf.

—It's important to some people. It wasn't important to us. It's up to each couple.

She regarded Hannah for a moment.

—Are you seeing someone?

—How did you know? You're like a genius!

Bets shook her head.

—Doesn't take a genius for these things. Who is he? I'm sorry. Who are they?

Bets winced. She was slowly learning the language of gender neutrality, but it didn't feel natural yet. *Too bad we can't print up whatever we're about to say*, thought Bets, *and edit before speaking.*

—It's a boy, said Hannah, glowing. He works at the store.

—So your parents know him?

Bets realized she didn't know many details of Hannah's life, beyond the visible blend of earnest intelligence and physical chaos, or the small tidbits she sometimes supplied, quickly deflecting back to Bets.

—Yes.

Hannah turned back to her cupboard, removed some wine glasses as she continued.

—His parents are friends with my parents. But Nate goes to a different school, so I hadn't seen him in years.

—That's your man? Nate?

—Yes.

—How long?

—We've been working together at the store for a few months, but we just started dating a month ago. Hannah, closing the cupboard, resumed her hair twirling.

—Hannah, said Bets despite herself, please stop with the hair. Hannah froze.

—What?

—The hair.

She pantomimed twirling, stroking.

—Why?

—Too many of my trainee nurses do it. It feels, I don't know. It feels bimbo. I'm sorry, I don't want to insult you.

Hannah reached across and took Bets' hand.

—Bets, you aren't insulting me! I respect your opinion! I definitely don't want to be a bimbo.

She tapped her glasses.

—While we're at it, what is with the glasses? Are they too big? Is your nose too vertical?

Hannah laughed.

—That's a bad habit. It drives my parents crazy. I'm trying to stop, but it's so annoying when my glasses slip!

Bets looked at their hands, clasped on the countertop. Hannah quickly withdrew hers.

—I'm sorry.

—Why are you sorry?

—I know you don't like to be touched.

How did she get that message? What vibes am I sending out? The truth was, the touch of Hannah's youthful hand had made Bets realize she had not touched anyone in a non-clinical sense for a long time. That she did, in fact, like to be touched, but felt uncomfortable with it, leaving her awkward and prickly.

—I'm okay being touched, said Bets, I've just sort of lost practice.

—Okay, now I've told you my secret, which you already knew, said Hannah, it's time for you to tell me a secret, too. The story of Raz's name.

***

Raz was very aware of people's perceptions of miners. Many pictured pick-axes and lanterns, possibly dwarves; a low-ceilinged dirt tunnel, punctu-ated with worms or tree roots. Many had no concept of an underground world that extended for kilometres, with overhead lights in places, with roads and people driving around in pickup trucks, with robotic machin-ery. It was second nature to him, but he knew that for most people outside of mining communities, it was not.

Some miners, for sure, were not well-educated. Many came in straight out of high school, attracted by a steady job, excellent wages, and benefits; some just wanted to avoid ever setting foot in a classroom again. There was a disconnect, sometimes, with the people in charge, who were often mining engineers with years of education, but who didn't have a clue about the workings of an actual mine, and what it was like. Raz thought every person up top should work at least one shift underground, maybe in the raise, so they would understand, but he also knew they could never do it. You couldn't go from sitting doing equations all day to climbing ladders with 150 pounds of equipment on your back. You couldn't go from being warm and dry to being soaked to the skin for hours. There was a toughness you needed to survive underground, a restlessness, and the long days of hard physical work and the long days of classroom activity just didn't go together; he knew that very well.

Raz had started out in engineering. No one in his family was university-educated, and there was really no reason for him to go, but his cégep teach-ers became excited about his math marks and his aptitude for physics, and said it would be a "waste" for him to enter a trade. His calculus teacher had even phoned his parents about it, perhaps the only phone call they'd ever received about him that wasn't reporting some kind of grievance. Normally, it was: Jean-Marie left the school without asking permission, Jean-Marie didn't return after lunch period, Jean- Marie and his friend disrupted the classroom. When this call from the teacher came, his mother and father sat staring at him like a specimen in a museum. Finally, his father had spoken.

—*Alors, veux-tu y aller, Jean? À l'université?*

Raz stared at his plate. Shrugged slightly. What did he know about university? How was he supposed to know if he wanted to attend?

—*Je ne sais pas.*

His father folded his hands and stared until Raz looked up.

—*Tu dois savoir. Ça coûte cher.*

—*Je sais.*

—*Alors?*

—*Oui, je veux y aller.*

—*Eh bien.*

The evening had gone on, as if that was that, and there was no further discussion about it. There was no question of who would pay, since his parents had no money to spare, and Raz's job paid well, working in the mine in the summer. In the end, paying his own way saved him.

The school itself was fine. He loved the age and austerity of the place, the buildings that truly felt like hallowed halls, so different from the sterility of high school with its rows of lockers and beige colour scheme, and the perpetual odour of hot dogs and adolescent feet. He got along well with the other students, engineers being a rowdy bunch historically, his class being no different. He found a lively group that enjoyed a drink and a laugh. He admired the women in the group, intelligent women who not only knew more than most of the men, but deftly sidestepped the constant propositions and suggestive comments tossed their way.

He had long ago dropped the "Marie" from his name. As Québec, and Raz, became more secular, some people found the name Jean-Marie a good excuse to delve into his religious history and ask questions about Catholicism in times of corruption and abuse by priests. To those, he usually replied, "I didn't name myself, you can ask my parents." In the right company, he added *Tabarnak*, just for good measure, which either got him a laugh or ended the conversation abruptly.

So, in university he was simply Jean Laframboise. English-speaking students and professors still thought he had a girl's name, but at least the Francophones and knowledgeable Anglophones knew how to say Jean.

A few in his group tried to translate last names one day.

—Yves of the father, one said, and Yves Dupère smiled.

—You'd think my mother would get more credit!

He endured a few good-natured insults about his mother.

—What about you, Jean Laframboise? John the strawberry? asked Brad, causing Yves to spray his coffee.

—It's a *raspberry*, he said, smacking Brad upside the head. *Maudit colon*, a framboise is a raspberry, not a strawberry.

Brad encouraged the name John the Raspberry, but clearly too long and cumbersome, it quickly shortened to Johnny Raz, and then Raz. Raz shed his old name and stepped into his new one as easily as a set of clean clothes.

—What did you say your name was? People asked him, newly introduced.

—Raz. As in, raspberry.

Or,

—Raz. It's a nickname. Sometimes, Raz left it at that, enjoying the quizzical expressions in his wake. Sometimes, especially if he thought the person might know some French, he just said, my last name is Laframboise. Either their eyes lit up with the shared joke, or they looked just as confused as before, in which case he redirected the conversation.

In the end, university was not for him. His classes felt pointless, his mind wandered, he longed to be outside, to be active, to be doing, rather than thinking about theories or doing calculations. He dropped out after second year, after his summer mining supervisor told him they were looking for full-time raise miners. His parents never said, *I told you so,* but it was there, in the set of their mouths as he explained, in the arch of their eyebrows, his father smoking, his mother moving around the kitchen. His mother didn't want him to be a raise miner, a dangerous profession that robbed many men of their youth, even with unions and safety laws. On the other hand, it had been difficult for them to understand his desire for higher education, and the associated costs, with no clear outcome or visible skill at the end. They let him come back and live at home for a while, but Raz had the taste of independence on his tongue and longed to sample it again. As soon as he could afford it, he moved into his own apartment.

Mining was perfect for Raz. Active all day, he needed skills, concentration, and problem solving. He could work with others, or alone. Even the shifts didn't bother him, although they seemed to be more difficult for other men. Even in winter, going in to work at 4:30 am, in the dark, getting out at 4:30 pm in the dark, Raz never got the exhaustion, the depression, or the physical ailments that plagued fellow workers. Once he moved in with Bets, he told her the shifts were more difficult, only because he wanted to be with her; when they were off-shift with each other, one on nights and one on days, that was the only time he wished for something else for his livelihood, something that would allow him to be there when she got home, to eat supper with her every evening, to watch TV together and go to bed together and be a regular couple.

***

—But you don't *have* to do shift work as a nurse, do you?

Hannah was balancing her notebook on her head, fairly successfully.

—No, said Bets, but it's different work if you don't. Public health, doctor's offices, outpatient mental health, that kind of thing.

—Did you ever wish you worked only days? asked Hannah, as she wrote the types of work not requiring shifts.

—Sometimes, admitted Bets, but on maternity—in most areas of the hospital, actually!—the interesting stuff usually happens on night shift. It's just one of those rules of the world. Write that one down.

Hannah bent over her notebook again, then looked up and rapped the pen on the book.

—What's a raise miner, anyway?

Bets laughed.

—I had to ask the same thing, many times. I'm not sure I can really do it justice.

—You can try!

—Well, they work in the raise. Drilling from drift to drift underground. This makes no sense, right?

—Right.

—Here.

Bets wiped her dusty hands on her pants. She gestured for Hannah's notebook.

—Are you sure you want to know this?

—Nate mentioned it one time. As a possibility.

Bets sat down at the table, turning a fresh page in the book.

—Okay. There's the central shaft, where the cage goes down… that's the elevator.

She drew two vertical parallel lines, with a small box inside to represent the cage.

—Then there are the drifts, those go sideways from the shaft.

She drew horizontal lines going out the sides of the main shaft at right angles.

—Then, in between the drifts, there are the raises. She drew angled lines joining the horizontal drifts. The raises follow the veins of mineral and join the drifts.

—The veins of gold?

—Sometimes gold. Around here, lots of other minerals, too. Nickel, silver, cobalt, zinc.

—How far down do the shafts go? asked Hannah, peering over Bets' shoulder, her hair falling onto the notebook.

—Far. Thousands of metres. I don't like to think about it.

Hannah traced Bets' drawing with a finger, trying to picture the mine.

—I have a lot more questions, said Hannah, is that okay?

—We're going to need more time, said Bets. Also, we're definitely going to need Eddie.

***

Eddie was tall and wide-shouldered, with spade-like hands and a square jaw, built as though curved lines had not yet been invented. Bets watched Hannah take in the crew cut hair, the earring, the tattoos winding up his muscled forearms, the extra-large takeout coffee in his hand. Raz had trusted this intimidating mining partner with his life.

Beside Eddie, Hannah was like a bird, a squirrel, something he could pick up and drop into a pocket. Bets well remembered her own response, meeting the enormity of Eddie, glancing at Raz, thinking *this* is the man you climb ladders with all day? She remembered Raz's smirk, accustomed to the dropping jaws that trailed behind Eddie, and wondered if she wore the same smirk now.

—Hannah wants to know about raise mining, as I told you, said Bets, as they spread themselves among the couch and chairs. I'm obviously not up to the task.

—You want to be a miner? asked Eddie. Hannah laughed.

—Well, no. I was asking Bets about Raz, and I wanted to know more about his work. And my boyfriend might be a miner. Maybe.

—Your Dad's not a miner?

—No. He's... we have a store.

—Shopkeeper! That's like torture. You could be a miner, you know, lots of women down there now. You're maybe—he cleared his throat—kind of small.

He glanced at Bets. *Am I doing this right?*

—I'm not going to be a miner! I want to be a nurse. Like Bets.

There was a silence. Eddie sipped his coffee. *Was this a mistake?* It felt like a bad blind date.

—Tell her about a day, Eddie, Bets suggested. Maybe the day Raz threw the stoper? For a little drama?

Eddie released an unexpectedly high-pitched giggle. Then he looked stricken.

—But that was...

—Yes. Right after our last miscarriage. It's okay, Hannah knows about that. Eddie glanced at Hannah, cleared his throat again.

—What's a stoper? Asked Hannah.

—It's the big drill they use to create holes for the explosives, said Bets. Eddie, you tell it, why am I explaining this? I don't know anything. Start from the beginning.

Eddie took another swig of coffee and leaned forward in his chair.

—Okay, well Raz, he was a pretty positive guy. He was always joking; he didn't like guys complaining all the time. Their wives, their kids, their sore backs, their white fingers. He'd say "Life's good! Let's make a wage!" or "Hey Debbie Downer, tell us a joke!" Sometimes he really pissed the other guys off, they needed to vent. But man, you could tell when he was off. He could work hung over, up all night, didn't matter. But not that day.

—I tried to get him to stay home, said Bets, but he wouldn't. Same as I wouldn't; we were both stubborn that way. Better to be busy.

—He wasn't himself, said Eddie, he wouldn't say why.

Eddie could tell Raz didn't want to go to work, was dragging himself in.

Why was it taking so long to get dressed, Raz had wondered out loud, when he did the same thing every single day? He was in the locker room, also called the clean dry, in clean underwear, socks and T-shirt (you could only re-wear the base layer so many times before the sweat and mildew stink hung around you like a combination of corn chips and damp dog). Raz and Eddie went into the dirty dry, feeling a blast of heat along with the smell of oil and sweat. They slipped their chains off the hooks, releasing their gear, which hung from the ceiling; climbed into coveralls, stiff from drying overnight. Raz pulled on boots, broke his lace, swore. Eddie passed him a spare, watched him re-thread, waited for an explanation for Raz's mood, but nothing was forthcoming. Hard hat, safety glasses, earplugs from the bin in the corner, external hearing protectors. Gloves, safety belt, wrenches hanging from the belt, backpack with water and extra eyebolts. Chains. Together, they got their headlamps, and their safety cards.

The safety card was the same every day: you will be working at heights. You will be exposed to falling items. You will be in a noisy environment. You will be exposed to cold, moisture, fumes. Things may be wet and slippery. Protect your eyes. Protect your ears. Lift properly. Communicate. It was like the safety demonstration in an airplane: they could understand why it was done, but after a while, no one was listening. Or reading, as it were. And did they really need to be reminded, every single day, that they were risking their eyes, their hearing, their lungs, their health, their lives?

They got their assignment from the shift boss: one of the raises nearing completion. That meant lots of climbing, and when they were told to bring up a new stoper, that only one had been operational up top, Raz swore quietly again. Eddie glanced at him. Clearly, carrying the heavy drill was an issue, even for Raz, who rarely complained, who protested against complainers, and who was easily strong enough to manage the drill.

Raz was listless during the mandatory stretches, and the shift boss shouted at him. Normally, Raz pretended right along with the rest of them, acting like an aerobics instructor, mocking the exercises meant to prevent injury, which instead felt ridiculous to them all.

They filed into the cage, a group of identically dressed men of varying heights, thirteen per level, three levels to the cage, to descend into the depths of the mine together. Most of them were lost in their thoughts. Eddie sometimes tried to get a song going, but today that seemed like a poor idea.

Their assignment was raise 610, which they'd been working off and on for weeks. It was nearly complete, and therefore almost one hundred fifty feet high; they only put guys with experience in the long raises. It didn't take them long to muck out the fallen rock from the previous night's blast, which seemed like a bad sign.

—There should be more, commented Eddie loudly. Raz would normally have had a witty reply, but he was silent. Maybe one of the blast rounds had failed. They'd have to go up and see.

Most of the equipment was still up top, but they had the new stoper to bring up, in addition to the usual daily gear. Raz had a couple of water bottles, some lengths of chain and some eye bolts in his pack, and they did rock-paper-scissors for carrying the stoper, as they always did for heavy items. Raz cursed as he lost yet again. He'd tried multiple strategies, insisted on best of three, and Eddie still consistently beat him.

—I'm in your head, big boy. Eddie wiggled his fingers at Raz before putting his glove back on. I'll take the ladder, just to be nice.

Eddie looped the spare ladder over one shoulder, shook the loose rock off the ladder already bolted to the foot wall, and climbed into the darkness above, banging and rattling as he went. Raz grunted, heaving the eighty-pound stoper onto his shoulder, pressing onto his backpack, reinforcing the importance of stainless-steel water bottles instead of plastic.

As Eddie climbed, shaking out each ladder in turn, dust and rock fell onto Raz, ascending one-handed below him, and periodically he called out,

—Loose coming down!

The first rule of raise mining was "Don't look up"—resist that urge to see what's falling, or you'll get it full in the face. Even a small piece of loose rock could do serious damage when it came from 200 feet up.

Eddie and Raz climbed one ladder after another. The air felt thinner, and had a damp mineral smell, combined with wafts of Eddie's sweat coming off his coveralls. Eddie passed a long, loud fart when Raz came close under him.

—*Câlisse*, you bastard, shouted Raz, and Eddie had to stop climbing for a moment and hang onto the ladder until his laughter passed.

Once they passed 100 feet, there was no fooling around. They couldn't secure themselves yet, and needed every sense focused on climbing, on ensuring the ladders were safe, on listening for rumbling above them. The tapping of boots on rungs, the clanging of Eddie's spare ladder against the climbing ladder or the raise wall, the plinking of falling rocks, and the hiss of the air hoses were the sounds following them up the raise, climbing within their circles of light in the darkness.

Eddie, looking down at Raz, could see the stoper was digging into the side of Raz's neck, but he didn't stop to adjust it. Eddie understood: better to get to the top and get the damn thing off. Both men were already soggy with sweat. Having to do the climb right off the bat meant they'd spend the day soaked even earlier than usual.

Eddie reached the top and aimed his light at the blast site from the night before. All the equipment was intact, thank God, hanging safely chained to the side wall. There was one obvious rock chunk clinging above, but overall, the site looked pretty clean. Eddie reached for the scaling bar, and Raz grunted with relief as he used equipment chains to hang the heavy drill under the other stoper. He rolled his neck a couple of times.

—Get ready! yelled Eddie, taking a jab at the lone rock jutting out, releasing a shower of dust, but the rock stayed in place.

—Are you attached? Called Raz, and Eddie pointed at him, set down the scaling bar, and looped the side rope through the metal ring on his belt, so that the rope would catch him if he fell. Raz, lower down, used the safety rope beneath him, then climbed back up. He'd fall further than Eddie if something happened, but eight feet was better than 150.

Eddie applied himself again with the scaling bar, this time trying to pry loose a corner of the rock. Another shower of dust.

—It's coming! FLATTEN OUT!

Raz pressed himself against the foot wall, head tucked, making himself as flat as possible. As Eddie gave the rock a final lever, it came loose, enormous, striking the far side of the raise and ricocheting back several feet below Raz, then crashing to a final decisive thud.

—Shit! shouted Eddie. That did not go where I expected. Sorry, Raz.

Raz gave a thumbs up but did not look up. More loose would follow a big rock like that.

Eddie scaled until the rock stopped falling, then climbed further until he was at the face. Raz climbed up behind him, both now on the same eight-foot ladder, with sixteen more ladders below them in the darkness.

Eddie tapped and poked at the face. Tok-tok-tok. Tok-tok-tok. Showers of pebbles came down, tiny pings down the raise, swooshes of dust, then in one spot, tok-tok-thunk. He poked around the spot. Thunk-thunk-thunk.

—Drummy here, get ready.

Again, Eddie reached with the scaling bar, jabbing and prying until the loose piece separated, much smaller this time, falling straighter and without incident. He finished scaling the face, and all seemed sound.

—I think we're good to go, he yelled.

—I can hear you, idiot. I'm right here.

Raz unhooked the hose and handed it up to Eddie, who sprayed the rock face to reduce the dust, then handed the hose back down. Both men were now covered in sweat inside their coveralls and soaked with water outside. Raz took off his gloves and emptied out the water, pulled out a chamois for the safety glasses, which were covered in muddy film.

—OK, all set. Eddie had cut the fingertips off his gloves so they could drain on their own. They were both surprised Health and Safety hadn't called him out on that.

They set up the staging. Raz handed equipment, already hanging in pieces from the previous day, up to Eddie, who drilled new bolts and chains so they could hang wooden planks. Raz handed up the pieces of lumber one by one, going up and down the two upper ladders, and Eddie set them up and when he received the pile of three-by-eights, he nailed them all together crosswise, completing a wooden platform eight feet long and six feet wide, hanging from the chains, strong enough to support two men and two heavy drills. Eddie walked along it, still connected to the foot wall by the rope in his belt, and jumped up and down experimentally. Raz detached himself from the lower side rope, and climbed up to Eddie, attaching himself to the upper bolt, and they sat side by side on the staging, each in his own personal aureole of light. Both were soaked and filthy with dust, and both downed a full water bottle in about two minutes, flexing pruney fingers, stretching necks.

Raz took off his safety glasses to wipe them down again, a mask of white skin around his eyes contrasting with his dust-darkened face, like a raccoon in reverse. They enjoyed the break, listening to the nothingness of the raise, the hiss of the air hose, the drip of water, the otherwise thick silence.

—What d'you think, lunch or drill? Eddie shouted.

Raz compressed one nostril and blew out the other over the side of the staging.

—Lunch, said Raz, replacing his safety glasses.

—Perfect. I need to take a dump, anyway.

—Classy, replied Raz, and they both started back down to drift level.

—He seemed more like himself, then, Eddie said to Bets and Hannah. He was joking, he was more normal again. But it didn't last.

After they'd eaten and Eddie found himself a porta-potty, they packed to head back up, trying to think of everything they could possibly need, to avoid having to come back down and face the climb multiple times. Raz reorganized his backpack—emptied onto the staging above—with steel bits for the drill, while Eddie packed the bag of blasting sticks by unspoken agreement, since Raz had hauled the stoper. Raz was ready first and started back up into the darkness. The raises were built on angles, following the mineral veins, but the climb still took significant energy.

They always had caffeine at lunch to avoid the post-meal sleepiness that made them want to nap instead of climb. They knew what could happen when guys lost focus: they looked up; they didn't hook onto the foot wall; they dropped things on their partners; they didn't check the strength of the chains; things fell, people fell.

—He told me later, said Eddie, all he could think about was his kids. He could picture them in his head, and they were fading, like a photograph, and he knew there wasn't anything he could do about it. I remember that so well, that description of the fading photograph.

They set up the drills with two-foot steel bits, and once they were both ready and they were both on the safety rope and had all their gear covering eyes and ears, they nodded to each other and prepared to drill directly above their heads. Eddie's stoper kicked right in, smooth, no issue. Raz started his drill, but the bit didn't cut into the rock smoothly, and the steel screamed and bent, causing the stoper to buck.

—FUCK you FUCKING PIECE of SHIT!!! He hurled the stoper off the stage, and Eddie stopped drilling, and they both stood listening to the crunch and smash of the stoper making its way down, down, down to drift level, followed by a clang, and silence. Raz sat down heavily on the staging, and Eddie put his stoper down and sat beside him.

—You okay, Raz?

He didn't shout this time. He could see Raz's eyes fill with tears, something he'd never witnessed before.

—*Câlisse*, Raz said, wiping his safety glasses, turning his face away from Eddie.

—You want to talk about it?

Raz later told Eddie he pictured himself shouting about his wife's miscarriage in the middle of the raise. Talking about the children that he wanted, but now couldn't have. Pictured Eddie raising his ear protectors, WHAT? WHAT?

—I'm good, he told Eddie. I dropped the stoper. *Tabarnak.*

Eddie aimed his headlamp downward.

—Kind of looked like you threw it.

—Threw, dropped. You English people and your words.

—Hog's going to kill you, Eddie said, referring to the equipment supervisor.

—Yeah, well. Maybe I'll kill him first.

Harley Hogg, in the equipment repair office at the mine for years, insisted his surname was pronounced "Hoag." They all called him Hog, but they had to be careful. Harley was known to hold a grudge, and report people who damaged too much equipment. Some had been fined a lot of money because of his reports.

After their shift, Harley stood in the window of the office, all greasy hair and small flinty eyes and thick glasses, balancing the stoper with his meaty hands, turning it, frowning.

Eddie watched Raz quietly add a couple of pieces of it he had gathered from the ground, placing them on the countertop between them. Hogg looked at the pieces and again at the stoper, looked at the warped steel, the dents on several sides, and peered at Raz.

—What did you say happened to this?

—It fell. From 150.

—It fell.

Hogg stared him straight in the eyes through his thick lenses. Raz didn't move an eyelash, meeting Hogg's gaze head on. Hogg grunted finally, prepared an equipment repair sheet, typing with two fingers thick as sausages. He handed the sheet to Raz.

—You should be more careful. The equipment is expensive.

—Yes. You're so right. Thank you.

Once he had signed off on the repair and they'd returned their lights and were safely in the dirty dry, Raz sat down and started laughing, softly at first and then harder, covered head to toe in sweat and dust, a puddle forming under his boots as the water drained off him. Eddie sat with him, shaking Raz's shoulder.

—Holy shit, Raz, you've lost it completely! "You're so right, thank you"?

Raz started into fresh waves of hysterics, slapping his knee, tears making clean pathways through the dust on his cheeks. Eddie joined in, giggling. Men shook their heads as they passed the two of them, smiling in spite of themselves, knocking on Raz's hard hat, kicking his boots. There was only a shower to go, then clean clothes, then daylight, and the end of that interminable day.

—See you on the other side, said Eddie, who was already naked and ready to shower. Go for a beer?

—Sure, said Raz, okay. Maybe one.

—You can tell me about it.

—About what?

Eddie glanced around to confirm no one was listening.

—About why you threw the stoper.

He slapped Raz lightly and disappeared around the corner to the showers.

***

—You knew all along! Said Hannah, lying on her back with her legs up the back of the couch, her head hanging over the edge, hair pooled on the floor.

—Yep, said Eddie. Raz didn't hide his feelings very well. It was all right there on the outside. But he thought he was really mysterious. We talked for a long time that day.

—I can't believe you did all that climbing, and carrying, and drilling, it sounds so *hard*, said Hannah.

—It does. I don't think I'd last a day, said Bets. I went down with him once, and I could barely stand up once I had all the gear on.

Hannah sat up abruptly.

—You went down with him! Can you do that? Could I do that?

She turned to Eddie, who shook his head.

—I don't think so. It was just something they did for the families one time, so they could see where we worked, and how we worked, so they could understand better.

—Which also made it more stressful, said Bets. It's so far down and feels so dangerous. Maybe you could go into a different mine. I'm sure there's one around here that offers tours.

Hannah wrote that down in her notebook.

—Um, did that help? Asked Eddie.

—A lot. I don't know how you do it.

—Well, I don't anymore. They've kind of phased out raise mining in most places now, anyway. Too risky. Not too dangerous for us to do it for almost forty years, but too dangerous now. Better to use robots, I guess.

—Do you miss it? Hannah asked.

—Well, he said, after a pause. It was never the same. After.

He glanced at Bets and didn't finish his sentence, reached for his cup. Bets willfully ignored Hannah, who tripped over the room divider while returning a tray to the kitchen. She tried, as she had many times, to picture Hannah as a nurse, but the image inevitably turned to dropped sterile instruments, IV poles crashing to the ground, Hannah sliding across the floor in a puddle of amniotic fluid. Bets shook her head and laughed quietly to herself as she touched Eddie's decorated forearm.

CHAPTER TWELVE

Back in the day, Bets asked herself why she hadn't told Raz immediately about Roxie's pregnancy and termination. She was so proud of their relationship, their open communication, and yet, now and then, a situation like this arose that she tucked away within herself.

The secret of Roxie's pregnancy hardened inside her, a sharp kernel that burrowed and festered. She was always aware of it, like a toothache, and occasionally it flared and she had to push it down deeper and distract herself. She was quiet, and when Raz put his hands on her shoulders to nuzzle her neck while she did dishes, she shrugged him away.

—What's wrong? He asked, watching her scrub the same perfectly clean pot again and again.

—Nothing, she said, not looking at him. *Why did I just say that?*

—Nothing, he repeated, watching her a while longer before he shrugged and left the room.

Bets allowed herself two tears and two minutes standing with her rubber gloves dripping, staring out the window at the darkness, before she resumed the dishes.

The secret felt heavier when Bets went to work, where she chastised co-workers who weren't getting their tasks complete. The women in labour seemed extra needy, and their noises made Bets feel like an animal having its fur rubbed the wrong way. She wanted to tell them to hurry up, to stop fussing, to appreciate their luck, to honour the importance of this event in their lives. On the outside, she was smooth and calm and professional... mostly. On the inside, the kernel burrowed deeper and deeper, growing and increasing the pressure, demanding attention.

The washing machine broke down, and she and Raz called in an appliance repairman after they drained it and checked the hoses and took off the top and poked at it for a while. The repairman stood and looked at it, sucking his teeth, and told them it wasn't worth spending the money for replacement parts.

They were both off work on Saturday, so they went to get a new washer. Bets tried to feel interested in the different brands and styles and their minimally distinct features, but was barely paying attention. Hoping to make her smile, Raz nudged her and tilted his head toward a woman looking at the dryers, accompanied by a young boy. The child was talking in a sweet, high voice, a steady stream of consciousness, and after each sentence he touched her leg and said, "Right, Mummy?" until she acknowledged his comment.

—We need a dryer. To dry the clothes. Right, Mummy?

—That's right, sweetheart.

—We can choose one at the store. At this store. Right, Mummy?

—That's right, sweetheart.

—This is the store that has dryers. Right, Mummy?

The mother looked at price tags and inside dryer drums, responding absently as she patted his hand. The little boy had thick, dark, curly hair, and enormous brown eyes. His skin was olive, just like Raz. They watched for a moment, and Raz said softly,

—That's what our baby might have looked like. He kissed her cheek.

A peripheral part of Bets felt the purity of his intentions, but his words penetrated deeply inside her, and the kernel ruptured toward the surface. Bets felt intense heat, felt she was breathing razor blades, and all she could think about was to escape before she lost control.

Raz found her in the car, eyes closed, deep breathing, cheeks wet with tears. He got into the driver's seat and waited.

After a few minutes, Bets was able to speak.

—Sorry, she said, searching under the seat with one hand, producing a squashed box of tissues. She pulled one out, blew her nose.

—Are you sick? What's going on?

—Not sick, said Bets. I didn't want to do this in the store. It's been building.

—Is it work?

His face was an open doorway she could walk through, welcoming, inviting. He really did look like a grown-up version of the little boy in the store.

Robin. Riley. Mitch. Cory.

—I saw Roxie, Bets said.

—Roxie!

—Yes. At the hospital. A few weeks back.

Bets took another tissue, spread it on her knee.

—She was pregnant.

—Pregnant.

—Yes. Coming in for a termination.

Raz sucked in his breath.

—What happened?

—I asked her to keep it. For us.

Bets folded the tissue, spread it again.

—Oh, Bets, said Raz. And she said no.

—She said we wouldn't want her baby, anyway. That it wasn't really a baby yet. That she'd done it before. She didn't even consider it. Not even— not even for a minute.

Bets could feel Raz testing out words in his mind. They looked out the windshield, where other people were driving in and out of parking spaces, walking to and from their cars with boxes and carts, as if it were a perfectly normal day.

—Bets, he said finally, taking her hand, you know I want a baby. Wanted. Our baby.

—Yes, she whispered. *But.*

—But Roxie can't have a baby, Bets.

—She can! She was pregnant!

—That's not what I mean. I mean she is… I don't know. Unwell. She can't go through a pregnancy. She can't even take care of herself.

—But maybe we could have made her! We could have had her committed! Said she's a danger to the baby. This could have been a chance. For both of them! For us!

Bets heard and hated the shrill sound of her voice. Raz lifted their clasped hands, lowered them down again, tapping the console with their single fist. Was he crying? Bets looked straight ahead, saw only his outline at the edge of her vision.

—Bets.

—I know, she said quickly. It's crazy. I'm crazy. I know.

—You're not crazy. It just wouldn't work.

—I know. I know it wouldn't. It just sort of felt possible. For a moment.

They sat, each locked into their own confined space of loss. Gradually, the edges softened, blended together, and Bets felt some of the tension leach away, as Raz's fingers relaxed within hers and their breathing slowed together.

—Maybe we should try again. See a specialist.

—I want to. Bets' voice was nearly a whisper. But I can't. I can't lose another one.

It was an old discussion, words repeated so often they were like a deer run in the woods, the earth packed down from frequent use, the brambles and leaves trampled and torn.

—We could still adopt. Not Roxie's; another baby. One that needs a home.

Another old one, worn like a carpet stair runner, faded from so much treading, over and over and over. The old arguments remained, without even talking about them out loud: babies scarce. Young mothers changing their minds. Unknown genetics. Older infants already suffering from irreversible damage. International adoptions with long waits, high costs, greedy agencies. Not impossible, not a problem financially, just not the best option for them.

—Nothing has changed, Raz. Nothing has changed, except that I saw my sister and she was pregnant, and I went a little crazy. I'm… I'll be okay. I'm okay now. I needed to release it, I guess.

Raz got abruptly out of the car. Bets, puzzled, watched him walk around behind the vehicle, appear outside her own door, and open it.

—What are you doing?

He extended his hand and said, Come out.

—I don't want to go back to the store.

—Do you think the washing machine matters right now? *Mon Dieu.*

Bets got out of the car and Raz pulled her to him and she managed a tiny laugh, small and light as dandelion fluff. She allowed herself to relax in his embrace, head against his shoulder, ignoring the mix of odd and tender looks from customers entering and exiting the parking lot.

A woman came out of the store, pulling at the hand of a little boy, who was crying loudly. The woman looked straight ahead, jaw set, and the little boy shouted, No, no, no! Large brown eyes full of tears. Curly dark hair rustled by the wind.

CHAPTER THIRTEEN

Initially, after Raz was gone, and they didn't want her to work so she could recover, Bets walked a lot. She went to the trails, since they were close by, and she was less likely to run into neighbours who both would, and would not, want to speak to her. So terrible, they said, so young. What a waste. What a shame.

Bets had nothing against her neighbours, but she just wanted to walk and not talk about anything, and the woods allowed her that. In among the conifers, she let her mind wander, changed its direction if it veered toward maudlin. The woods brought Raz closer, since he believed in the force of nature, the cycle of life returning everyone back to the beginning. That thought comforted Bets more than any concept of Heaven, in which it was impossible to picture Raz doing his lisping Frenchman routine, Raz swearing his religious-themed French expletives. There was no way he was strumming a harp somewhere. *Tabarnak! Faudra d'abord me tuer!* She could hear him in her mind.

Bets imagined Raz's spirit swirling through the woods; he'd love to be there, to finally know where the birds went in the cold, to understand the hundred calls of the ravens, to see the patterns of lynx, foxes, rabbits, bears.

—Look at those tracks! He'd said, out in the woods in the winter.

A huge, crazy maze of overlapping prints in the snow, hundreds of them, in all directions.

—Is that a hundred rabbits, or one insane rabbit? What is it doing? There's nothing chasing it—look, no other prints anywhere.

He'd looked at them with awe.

—Maybe it's a meeting, a rabbit conference! *Le Réunion des Lapins.* Think of the important decisions being made.

He'd laughed, he'd walked on, awkward in his snowshoes, leaving Bets behind for a moment, thinking—would I notice those tracks, here on my own?

He'd shown her that chickadees were tame, if you put sunflower seeds on your hand, or your mitten, if you stood perfectly still, or made a little chirping call. They'd fly in, look at you, grab a seed, sometimes even linger for a moment before flying off. She felt more present at those times—those stolen, perfect fragments—than at almost any other. It was like watching a baby emerge, a similar almost-miracle. She could picture Raz as the wind— his spirit, his essence— watching the chickadees, supporting their flight.

Usually, she walked until she reached the creek, where there was a large, smooth rock in a clearing, warm from the sun; a natural resting place. She sat there in stillness, sometimes for an hour or more, listening to the wind in the trees, the crackles and rustle of the undergrowth, and in the warmer months, the bubbling of the creek itself. People walked by fairly often, or skied, or snowshoed, or biked, or jogged, making her wish she could set up a video camera and do one of those time-lapse movies, where flowers open and close and suns and moons drop and rise in an instant. How many dogs bounded up to her, sitting on that rock, how many leaves swirled around her, how many snowflakes, how many raindrops?

Time was suspended; it stopped, but also continued. It was hard to keep track.

***

Bets was standing frowning at her front garden when Hannah arrived. At each end was a juniper, not wrapped for the winter and now completely mussed, as if just out of bed. One had a large crater in the middle, as if struck by a meteorite, while the other had all its branches squashed to one side like a hand bent at the wrist. Bets and Hannah stood looking at the mass of brown, withered hydrangea blossoms, tangled branches, long skeletal brown leaves, clots of brown slime that had once been plants, and two takeout coffee cups that had blown into the bushes over the winter.

—Your garden is lovely, said Hannah.

Bets, lamenting her lack of autumn preparation, feeling overwhelmed at the work to be done, laughed out loud. Once she started, she couldn't stop.

—Your garden is *lovely*! She shrieked, clutching her stomach, putting out her hand to lean on Hannah, who was giggling too, although tentatively. Bets tried to stop, managed to wipe her eyes and stand up, but as soon as she saw the garden, she was off again. Hannah watched as Bets' fit went on; smiling, uncertain, she hitched up her backpack, glanced around. Finally, Bets was able to stop, wiping her eyes again.

—Whew, she said. I needed that.

She looked at Hannah, at her expression, and patted her arm.

—It's okay, Hannah, I'm not completely off my rocker. Not yet.

—I meant, I can see it *will* be lovely, protested Hannah softly.

They went for a walk, Bets having spoken of the trails, and Hannah rarely using them but interested in seeing the things Bets described. As they walked, they talked for a while about seniority, which Hannah had heard about but didn't quite understand.

—So if a job came up and we both applied, you would automatically get the job?

—Well, not automatically, but probably, if I was already working at that hospital.

—Even if I had better qualifications?

—Probably. Although your qualifications would unlikely be better.

—But that makes no sense.

—Well, it's like a reward. It's like saying, you stuck it out here, so you get dibs.

—But maybe I'd do a better job!

—But you haven't done the time.

Hannah had picked up a branch, and she tapped it against tree trunks as she walked.

—I don't like it. If I graduate and I'm looking for a job and I'm all energetic and enthusiastic, I can't get a job because someone who's old and worn out and ready to retire gets the spot?

—Watch it, said Bets, pushing Hannah's shoulder. But yes. Exactly.

Hannah threw the stick like a javelin.

—I have a new topic, she said. Have you ever been camping?

—Camping? That's what you want to talk about?

—Well. Nate wants me to go camping with him for May Run.

May Run—also known as Victoria Day Weekend—was extremely popular for camping in Northern Ontario, despite the distinct possibility of snow or rain. Determined to get out onto the land for this first long weekend of spring, people congratulated themselves on their toughness, compensating for poor weather conditions with equal parts bonfire and firewater.

—I've been camping, said Bets. But not May Run, it's too cold.

—I know, agreed Hannah, that's worrying me. I don't like being freezing.

As if to prove her point, she was wearing a heavy knitted sweater over her leggings once again, and her omnipresent enormous scarf. Her hair, loose and voluminous today, was another protective layer. Her face seemed tiny amid the fabrics, hair, and lenses.

—I really want to go, said Hannah, it will be fun, but I don't know how to camp. My family never went.

—And your parents are okay with you going? Hannah shook her head.

—No, not at all. I'm supposed to work all weekend.

Bets waited, listening to their feet, weaving around slushy sections of trail and puddles of mud.

—I'm telling them I'm going with Kayla, said Hannah finally. You think I'm terrible.

—Are you terrible?

Bets bent to toss a dead branch aside.

—No! I just want to do what I want, sometimes. I want to do something other than work at a deli. And they won't let me go if it's with Nate.

—I thought they liked Nate.

—They do, but not, you know. Overnight.

—Right. Said Bets. *Probably with good reason.*

She wrestled briefly with her urge to give unsolicited advice; should she discuss birth control, safety, first aid, alcohol, drugs?

—Well, camping's not difficult, she said finally. As long as someone can build a fire and put up a tent, there's not much more you need to know. And there won't be many bugs this time of year.

—That's true! That makes it better!

—And a warm sleeping bag. You need that, the nights will be cold.

—Nate has all that stuff.

—Well. Sounds like you'll have a great time, said Bets, smiling at Hannah, turning to walk with her hands in her pockets.

Did I once walk around with a dreamy look on my face like that? No. No way. Maybe.

***

Bets had been pretty sure Raz was testing her the first time he took her on a camping and fishing trip. He was like a small child, talking rapidly, mixing his French and English, taking her to get her fishing licence, to borrow a smaller life jacket, to pick up worms and leeches. He showed her his tackle box and the various bits of metal and twine and beads he used to make lures. She saw, in his calloused fingers, the care he took, selecting each bead, telling her its importance, knotting the ends as expertly as the surgeons during c-sections.

He packed them a lunch, making his specialty: loaded sandwiches, buttered and bursting with vegetables, smoked meat, brie, and condiments like hot pepper jelly and sliced pickles, where Bets always just used mayonnaise, or plain mustard. He included snap peas in the lunch, and cherries, things that Bets passed by in the supermarket due to the exorbitant prices. He packed dark chocolate, and frozen bottles of water to keep everything cold, and a small flask for each of them, which she asked about, but he only wiggled his eyebrows at her and hid the flasks away in the pack.

The morning of their departure, he got up at 5 am to make a thermos of coffee, and presented her, when she yawned her way into the kitchen, with the thermos, a small container with two hard-boiled eggs (already peeled and salted), some grapes, and a croissant.

The drive to the pre-selected prime spot was long and bumpy. The roads seemed smaller and narrower with each new section.

—What if we meet someone going the other way? Asked Bets, bouncing as the truck went over holes in the road, around huge puddles, swerved away from branches.

—We won't meet anyone! Laughed Raz, and they didn't.

—Are we lost? Bets ventured after another long period of bouncing and swerving.

—Just wait, said Raz, just wait.

Looking for his good spot, he said, a remote spot, untouched by people with their cottages, their music, their pontoon boats, their motors and wakeboards and Sea-Doos. A spot where fish waited beneath the surface, if only you knew where to look, the surface itself calm and smooth. Soothing to the spirit.

As they drove, as the roads became worse and worse, Raz told her he was being transported back in time, into a tiny vehicle with his family, with roads becoming gravel, then two tracks in the grass, grooved tracks that sometimes dug so deeply into the earth that a large hump was created, scraping under the car and threatening to leave it stranded and teetering like an upturned turtle. The branches got closer and closer, until toward the end, they scraped the vehicle like long sharpened fingernails, and he and his sister ducked to the side as if the branches would poke into the windows and scratch their faces, as if the trees were blocking their way, saying, who asked you here? Not us.

They bounced and jarred in the back seat, Raz and his sister Josée, shrieking if their heads hit the ceiling—no seat belts of course—and the dog, he vividly remembered the dog, who at the start of the ruts (or even the gravel road) knew where they were going and began whining and jumping around the car in excitement, scratching everyone's legs, provoking cries of *Vas t'en!* Until finally Raz's father cursed and stopped the vehicle and dropped the dog out the door, leaving him to chase them the rest of the way, the children anxiously watching out the back to make sure he was not lost, or struck, but he was too smart for that. Usually, once she had looked backward too many times, his sister would shout *Arrête!* And their father slammed on the brakes just in time for her to open the door and vomit. Félix, that was the dog's name. Which made them laugh, since of course Félix was supposed to be a cat.

Finally, they came to the clearing where the tiny family cabin stood, where the campfire pit sat darkened, where the old boat waited, stashed under an ancient tarp, motor and all, because who in their right mind would ever come all the way into these back woods just to make off with someone's ten-horsepower motor?

The worst part was unpacking the car. Raz and Josée wanted to be off, down the path that led to the lake, but they first endured endless trips into the cabin, with bedding and food and coolers and cases of beer, the tasks interminable and frustrating, after such a long trip, with such possibilities waiting.

As soon as they could, they were in the boat, lines in the water, Raz and Josée proudly handling the bait, Raz fascinated especially by the leeches, which twisted around with their tubular mouths, looking for something to suck, attaching to his thumbnail even as he pushed the hook through their twisting, undulating bodies. His father knew when and where to jig, or troll, when to let the line fall right to the bottom with little sinkers for weight, when to use the pickerel rigs that spun and flashed and therefore were favourites of his sister. They didn't always catch something, but they caught enough to keep it exciting, enough to have a story to tell their mother, about the fish that broke Raz's rod, or got away because someone was too slow with the net, or flopped suddenly in the boat when they thought it was dead, making Josée scream.

Just being out on the water when it was quiet could take Raz back to the promise, the adventure, he said, of being young. It reminded him of the smiles exchanged between his parents, who fought so much at home. Of time alone with his father, who said he was proud of him if he untangled the line, or baited the hook well, or pulled in a large fish. Mostly his father sat silent, with a cigarette, or a beer, every so often grabbing the back of Raz's neck or elbowing him with a smile, so that it felt like they were friends instead of father and son, normally at odds, with not much in common.

In the evenings, they built a campfire. Some days they cooked on the fire, frying up the fish from the day, or making spider dogs by slicing the ends of wieners lengthwise, and watching the ends curl up as they cooked. Raz and Josée were sent to collect wood and rocks to make a proper border on the fire pit, somewhere to sit the pots or dry the damp logs and shoes. Josée liked to come back with armloads of kindling, creating an impressive roar of flames, smoke whistling and sucking upward, but gone in moments. Raz preferred to aim for fire for the evening, seeking large logs, dry pieces, and as he got older, he was allowed to use the hatchet to split the wood, or to shorten logs too long for the fire pit.

Around the fire, Raz said, it was easier to be together. The conversations were wide-ranging and detailed, unlike the minutiae of suppertime conversations at home: who emptied the milk and didn't get a fresh bag, who kept using up the toilet paper, who had a sports practice that week. At the campsite, the topics were larger, and less definitive: why did some people hate francophones? Was religion important? Were people, in the main, good people who should be trusted, or bad people who should be feared? Around the fire, as it crackled and illuminated their faces fleetingly in the darkness, it felt possible to speak without ridicule, to say things unsaid in the light of day, looking someone right in the eyes. There were arguments, of course, and expansive hand gestures, and more than once someone (usually Josée) would leave the fire in a huff and go into the cabin. Raz's father shook his head at those times, and said, *Si sensible,* which meant she was too sensitive.

Sometimes they sang, French folk songs mainly, but they were not musicians. They clapped hands or slapped knees and Raz's father joked, someone was in tune there! Who was that intruder? Sometimes, especially if they had splurged for wine or whiskey, Raz's parents got up and danced together while Raz and Josée kept the beat.

Even now, with his parents long gone, Raz said he could picture them dancing together at the side of the fire, shadowy against the blue-black of the night sky, with frogs gulping in the background, and crickets chirping, with the fire's crackles and sparks whirling into the air, and the smell of smoke and pine. He'd asked Josée, once, if she did any camping with her kids, on alternating weeks, after she and her husband were no longer together. She seemed perpetually exhausted and prematurely old, and she said no, why would I? It was horrible. I always threw up on the way there; the bugs were bad; the water was freezing; we had to wait forever for supper, and eat fish all the time, and you and Dad were always making fun of me. Why would I subject my children to that? Raz marvelled at the nature of memory, and the difference in their shared experience.

—What about you? He had asked Bets as they drove on and on. Did you have a camp?

Bets' family did not have a "camp," as people called them, they did not fish or hunt, or use ATVs or snowmobiles, or boats. She and Roxie learned to swim at the local swimming pool, and one summer, after a lot of begging, they both attended sleepover camp just outside of town. They had to borrow a lot of gear, their mother having no interest in shopping for sleeping bags or bug spray, and not really understanding why they wanted to go in the first place. They got a ride to camp from Bets' friend Katie and her mother, and when the time came to leave, their parents briefly hugged and kissed them, and waved. When Bets looked back, her mother had already returned to gardening, and her father had gone into the house.

Katie's mother said to call her Barb, and was very enthusiastic, asking lots of questions, stopping for cans of pop on the way as a treat, singing along to the radio or just random songs, while Bets (still Betsy at that time) and Roxie sat in the back seat and watched her in silent wonder.

It turned out that many of Barb's songs were camp songs, ones she herself had learned way back when, some of which showed up again around the campfire the first night. Bets didn't know what to make of the loud chorus of voices, the frantic gestures that went with some of the music, the clapping, and the harmonies, but it didn't take her long to join in. By the third night she felt part of it, and found she enjoyed singing at the top of her lungs, waving her arms, or peering around as if shading her eyes from the sun. Her cabin mates, who felt too loud and boisterous at first, took her in and helped her to understand the schedule, the activities, the rhythm of living at the camp, and Bets found herself dirty, fatigued, and happy.

Besides the singing, Bets sat in a canoe for the first time, fearful and wobbly at first, then laughing hysterically with everyone else when they tipped it on purpose and learned to right it again. Within a couple of days, she could paddle reasonably well, in awe of the girls who knew how to steer, and pull sideways, and turn on a dime.

The lake was spring-fed and therefore intensely cold, but they played games in the shallow sandy stretch which made them forget the temperature for a while. One day, Bets got so chilled her fingers turned purple and she couldn't stop shivering, and Katie took her to the camp nurse, Margaret, who clucked over Bets and wrapped her in a gray scratchy blanket and made her a cup of tea, adding lots of sugar. The only "adult" beverage Bets had ever tasted was a sip of her mother's coffee, unsweetened and dark and bitter.

Bets tried archery for the first time, finding the bow much stiffer than expected, finding the bowstring hurt her fingers, and the first few times the arrows just fell in front of her, making Katie shriek with laughter. As soon as she got the hang of it, arm straight, pull back, hand steady, she sent several perfect arrows into the target, surprising everyone, most of all herself. The instructor applauded Bets' release and called her Bull's Eye.

She had just discovered the culinary pleasures of cinnamon toast and was wolfing down her third slice when the camp director appeared at her table and told her she had to go home.

Bets was peripherally aware that Roxie was not loving her camp experience. Being Roxie, she'd made friends immediately, but then had looked pale and unhappy. Word circulated that she'd thrown up and had to go to Nurse Margaret, but Bets, having enjoyed the attentions of the nurse, felt no anxiety about that, nor any guilt about failing to check on her.

It turned out that Roxie was not only vomiting, but, in fact, had salmonella poisoning and had to go home. It turned out that Bets' parents wanted neither of their children remaining at a camp where such a thing could happen, nor returning there in the future.

Bets begged the director, and her parents, when they arrived, to remain at camp for the full ten days. The director said it was up to her parents. Her mother said she was leaving, and there was no use crying about it. Katie came to see her off. The adults packed Roxie into the car with a can of ginger ale and a basin in case she felt sick. Nurse Margaret hugged them both goodbye.

—I hope you'll be back next year! She twinkled at Bets, who climbed in and put on her seat belt, looking hopelessly out the car window at Katie, who sat stabbing a stick into the ground.

—I hope you'll be back next year, mocked her mother as they drove away. That dirty place?

She shook her head. Bets looked out the window, landscape blurring from her tears, then turned and pinched Roxie as hard as she could. Roxie's only reaction was to look at her sadly, her eyes underlined with dark circles, and turn to look out her own window.

That first time going camping with Raz, after they shared these stories during the long bumpy ride, they had pulled through a dense area of bush into a clearing, and Bets had opened her window to get a clearer view. A pristine lake lay before them, fully surrounded by trees, with a small beach area stretched in front of the truck. There were no other vehicles, no cabins, nothing but trees, and water, and the two of them, and a beautiful sunny sky, and the sound of wind, and a loon calling out from the surface of the lake.

When she stepped out of the truck, the air, the trees, the lake, the loon, all brought back, in a rush, the memories of camp, tucked away for years. Raz looked to her for her reaction, excited as a child, then fading slowly.

—Are you crying? What's wrong? Don't you like it?

Bets smiled and wiped her eyes.

—I like it, she said. I love it. It's my happy place. I just forgot about it.

Raz came around the truck, took her face in his hands, kissed her, softly at first, then more deeply, and then he unzipped her jacket, moved his hands under her shirt, and she unzipped his pants, and without fully undressing they were both touching, and their cries joined the sounds of the woods. A beaver, uncertain, slapped his tail on the water and dove to escape this new and questionable threat.

***

Bets told Hannah only bits and pieces about fishing with Raz. She knew the trip Hannah was proposing would be entirely different from the Zenlike experience of silence in the bush; most likely, the teenagers would have music blasting the entire time, and would be lucky if the weekend didn't finish by burning all the equipment, or two boys in a fistfight. Hannah was imagining something somewhere in between, most likely.

—I think it will be so beautiful, and so different from anything around here, said Hannah.

—There are a lot of lovely spots, agreed Bets.

—People should give birth in the woods! Did you ever think of that? She spread her arms, indicating the trees that surrounded them.

—Think how peaceful it would be! You could have a stream in the background, or a waterfall!

—You're not the first to have that idea.

—I'm not?

Hannah climbed up onto a boulder, looked around her.

—No. There's a whole movement toward nature-based births, and self-delivery.

—Self-delivery?

—Women going off on their own to deliver their babies.

—But isn't that dangerous? I meant, more like, set up the whole maternity unit in the woods.

—That would be beautiful, a maternity unit in the woods. I like the image. And yes, it's dangerous to self-deliver.

—Did any of your patients do that?

Bets paused.

—Yes.

—And how did it work out?

—Well, at first, I didn't know all the details. Bets skirted the question.

—But then?

—But she told me after. We spent a long time talking about it.

—And how did it turn out? Persisted Hannah, sitting down on the boulder. Around her, the trees rustled. Bets leaned against the rock.

—It didn't turn out well, she said. The baby died. The mother almost died. Let's leave it.

The young woman had staggered in through the front entrance of the hospital, with her hair in disarray, her face streaked with tears, covered in impossible amounts of blood, holding a baby that was deep purple in colour, the umbilical cord still attached, dangling from beneath her stained dress, blood running down her legs and pooling on the floor as she walked. The ungodly noise coming from her: keening, wailing, no word covered it properly, but it signified that she already knew. She knew what her choice had cost her.

Bets closed her eyes to the image and said nothing to Hannah, who sat resting her head on her folded arms.

—I don't know how you do it, Hannah said.

—How I do what?

—How you see terrible things, sad things, and keep going back. I don't know if I can do it.

Bets touched Hannah's foot.

—Most of the time it's happy, Hannah. Birth is happy! Hospitals have lots of sadness, but on the maternity unit, there are so many good things. I just keep dwelling on the negative ones, maybe because they don't actually happen that often. They stand out.

—It feels difficult.

—It is difficult, sometimes, said Bets. But it can be wonderful, too. Miraculous.

—Maybe, said Hannah.

CHAPTER FOURTEEN

Bets scraped away at the brown detritus in her garden with a trowel, revealing green shoots pushing their way out from underneath. *Well, look at you, all alive under there.*

Hannah watched as Bets pulled away dead leaves, beheaded hydrangeas, and deposited everything into the wheelbarrow with her wiry, capable arms.

—Can I help?

Using the back of her wrist to scratch her nose, Bets took in Hannah's long sweater, the ubiquitous leggings, the mass of hair held back with a bandana.

—I'm afraid you'll get yourself dirty.

—That's okay, this is an old sweater.

Hannah smoothed the sweater over her hips. It was off-white and seemed high risk to Bets. She wondered if Hannah ever did her own laundry.

—Come on then, I'm happy to see you.

Bets tossed Hannah an extra set of gloves, and they set to work side by side. Within moments, Hannah's hair was tangled in the hydrangea bush. She stood, bent from the waist, giggling as Bets unwound her hair, tsking but smiling.

—Maybe you should just sit on the steps and entertain me.

—No, you sit on the steps and I'll do this!

Hannah produced a hair elastic, pulled up her hair and expertly braided it, repositioning the bandana overtop. She bent to the hydrangeas again.

—Well, I wouldn't mind a break.

Bets removed her gloves, sat heavily on the step.

—So, how was the camping?

—It was pretty good. Nate's friends were nice, and the weather wasn't too cold. We ran out of food; the boys really eat a lot. They made up for it with beer.

—And was that okay? Asked Bets, sensing something in Hannah's voice.

Hannah didn't answer right away, absorbed in pulling up parts of a dead Hosta. She sat back on her heels.

—Nate was a bit, I don't know. He got mad if I spent time talking to his friends. But he got over it, it was okay in the end.

Bets waited, expecting more, but Hannah resumed her gardening. Bets dusted off her hands on her shorts and joined in.

Bets kept expecting Hannah to lose interest in her nursing project, to drift away, to cancel or not show up. They'd been talking for months now, Hannah had a boyfriend, and surely a seventeen-year-old girl had better things to do than hang around a sixty-three-year-old woman. But just when she thought the whole thing had run its course, there was Hannah, jumping up the steps, hair flying, objects spilling, pulling Bets into fierce spontaneous hugs. Bets found herself choosing items at the grocery store because she thought Hannah might like them, or storing little tidbits of information during her day that might help a future nurse.

This can't last much longer, she'd thought while at the A&P, then added a pomegranate to her shopping basket, in case Hannah had never tried one.

After their gardening, as they passed through the hallway to the kitchen, Hannah lingered as she often did before the pictures on the wall. One showed the sisters on the day of Bets' high school graduation. Bets, turning to look at Roxie, held her mortarboard on her head with one hand, and Roxie, head tipped back, laughing, was trying to push the mortarboard off.

—She's so beautiful, said Hannah, tracing the women with her finger. You guys look so happy.

—Yes.

—Will you tell me more about her? Why don't you talk about her?

Bets looked at the photo for a moment and put her hand on Hannah's shoulder.

—Hannah, there are a lot of sad stories. Remember how I skipped the last one, that birth in the woods? You're young, you should have happy stories.

—But I always learn.

—True. But lessons don't always have to be hard. Do you want a snack?
Bets was carrying a plate of nuts and dates.

—What are those?

—Those? They're dates.

—They look like beetles! Hannah pushed the plate away.

—I guess they do look a bit like beetles, Bets conceded, but they're sweet.

—You eat weird stuff.

—Maybe *you* eat weird stuff. No notebook today? No nursing?

—I don't need it if you are going to tell me a story about Roxie.

Bets took a date, chewed as she was thinking.

—Okay, Hannah. I'll tell you some things about Roxie. Then you can
decide if you want to keep going or not. I have a question for you, though.

—What?

—It's summer! Don't you want to be with your friends? Or Nate? Or
don't you need to work? Not that I mind, she added quickly. I was just
wondering. Let's sit out back.

They went through the sliding doors and settled into the chairs on
the patio.

—It's once a week, Hannah pointed out. I can be with them other times.
Anyway, my friends? I don't even know if we're really friends anymore,
nothing's new there. And Nate's working now, but my parents don't need
me until later. And I like coming here!

She took a handful of nuts, leaned back in her chair.

—It's peaceful. It's interesting.

—Do you want to talk about your friends?

—Not really. I'm tired of the drama. I come here to be away from it.

—Well, Roxie then. Where did we leave off?

—She was more popular than you, and you were jealous, said Hannah,
impressing Bets with her attention and memory.

—-Right. You should know that Roxie started drinking a lot, and she
was pretty promiscuous in high school.

—Wild child, said Hannah.

***

Roxie was out more and more. It was like looking for a shadow, or a ghost. Bets saw the bread on the counter and knew Roxie had been home; a towel on the floor of their shared bathroom, a pair of shoes that came and went in the entryway. Small items went missing: Bets' hairbrush disappeared and she spent days trying to figure out where she could have left it. She heard her mother ask her father if he'd seen the ancient fleecy blanket from the couch, which was nowhere to be found.

Her father asked Bets if she'd seen his watch, which he removed each night when he came home from work and laid on the shelf by the door. Bets ran upstairs to her room, feeling a sense of foreboding. *Would she? Would she really?* She pulled open her top drawer, where she kept a wooden jewelry box with her few items of value: a necklace from her parents, a gold bracelet from her sixteenth birthday, a pair of pearl earrings from her grandmother, each one set with a tiny diamond, that Bets was saving for graduation. She knew before opening the box that it would be empty, felt herself equally hollow. Her father appeared at her bedroom door at that moment.

—Your mother's jewelry is missing.

Wordlessly, Bets held out the empty jewelry box to her father. He looked at her, looked at it, frowned. He went downstairs and called the police.

When they brought Roxie home, Bets stayed in her room and listened as her father thanked the officers. He told Roxie, right in the entryway, she was not to go anywhere except school, and she would work as well, to pay for what she had taken.

—Mind if I smoke? Asked Roxie.

Bets felt like a rabbit in the woods: afraid to move, hyperalert, aware of every breath.

—Of course, I mind, snapped her father, barely able to form the words. You will not smoke in this house. You will not smoke at all! Give me your cigarettes right now!

Silence.

—I was just joking. I don't have any.

She walked away, up the stairs, and Bets heard their father bellow after her.

—No more of this, Roxanne. No more!

Roxie's footsteps came down the hall and stopped in Bets' doorway. Bets, sitting at her desk, looked straight ahead.

—Hiya, Bets.

No reply, no movement.

—What's up?

Roxie came into the room and was about to flop down on the bed when she saw the empty jewelry box.

—Hey, listen Bets, sorry about your jewelry. I'll get it all back for you. It was just, I needed money for something.

Bets turned. Roxie's smudged mascara making her look like she had two black eyes. Her tousled hair, her clothes the way she'd looked at age ten after a day of climbing trees.

—I can't believe you stole from me, Roxie.

Roxie picked up the wooden box, closed the lid, placed it back on the bed.

—Well, I didn't really *steal* it. More like borrowed it, just for now, until I can get it back.

Bets snorted and turned back to the wall, picked up a pencil lying on the desk, rotated it around her fingers.

—Don't be a jerk, Roxie, we both know you're never getting it back. What did you spend it on, anyway? Pot? Booze?

—No.

—What then?

—Other stuff.

—Other stuff.

—Yeah.

Bets suddenly, at the same moment she was asking, didn't want to know. Didn't want to know what a fifteen-year-old girl would buy with a few hundred dollars' worth of items from her family, didn't want to know who would buy the items from her for cash, didn't want to know where she'd been, what she'd been doing, who she'd been with.

—Roxie, you need to stop, you'll screw up your future.

—I'm not super worried about the future, Roxie said from where she now lay on the bed, stretching her arms up to the ceiling, lowering them down the sides, raising them again. I'm mostly interested in getting out of this house, being out on my own.

—So go to university, like me! Then you'll be out!

—Not really. You'll still be under their thumb. You'll still have to come home, and you'll owe them money.

Roxie sat up and crossed her legs.

—I mean it, Bets, you should leave, too. We should both go.

—What's the rush?

Roxie's intensity confused Bets. It was unlike her to be so serious. Roxie held Bets' eyes for a beat, then jumped up.

—I gotta go. I'll see you, Bets.

She paused in the doorway, looked back for the briefest moment.

—Sorry.

She went into their shared bathroom, and Bets heard the shower start. She picked up the wooden box, which had fallen off the bed, smoothed the lid, and replaced it in her top drawer.

A few days later, Bets had to stay late at school to work on a group project. (How she hated group projects—the motivated members of the group, those with actual aspirations, doing all the work, dragging each of the others along like a personal albatross). She arrived home at the same time as her father, who was just pulling into the driveway. He parked, got out, nodded to Bets.

—Elizabeth.

—Dad.

They walked in silence to the front door, which was unlocked. Her father frowned.

—I thought your mother had that meeting tonight.

Inside, there were some noises coming from the kitchen.

—Hello? Said her father, craning his neck but unable to see into the kitchen. They went down the hall together, and her father pushed Bets very gently ahead of him.

She thought about that nudge, afterwards; one might expect a father to tuck his child behind him, to keep her safe, but instead she was first to see what was happening.

What was happening was Roxie, sitting on the kitchen counter, blouse open, breasts exposed, skirt hiked up, legs spread, with what appeared to be a teenage boy bent in front of her with his head between her legs. Roxie was gripping the boy's curly hair and moaning slightly, and at their father's sudden bellow the boy jumped up, wiping his mouth with his hand, eyes wide with panic, and Roxie opened her eyes, more lazily.

—Go, she said to the boy, who dodged Bets and her father. Roxie jumped down from the counter, smoothed her skirt down, began buttoning.

—Roxanne, said their father, his voice more menacing than Bets had ever heard him. Get. Upstairs. I can't even look at you.

—What's wrong, Dad?

Roxie finished buttoning, picked up her shoulder bag. She cocked her head at her father.

—Jealous?

The slap was so immediate, so unexpected, that Roxie staggered and fell over a chair, and Bets let out a shriek, reaching out, grasping at nothing. Her father doubled, tripled in size as he stood over Roxie, hand still in the air.

—You… you… he sputtered, both girls fully focused on the raised, wavering hand. Abruptly, he regained control, returned to regular size, straightened his tie with both hands.

—Get out, he said simply. Get out of my house. I don't know who you are; I could never produce such a whore.

—Dad! Shouted Bets.

Roxie got up, touched her cheek—already fiery red from the slap—picked up her bag again.

—No, it's OK, Bets, said Roxie, eyes fixed on their father with—what was it? Triumph?

—I'm out of here, anyway. Now, they can't make me come back.

She pulled Bets into a one-armed hug as she passed her, kissed her cheek.

—Sayonara, Bets. Get out soon.

She walked past them and picked up a duffel bag from the entryway.

—Oh, and Dad? She called over her shoulder. Go fuck yourself.

Bets and her father stood in the kitchen as the door slammed.

What just happened?

Her father cleared his throat.

—Elizabeth.

—Yes.

—Do not speak of this to your mother.

—What?

Bets looked at him, incredulous.

—What are you talking about? You just kicked her out!

—I said, he repeated evenly, as if Bets was very young or very stupid, do not speak to your mother about this.

Mom won't notice that her youngest child has left home?

—Ok, Dad, whatever you say, she said.

—Good, he said, patting her shoulder awkwardly.

He turned and left the kitchen. She heard him go into his study down the hall and close the door.

***

—But your mother found out, said Hannah. Right?

—Of course! I don't know what my dad was thinking. Roxie was gone for a few days and then the police brought her back. She wasn't even sixteen. But my dad never spoke to Roxie again.

—Even when she was still at home?

—No. He'd talk over her, around her, but never directly to her. Then, as soon as she turned sixteen and could become a ward of the state, she moved out.

—Did she steal again? From you?

Bets ran her hands through her short hair, locked them behind her neck.

—We tried to keep everything valuable hidden away. But yes.

Hannah had pleated one of the paper napkins into a strip, which she now folded into a fan.

—But wait, she said suddenly, what about the picture?

—What picture?

—The one in the hallway! You're at your graduation, and she's there!

—This all happened during my final year of high school. She didn't turn sixteen until the fall, when I had already left. So she came to my grad.

—She was drunk, added Bets. She let out a really loud cheer when I crossed the stage to get my diploma, when everyone else was just getting polite applause. And she kept grabbing me and yelling to everyone that she was so proud of me. My parents were mortified.

Hannah smiled, fanning her napkin.

—Were you mortified?

—No, not really. It was just Roxie—she'd always say and do things I would never say or do. Even the photo was supposed to be a formal grad portrait, but she kept jumping into it, hugging me, saying she wanted to be in the moment with me, and in the end the photographer just took it of the two of us.

—It's a great photo! Much better than a formal portrait.

—I agree, said Bets. Funny how that works, isn't it? Hannah hugged her knees with her arms.

—So what happened after that?

—After that, we didn't see each other for a while. I left for school, and by the time I came home she had left, and after I finished university and found a job, I moved into my own place, and I didn't even know where she was, or if she was still in town. And then I was all caught up with Raz—Bets smiled briefly at Hannah—and he occupied a huge space in my life, and I didn't think about Roxie much. Until she showed up one day.

***

Raz had called out a greeting as Bets arrived home, then came into the front entryway wiping a plate with a dishtowel. He kissed her, stepped back as she removed her shoes.

—How was your day? He asked.

—Long. I'm zonked.

—We have a guest, he said, slinging the dish towel over his shoulder, holding the plate against his chest.

—A guest?

He looked at her in a way she couldn't quite understand, and then she heard footsteps and knew who would appear.

—Hiya Bets!

Bets' first thought was, she's so thin. Roxie was smiling widely, and Bets noticed that her beautiful teeth were stained yellow. Her hair was piled up on her head, tousled yet somehow chic; short skirt, cropped shirt, leather-ish jacket. And her eyes—there was something about her eyes.

—Bets, prompted Raz, can you say *high*?

Emphasizing the last word, widening his eyes at her as she stood frozen to the spot.

—Hi Roxie, said Bets at last. This is a surprise.

—I know! Roxie threw her arms around Bets, rocking her. Isn't it great? I found you! You moved! You moved in with this dishy man!

Indicating Raz, then knocking him with her elbow.

—*Voulez-vous coucher avec moi*? She gave an exaggerated Pepe Le Pew laugh, *hmm hmm hmm*, and draped her arms around Raz, who stood with his hands full of dish, tolerating the hug, managing to shrug at Bets at the same time.

—Is there food happening? Asked Bets, in a chirpy voice completely unlike her usual. I'm starving!

Roxie let go of Raz and clapped her hands.

—Yes! Dishy man cooked for us! A man of so many skills!

Roxie swirled into the kitchen, leaving Raz and Bets alone in the entry-way looking at each other.

—How long has she been here? Asked Bets, sotto voce.

—Long enough to proposition me and drink a bottle of wine. Maybe half an hour.

—Oh God.

—Do you need time to shower and recover a bit?

—Well, now I'm afraid to leave you two alone, said Bets, trying to laugh, but it came out as a high-pitched squeak.

Raz snapped her with the dish towel, and she felt a bit of herself return to her body.

—Okay, she said. I'm coming.

Raz kissed her again, the lightest sweep of lips on hers, sauntered back to the kitchen as Roxie began a loud, off-tune version of "All by Myself."

Roxie ate little but compensated with wine. She talked nonstop, going off on tangents, not always making sense. She stopped, said "I'm talking all about myself!" then launched into another stream of consciousness. She was restless and jumped to her feet several times during the meal, pacing the kitchen, sitting, jumping up again, sitting with her feet tucked onto the chair, turning the chair around, sitting back down. Finally, she paused, took one of Raz's hands, one of Bets', smiled at them.

—Look at you two. Just look at you. Playing house together. All grown up. You're so cute together! I love this! I love that you're together! I love that this man won't sleep with me! Roxie laughed, throwing her head back, squeezing their hands. Just as quickly, she was up and pacing.

—Now that I've found you, we can spend more time together, she said. I'm in need of somewhere to stay. And I'm in what you might call a cash-poor time of my life.

She returned to her backward chair, turned it forward, sat, looked from Raz to Bets.

—What do you say? I could stay here, help you guys out a bit, maybe you could pay me! What do you say?

She smiled her heart-splitting Roxie smile, so familiar other than the yellow teeth, other than the expression in her eyes, the edge of desperation in their full gaze. Bets opened her mouth to say of course you can stay, even though she knew she should not, even though she knew this wasn't even Roxie herself talking, but some other substance using Roxie as a spokesperson.

Before anything further could happen, Raz took back Roxie's hand.

—Roxie, he said. We are so very glad you came. I've heard so much about you! We can't take you in, but wonderful to see the real thing. You are every bit as beautiful as Bets described.

—Did she say that? Really?

Roxie turned to Bets, her expression unreadable.

—Did you say I was beautiful? Bets, recovered a bit, forced a smile.

—Of course. I always describe you that way.

Roxie reached over, touched Bets' face. Bets held Roxie's strange gaze, felt she was facing a wild animal, something she had placated for a moment, something that could turn on her and clamp onto her throat.

—So, he speaks for you? Asked Roxie, a hardness in her voice, hand still on Bets' face.

Bets felt Raz tense beside her.

—No, said Bets carefully. But I agree with him.

She reached up to her cheek, put her hand over Roxie's.

—We can each make our own way, Roxie. We always have.

There was a pause, in which Bets was very aware of Raz, coiled like a spring beside her, and the knives in the knife block, and the forks on the table, and her own heartbeat throbbing in her ears, so loudly she could hardly hear. And Roxie, whose smile had faded, who held Bets' gaze, who was motionless for the longest time since she arrived, finally patted Bets' cheek, and smiled.

—Okay. She said. I thought, maybe family means more than romance. But okay. I want you guys to be happy.

She got up, finished the dregs of her wine, and this time Bets and Raz stood up as well.

—I'm gonna go, she said, weaving slightly as she walked out of the kitchen.

Bets and Raz exchanged a glance. Bets rubbed her fingers together at Raz: *get some money.* Raz frowned at her and she widened her eyes at him. He cleared his throat, pulled his wallet from his back pocket.

Roxie had stumbled into the powder room, and was now stumbling out again, holding the wall.

—Where are you going? Asked Bets. Can I call you a cab?

Roxie leaned against the wall for a moment and closed her eyes.

—Nah. I'll walk. I'm good. I'll find some people.

—Roxie, why don't I call you a cab. Maybe to take you to detox?

Roxie laughed, reached out to pat Bets' shoulder.

—Bets, she said, you'll never change. I love that about you. She stretched, arched her back.

—I don't want to detox, Betsy baby. I want to go out and get really, really high.

She stood inches from Bets, looked into her eyes with her off-kilter, still devastating, Roxie gaze.

—I'm gonna make things work, Bets. I'm gonna show you both.

Raz appeared at Bets' shoulder, placed some rolled up bills into her hand. Bets reached out to Roxie.

—Here. Here's some money.

Roxie took the bills, tucked them inside her bra, looking meaningfully at Raz as she pulled her shirt aside briefly.

—Well thanks, guys, guess I owe you one. Even if you don't want me to help out and earn it. Even if you don't fucking care.

She walked to the door, opened it, turned.

—You just live your happy little lives here, okay? Don't worry about me. Maybe I'll see you around.

She blew a kiss, left the house, pulled the door closed behind her. Bets leaned her head against the door, and Raz sat down on the steps, and they stayed like that until the sun finished setting and it was fully dark.

***

Hannah stood at the fence, looking out at the neighbour's yard.

—I'm sorry, Bets.

—Sorry for what?

—I'm sorry I said Roxie sounded like so much fun. I'm sorry I said how lucky you were to have a sister.

—Don't be sorry, said Bets. Roxie *was* fun, for a while. I felt lucky that she was sister. She showed me how life could be if you didn't overthink and analyze every action. The good and the bad of that.

Hannah didn't turn, and all Bets could see was the thick braid like a ship's rope that hung down her back.

—Why wouldn't she go to detox? Why didn't she want to change?

—I guess, said Bets, it's not that simple. It feels simple to us—just don't do this anymore!—but it's not like that in reality. The drugs make them feel something—or not feel something—and then that's all they want.

—But you gave her money.

—Yes.

Hannah turned to face Bets.

—But she probably went to buy drugs with it!

—Yes.

—So why give it then? Hannah was biting her lip.

—I guess that's all I really felt like I could do. What else could I do?

—You could tell her you won't give her anything! Hannah said, frustrated. You could tell her you won't pay for her habit! That it's ruining her life!

A pause.

—And what would happen then? Bets asked, softly. Hannah looked into Bets' eyes: pain, despair, sadness, loss.

—She'd tell you to f-off? Said Hannah, volume lowered.

—Now you see the problem.

—Did she come by again?

—Sometimes. If she wanted some cash. Not that often, considering she must have needed money all the time. Anyway, said Bets, changing tone, standing, that's enough about that. So depressing! New topic?

Hannah shook her head.

—Hannah, Bets touched her arm briefly. You're very young for all this heavy stuff. Just because my life has had sad moments doesn't mean you need to load it all onto yourself.

—You were living through this, at my age, not just hearing about it, said Hannah. Plus, honestly? I feel like you need to talk about it.

I need to talk about it? Did a seventeen-year-old just tell me I was holding everything inside? Bets stopped in the hallway, in front of the photo of herself and Roxie, laughing together. That stupid mortarboard. She felt like she should maybe be crying, but there was only emptiness.

***

After Bets saw Roxie in the hospital, after the pregnancy termination, she thought about cutting Roxie out of her life. *How is this relationship helping me? Why even stay in contact with this person, this person whose life is completely out of control, who gets pregnant and ends it on a whim, when I tried for years, and years?*

She asked Raz, of course.

—Why can't we have normal sisters? She asked, as they both lay awake in bed, many nights over the years.

—Who decides what is normal? His usual style.

—Lots of people get along with their sisters, or their sisters-in-law. It can be normal.

Raz placed his hands behind his head and laughed softly.

—What is it you want, exactly?

Bets considered for a moment.

—I guess someone to talk to. Someone who understands me. Someone to, you know, visit, and spend holidays together.

—Well, said Raz. Visiting. Holidays. You watch too many of those romance movies. Bets punched his arm.

—Plus, he added, you have someone to talk to, who understands you! *Un bel homme, ici dans ton lit*! He rolled himself on top of her unexpectedly, pinning her arms, kissing her nose.

Bets flailed and struggled.

—Get off me. You're too heavy.

He dropped his full weight onto her, then rolled off obligingly.

—You're being difficult.

—Difficult!

He shook his head.

—I'm trying to help you process your sister. She has addictions, and is unreliable, and you can't forgive her for the abortion. It seems very simple to me; you either want her in your life, or you don't. If you don't, then don't see her anymore. If you do, then you know what you are getting into, and you accept that as the cost of having a relationship with her. See?

He dusted his hands together.

—*Très simple.*

Bets knew he was being provocative, despite the logic.

—If it's so simple, then why do you complain about Josée? She snuggled against him.

—Ah, Josée, he said. Josée is a lost cause. She set her joy down somewhere and can't remember where she put it.

—But you want her in your life?

—Are you turning my own philosophy onto me?

—Absolutely. I demand consistency.

—Well. She's my sister.

He said it as he always did, without emphasis, without judgement, as if it explained everything.

Which perhaps it did.

CHAPTER FIFTEEN

Sometimes, after Hannah left, Bets looked at herself in the mirror, even though she knew better. Comparing herself to someone over forty years younger, how was that going to end well?

She saw a woman in her sixties. She was tired of the ads showing women with flawless skin and subtitles like "I'm fifty-three, did you guess?" or "Look ten years younger!" She saw wrinkles around her eyes and across her forehead, a few starting to rise from her upper lip. She saw her neck taking on a crepey texture, also a devastating find, according to magazines; she knew women who only wore turtlenecks, as if skin changes were deformities, as if people recoiled in horror at the sight of wrinkly necks. In the mirror, she saw blue eyes, so much like Roxie's, and yet so different; less disarming, with shorter lashes and less defined brows. She saw short grey hair, styled to one side, much the same over the last forty years, since cutting it off in nursing school. She saw points, and angles, jaw and cheekbone and collarbone, and was reminded of a man she overheard one day referring to his girlfriend as a bag of hangers.

Years ago, when Bets decided not to colour her hair anymore, she did so with the same trepidation she had felt when cutting it off in the first place. Was she ready to be considered old? *Who am I kidding? Roxie has called me an old lady since I was ten.*

It had taken a few months to grow the colour out fully, despite her short hair, and she felt like a rabbit transitioning to its winter white; occasionally, you spotted one in November with a brown body but white legs, its body not yet committed to winter camouflage. Did other rabbits mock? Were there some rabbits who transitioned effortlessly in a day, who never appeared motley? Were they the cool rabbits?

Once Bets' hair was fully gray, she had it cut and styled, and there was much oohing and aahing at the hair salon as they spun her chair to show her the back, as she sat with her little hand mirror. The hairdresser had changed the style a bit and sold her an outrageously expensive hair wax so she could maintain it.

—You're still young, keep it hip! Urged the hairdresser, Bets' favourite for years, who had a pierced nose, and whose hair was bright orange and spiked out like a puffer fish, her ears filled with lines of earrings like studded tires.

—You're so brave, said the other stylists, you look great! I wish I had the guts to stop colouring! Gorgeous gray! Look at the low lights!

Bets had no idea what low lights were. She heard, hiding under the word "brave," the word "crazy," but the positive feedback worked. She left with her wax, feeling like an invisible cord from the sky was pulling her head upward.

She had spontaneously gone to the drugstore to get a lipstick, to complete her transformation. The girl at the makeup counter—eighteen years old, by Bets' estimation—was surprisingly patient and helpful, and was done up very tastefully, inspiring confidence in Bets, who normally liked conservative people, hairdresser notwithstanding. With the girl's help, Bets was able to navigate matte lipstick vs. gloss, lip liner and colours that might match her skin tone. Soon she had a basket of tubes and packages, from which she selected two for purchase and headed to the checkout. She paused for some gum, her attention diverted when the cashier, swiping her purchases, asked if she'd like to use her senior's discount.

—Pardon me?

—I said, repeated the cashier, do you want the senior's discount?

—How old do I have to be to qualify? Bets immediately regretted her question.

—Sixty-five.

The cashier, young and shaggy, wearing a plaid shirt under his drugstore smock, stood behind his counter, face blank, passive as a cow. He was even chewing something.

Sixty-five.

Bets was fifty-two. There was a brief silence.

—Sure, said Bets, forcing a smile. Discount for sure.

He didn't ask for ID.

Sitting in the car in the parking lot, Bets had considered going back inside for hair dye. Instead, she went home, where Raz declared her *la plus belle au monde*, which helped, but the lipstick stayed in its bag until she found it a few weeks later and threw it out.

—I think you may need to trade me in for a newer model, she said lightly, as she and Raz prepared for bed that night. He furrowed his brows, flossing.

—Why? He mouthed around the floss.

—I don't know. The cashier at Shopper's asked me if I wanted the Senior's discount.

Raz rinsed his mouth, checked his teeth in the mirror.

—Did you take it?

—Yes.

—Well, then! He tapped her shoulder. Well done!

She shrugged him off.

—I'm not supposed to look old enough to get the Senior's discount.

—It was probably some teenager, said Raz, they think everyone over thirty is ready for a nursing home.

—True, she admitted. Maybe I should keep colouring my hair.

Raz ran his fingers through her hair, standing behind her, both looking in the mirror.

—If you want, he said, but your gray is wonderful. Your hair is perfect.

—Easy for you to say.

Raz turned her around to face him.

—Is this just because of some stupid teenager at the drugstore?

—I don't want to be old. I don't want people to think I'm old.

—Why not?

Bets paused.

—Well, because. I don't know. Old things are used up, not worthwhile. And don't say I'm like a fine wine.

—Damn, you stole my line.

Raz went to touch her hair again, and she pushed his hand away.

—Bets, he said after a moment, I don't know what's happening right now. I don't care how old you are; I don't care what colour your hair is; I don't care about drugstore morons. I just want you, and I want you to be happy.

Bets wanted to let it go, but persisted.

—But don't you ever wish you had one of those wives with the makeup, and the clingy dresses, and the high heels?

—I feel like you're not listening, said Raz, crossing his arms, leaning against the wall. *Chérie.* You are more like a pair of comfy jeans.

—I don't think I'm going to like this.

—Give me a moment! A pair of comfy jeans. Not new jeans, but the ones that are broken in just right, that fit in all the right places. The ones that can't be replaced.

Bets felt her despair lift slightly from her shoulders and neck.

—Maybe your friends, continued Raz, look at some jeans, say, wow those are so stylish! *Incroyable!* Or, those are so new! So different! But what do you want, every day, when you get home from work? What do you really want to wear?

He waited.

—The comfy jeans, admitted Bets. Raz smiled broadly.

—*Absolument.* The comfy jeans. Every day I come home just so happy to get into those comfy jeans.

He opened his arms, raised his eyebrows. Bets nodded, and he enveloped her into the hug.

—Only you, said Bets, could make a woman feel better by comparing her to a pair of comfy jeans.

***

—Here's what I'm thinking, said Hannah.

She sat across from Bets, licking the spoon as she conquered a yogurt in quarter-teaspoon sized bites, glasses sliding down her nose, hair looped up in a high elastic and cascading down on all sides.

—I'm thinking, you can start to train me as a nurse, and that way I don't look dumb when I start! Great, right?

—Train you? Hannah, you need background. You need school. You can't just randomly start.

—Why not?

Hannah put down her spoon and struck the table, knocking the spoon onto the floor. She bent to pick it up and hit her head on the table as she straightened.

Bets winced.

—Why not? Asked Hannah again, rubbing her head. You show me how to ask questions, how to, I don't know, feel a pregnant belly, or take a blood pressure. Right? That way, when I'm in school, everyone thinks I'm super smart.

—Why does it matter what other people think?

Hannah picked up her spoon again, took a micro-scoop of yogurt, turned the spoon upside down, sucked it clean.

—It matters, she said, gesturing with the spoon. It matters to everyone. Even you! Bets cleared her throat.

—Hannah, you're getting way ahead of yourself. You're not even ready to finish high school yet! You have all kinds of time to prepare yourself for your life. I thought our talks were to help you decide if you even want to *be* a nurse, not train to become one!

Hannah scooped again.

—Also, said Bets, *why* are you eating your yogurt that way? It's making me crazy.

Hannah paused with the spoon already in her mouth, upside down.

—Whah way? She mouthed around the spoon.

—Oh, Lord.

Hannah put down the spoon.

—Listen. When you have trainees, don't you like them to know something? Don't you want them to be quick, and smart, and helpful?

—It depends.

—It depends? Depends on what? Asked Hannah. How can it depend?

***

There were doctors who were there all the time: Dr. Jenna, when she wasn't having babies of her own, who used her first name because of the multiple g's and z's in her complicated surname.

There was Dr. Martin (surprisingly accepting of the footwear jokes), and Dr. McIlroy. But the three of them needed breaks sometimes, and babies just kept coming, and the midwife and the family physicians couldn't do the surgeries and gynecologic procedures, so they had to have visiting obstetricians—locums—each new locum bringing a unique style, attitude towards nurses, and level of competency. Some of them came once, in winter, experienced minus forty Celsius for the first time, and never came back. The third time a visiting locum missed a delivery because they didn't know to plug in their car, the hospital board prepared a handout, and called the single car rental company in town to remind them for God's sake to include an extension cord with the rental and explain about the block heater.

Some locums came from large hospitals in southern Ontario or Québec, and were completely unprepared for the lack of equipment, manpower, and services that they were used to, and new nurses could be exactly the same.

Breanna, young, excited to be working full time when she moved to town due to her husband's job, walked into the maternity ward radiating energy and ideas.

—Wow, you guys get your own scrubs! She gushed. We had to all wear the same colour, so that people could tell which department we were from! We had a dispensing machine to get them from each morning! You had to use your ID badge!

Bets was in charge of her training period. She toured Breanna around.

—Wow, you still have ward rooms? With curtains? Our new hospital had all single rooms on maternity, and I heard the curtains were contamination risks. Are these older beds? I haven't seen these ones before.

Bets demonstrated the use of the beds; side rails, brakes, controls to raise and lower.

—Hospital bed's a hospital bed, was her comment, even though she knew full well that each one had its idiosyncrasies—the nurses joked that each new bed had a slightly different mechanism to raise and lower the side rails, just to make them look like idiots. She didn't feel like sharing that with Breanna.

They toured the nursery, which apparently had much less high-tech equipment than at Breanna's old hospital, and the birthing rooms, with their special beds that came apart and allowed for different birthing positions.

—Oh, *here* are the beds I'm used to, said Breanna, smoothing one with her hand as if stroking a dog. We had the privates, right, so everything was done in the one room. The labour, the birth, the recovery with the baby. It was really great.

—It sounds great, said Bets, voice neutral.

—Where are the birthing balls? And the bathtubs?

—Patients bring their own balls. And we don't have a bathtub. Sometimes the midwife brings a portable pool.

Breanna's eyes widened, and she shook her head ever so slightly. Bets felt her neck muscles tightening.

Their day began quickly. They were the float nurses, so that Bets would have time to train, and they started off helping with the walk-in patients who arrived all at the same time. One young girl was complaining of a headache, and Breanna's questioning, manner, and diagnosis (probable pre-eclampsia) were so efficient and accurate, Bets had to take a moment to dismantle the mental folder into which she'd already filed Breanna.

—Great, so what next? She asked. Breanna ticked items off on her fingers.

—Start an IV, call the doctor, see if they want any lab work, get a urine sample, monitor the baby, chart the visit.

Bets showed her where to find the on-call doctor's name and number, after which Breanna looked at the list of names.

—How do I call the IV team?

—The what?

—The IV team. To come and do the IV?

Bets laughed softly. She left for a moment and returned with a plastic divided tray with a handle, setting it down in front of Breanna.

—Here's the IV team, she said. Have you done any IV insertions? Breanna looked at the tray of needles, swabs, and tubing, and at Bets.

—Not for a while.

—Okay, said Bets, no time like the present to get back at it.

Breanna needed very little guidance and had no trouble with the IV. She became quieter.

They were called in for baby care at a c-section, and as they put on their surgical gear, including the cotton gowns, Breanna commented that her old hospital had great Gore-Tex gowns that never stained.

—Where do we find the number for the neonatologist?

—Well, said Bets, we don't usually call the neonatologists, since they are in Toronto, or Ottawa. The pediatrician calls them if she needs help.

—When do we call the pediatrician? Asked Breanna, in a smaller voice.

—If something goes wrong, said Bets, or if we think the baby's in distress. This c-section is elective, everything should be fine.

—What if… it isn't? Asked Breanna, as they put on their caps and masks.

—Then let's hope you remember your neonatal resuscitation!

Bets patted Breanna's shoulder cheerfully and pushed open the operating room door.

***

—Okay, she was obnoxious, said Hannah. I'd have slapped her.

Bets threw back her head and laughed.

—Of course, you wouldn't have. I'm just saying…

—It's not always good to think you know everything?

—It's always good to show a little humility, to learn how things are, wherever you are. That's one for the notebook.

She waited while Hannah wrote.

—Breanna is a skilled nurse. We just didn't start off well.

—But, said Hannah, would you have *ever* liked her, if she was also dumb?

—Hannah, said Bets, rolling her eyes skyward. You're not dumb. You'll never come across as dumb. Besides, that's inaccurate speech. It means you can't talk.

—Oh, Lord. Hannah imitated Bets perfectly.

—I just want to jump ahead. I want to skip the part where everything's new and I look stupid all the time, and just be where *you* are, where you know everything and you've seen it all and nothing can upset you.

—Well, it's not quite like that. Did you just put that yogurt back empty?

Hannah retrieved the empty yogurt carton from the fridge, handing it to Bets.

—You learn, and you keep learning, said Bets, rinsing the container. It's a forever thing. You never know everything. Never!

—But that's so frustrating.

—That keeps it interesting.

—Okay, tell me about another nurse. One who had, what did you say? Humility?

Hannah jumped up to sit on the countertop, legs dangling. The jar containing a bouquet of wooden spoons toppled beside her.

***

Bets had three ladies in labour one shift when a tall, ginger-haired young man in a hip-length white coat, wearing a stethoscope around his neck, hovered by the nursing station. Bets went in and out of a couple of rooms, willing him to disappear, but when she returned, he was still lurking there, swallowing, and smoothing his hair to one side.

—May I help you? She asked.

—I'm, um, I'm a physician assistant student, I'm working with Dr. McIlroy? He said we had someone in labour?

The student glanced around, and there was a long groan from one of the labour rooms. He looked like someone had just mentioned an approaching tsunami.

—Well, I don't think Dr. McIlroy is here yet, said Bets, extending her hand. I'm Bets. You can tag along with me if you want.

—Adam.

He had a firm handshake. There was another shriek from down the hall.

—Sounds like we'd better go check on Mrs. Southwind, said Bets. Have you seen any deliveries yet?

Adam mutely shook his head. *Great*, thought Bets, *he's going to faint, and I'll have two patients on my hands.* She grabbed a package of cookies on her way past the ice machine in the hallway.

— Here, she said to Adam, eat these. Did you have lunch?

He nodded, confused, accepted the cookies.

—Follow me, she said, and headed to labour room two, where Desi was wailing loudly with each contraction, and grunting a bit. She had her sister Nel with her, holding her hands and trying to keep her focused.

—I think it's coming, said Nel.

—I think you're right. Desi, can I get you to lie down? That's the way.

Bets introduced Adam, and asked if he could stay, and Nel glanced at Desi, who shrugged and lay back heavily.

Desi had been only five centimetres, and now Bets' probing fingers felt hair.

—Oh yes, she said, baby's coming. Adam, press that white button on the wall there. Please? Thanks.

Desi whimpered again, grabbed for her sister.

—Adam, said Bets, take off your jacket and grab two of those plastic aprons on the table, and some gloves for each of us.

Within moments, Bets lowered the base of the bed, tucked a drape under Desi's bottom, put on her gloves and apron, and pulled the sterile cloth away from the delivery table to reveal the equipment.

—Call Dr. McIlroy, Desi's delivering. If he's at the cottage, he's not going to make it, Lexus or no Lexus, she called to Shannon, who had appeared in response to the call button.

Desi let out a mighty shout and pushed. Adam took a step back, holding his hands up facing him like a surgeon.

—Desi, you are doing really well. Baby is coming, said Bets. Adam, put your hands down, we're not in surgery. This is not a sterile procedure. Come here beside me.

Adam squeezed in beside Bets as Desi screeched and pushed again, this time emptying her bowels as the baby's head emerged a bit more and then slid back.

—Aaah, I'm having a crap! I can't hold it! Aaaah, she pushed again. Bets deftly reached for another drape, covering the soiled area, and guided Adam's hands to the baby's head.

—Don't worry, Desi, said Bets, happens all the time. You can't push one without the other.

There was a pause. Desi's eyes rolled back, and she stopped panting and breathed more heavily. There was silence other than the soft gurgly hum of the suction machine. The baby's scalp remained visible between Desi's legs, and Bets checked the fetal heartbeat—normal. Nel and Adam looked at each other, then at Bets.

—We're fine, said Bets. Her body's just giving her a little endorphin break before her final delivery. Her contraction will wake her up in a second. Adam, get ready: it's a myth that doctors and midwives deliver babies. Women deliver babies, and they are very good at it, especially fourth babies like Desi's here. Our job is to control the birth, so she doesn't tear from top to bottom, so we have to push against the baby so it eases out gradually. Got it? Ready to push?

Adam's eyes were panicky, and he appeared sweaty.

—Adam, Desi needs you, said Bets, but if you're going to faint, for God's sake sit down on the floor.

—I'm okay, squeaked Adam, just as Desi woke with a bellow and immediately pushed hard, teeth clamped, a long guttural noise following from her throat.

Bets placed her hands over Adam's, pushing against the emerging head. They could see more scalp, and more, and more.

—My God, said Adam, now visibly pouring with sweat.

—How big was last baby? Bets asked Nel.

—Nine and a half, said Nel, looking at Desi, squeezing her hand, guiding Desi's long black hair off her forehead. Desi rested once more, and Bets could see a third of the baby's head, staying in place. Point of no return. She checked the heartbeat.

—Next contraction we're having your baby, Desi, said Bets. Adam's hands remained locked in position.

—Adam's ready. Don't bear down, Adam, you'll get hemorrhoids. Just push against the baby's head.

When Desi pushed again, Bets and Adam gave counterpressure, the head slowly emerged, and once it was out, Bets guided Adam: one shoulder out, second shoulder out—get ready, Adam!—the rest of the baby in a rush onto the bed. Bets picked up the baby, already squalling, and placed her on Desi's chest.

—Your new little girl, Desi. She turned back to Adam, who stood with his face wet with sweat and tears, hands held up in front of him again.

—Beautiful, isn't it? She smiled at him. The miracle of birth. There's nothing like the first time.

—When can I do another one? He asked, giving a loud sniffle, and they both laughed.

—Let's finish the job here first, Adam. Then we can worry about your new career path.

They bent their heads together over the umbilical cord, the placenta, while Desi and Nel cooed over the new baby.

What advice should she give, thought Bets, guiding Adam along, helping him to take the cord blood. What does he need to know?

She heard the unit doors crash open, and the stampeding footsteps of Dr. McIlroy. I know, thought Bets. Don't get a cottage.

Or a Lexus.

CHAPTER SIXTEEN

Bets sat in the sun on her front porch, feeling the ache in her neck and knees after an hour of weeding. *In Northern Ontario, we appreciate summer*, she thought. Everywhere, there were people walking, or gardening, or mowing lawns; children's voices called and shrieked; bicycles whizzed by at regular intervals; dogs barked; smells of barbecued meat and backyard fire pits filled the late afternoon air. People loaded four-wheelers onto their trucks, hooked up boat trailers, called to each other across fences.

Hannah, sitting on the step with Bets, wore her hair tied back in a bun, unusually tidy, other than some strands that escaped and blew gently around her face. She wore a sundress and sandals, and a woven bag across her body. Her lips were bright red, and her eyes unusually prominent behind her glasses.

—What will you do on your date with Nate? Asked Bets.

—I don't know. Someone is having a fire out at the gravel pit, so we'll probably go there.

Hannah broke a piece off the cedar that reached out to her from beside the porch, bent off a branch, brought it to her nose.

—I love the smell of cedar.

—Me too, agreed Bets. I need to trim those. But look at me—I weeded! Remember the garden a few weeks ago?

They both laughed.

—Thank God for perennials, said Bets. It would still be brown sludge otherwise!

They sat in silence for a while, enjoying the warmth of the sun.

—So, you and Nate, that's been awhile, noted Bets. Everything good? No more jealousy?

Hannah peeled the bark away from her cedar branch.

—Sometimes. I'm dealing with it, though.

She played with the branch, bending it, twisting it into a knot.

—Can we talk about Raz today?

—Raz? What do you want to know?

Easy, Bets. Easy there. No need for high alert.

—I want to hear more about the mine. Or do we need Eddie?

Bets dusted her hands on her shorts.

—I think I should be able to manage. Eddie and Raz were always telling stories.

Are you good to stay here? Sitting on the step?

Hannah leaned against the railing, face to the sun, looking serene for a change, instead of scattered and frantic.

—I could sit like this forever, she said, closing her eyes.

—I know what you mean. If only it lasted longer.

Bets unfurled herself in a long, full stretch. Raz used to say, winter is for strength, summer is for wonder.

Hannah smiled without opening her eyes.

—I hope I marry someone wise like that.

—Well, said Bets, picturing Raz with his hair askew in the morning, or removing his dental plate to grimace at her. I don't know about *wise.*

***

Raz and Eddie were working together again, so it was a good day. Eddie was spot on with his jokes, the raise was halfway finished, which meant less climbing, and they were having one of those days where everything was in sync, where the blast had been clear, there was minimal scaling needed, and the drilling had been smooth and easy. They weren't getting in each other's way, no loose was falling, equipment was staying in place. They were sitting side by side on the staging enjoying a well-deserved water break when they smelled sulfur gas.

—Damn it, you smell that? Eddie pocketed his water.

Raz put his hard hat back on. Stench gas meant emergency, so they had to descend as quickly as possible and get to the refuge station. They could already hear commotion in the drift below them. Eddie flipped himself onto the ladder and started down, Raz right behind him. At some point in their rapid descent, Raz's boot connected with Eddie's hard hat.

—Ow! Raz! Watch where you're going, asshole!

—Sorry, sorry.

He slowed down, and once on the lowest ladder they both jumped, and joined the other men merging into the drift from various raises, arriving at the refuge station panting, some bending forward to get air, not used to the running. The supervisor, Denis, was in the station with his clipboard and a stopwatch, ticking off names as men appeared.

—Are you kidding me? Groaned Eddie. It's a drill.

There were protests all around. When the last worker had entered the room, Denis stopped the watch and called for order, his voice barely audible over the din of complaints. Denis's two-finger whistle, so piercing it penetrated even earplugs and headsets, finally achieved silence, after which he picked up the telephone and called in, listing off all the men he had in the refuge.

—You guys were slower than last time, and Meyers, Loranger, you guys took way too long. If there's an actual gas leak, or a fire, or whatever, I don't want to have to go out and find you. And if we should be sealing off the door, do you really want your co-workers to die because you took too long to get here?

The two men looked at the floor, like boys being chastised for stealing cookies.

—Okay, said Denis, remember, drills are important. They're for everyone's safety. Please take them seriously. Let's be faster next time. Back to work, everyone!

The miners began filing from the room, and as they shuffled forward, Eddie whacked Raz on the side of the head.

—Hey! *Câlisse*, what was that?

—That was for kicking me on the way down, said Eddie.

—Kicking you! You were so slow, I hit you with my boot! Raz kicked Eddie's boot, tripping him slightly.

—If I want to kick you, you'll know it.

—Oh yeah? Eddie shoved Raz with his shoulder.

—Oh yeah! Raz tackled Eddie around the waist.

They both went down, grappling for a few minutes before they were laughing too hard to continue. A pair of boots appeared beside them and they looked up into the unsmiling face of Denis.

—What are you guys, nine years old? We just lost half an hour. Stop dicking around.

He moved past them as they hauled themselves to their feet, both breathing heavily.

—Sorry I kicked you, said Raz to Eddie. I should have slid down and knocked your fat ass off the ladder.

They both felt more sluggish as they climbed back up to the staging, frustrated that their rhythm had been interrupted and was now unlikely to return. Eddie climbed first, then Raz, hauling the fifty-pound bag of Amex explosive over one shoulder, to save having to do it later. They were on the fourth ladder when Eddie stopped abruptly, nearly causing Raz to collide with his feet.

—*Câlisse*, shouted Eddie in imitation of Raz, I left my water bottle down there.

Raz, raising a hand to block the light from Eddie's lamp, looked up at him. There was no way to pass each other. Raz sighed heavily, knocked Eddie's boot.

—I'll get it. Here, take this.

It was punishment, in a way; he handed up the heavy bag of explosive to compensate for the descent and ascent that he'd have to do for something as minor—and yet as necessary—as a water bottle.

They had passed equipment up and down to each other hundreds of times, perhaps thousands, and they spent most of their days on ladders, so neither one could describe what exactly happened. Raz stretched the heavy bag above his head, Eddie reached down on his left to grasp it, shifted his boot for better positioning, lost the grip of his right hand, and fell.

Raz instinctively tried to grab him, despite still holding the bag, realizing afterwards it was a terrible strategy and would have resulted in both of them going down. Eddie tumbled past him, and Raz barely kept his own balance as Eddie's weight pushed him against the ladder on the way by.

—Eddie! He yelled. Eddie!

He couldn't see well, even with his headlamp. He climbed down, possibly faster than he'd ever climbed in his life, and put down the bag as he scanned with his lamp and found Eddie's body on the ground, silent.

—Shit. Shit, Eddie! Help!

He ran to Eddie, tearing off his gloves, throwing his earmuffs, his safety glasses, bending over his friend.

—Be okay. Eddie! Be okay.

He reached out, gingerly shook Eddie, tried to look for obvious injuries.

—Help! I need some help down here!

He looked at nearby raises, but no one was around. He turned back to Eddie. Best to assess the damage, then run for help. Maybe he needed to start CPR. He gently pulled on Eddie's shoulder to turn him onto his back. Eddie screamed, reached up, and grabbed Raz in a bear hug, laughing hysterically.

—OH, YES! I GOT YOU! I GOT YOU SO GOOD!

Eddie pounded Raz's back. Raz jerked away, jumped up, stared down at him.

—You—you were faking it? You're okay?

Eddie lay back, lifted his arms in victory.

—Whooooohoooo! He shouted, giggling again. You were awesome. He switched to falsetto. Eddie! Be okay Eddie! Help!

Raz bent down, elbows on knees, gathering emotions. Relief and anger wrestled for dominance, and despite his powerful urge to kick Eddie with his steel-toed boots, relief won out.

—You seriously okay, you *fils de pute*?

—Not bad. I rolled the landing.

Eddie giggled again, shining his lamp into Raz's face.

—You okay?

—You're lucky I didn't have a fucking heart attack. What the hell is wrong with you?

—Hey, hey, hey, Raz, said Eddie, getting up with a grunt, it's all in good fun.

—What if you were seriously hurt?

Raz shook his head and stood back up, swung his lamp to find his discarded gear. Eddie came and slapped him on the back.

—I won't be seriously hurt. Nine lives, man!

Raz shook his head again, knocked the ladder in absence of actual wood.

—Eddie. Just get your goddamn water bottle.

***

—Eddie sounds like an idiot in that story, observed Hannah.

—He is an idiot, but he is a very loving and loveable idiot. So that's something. That day, Raz wasn't much better.

Hannah stood, stretched, put one foot up on the steps.

—It sounds very repetitive. The same thing every day.

—Actually, Raz would argue that every raise, every vein you follow, every face you're drilling, they're each slightly different. He liked the variety of it. Same as nursing, really.

—It's nothing like nursing!

—Well, but your basic day is the same. Your tasks are the same. It's just that the order changes, or some crisis happens, and that mixes things up. The people change, you're with a different team, that kind of thing.

Hannah thought about it for a moment.

—Maybe I shouldn't be a miner, mused Hannah. Not that I was considering it. Maybe Nate shouldn't either.

—Nate will want to make up his own mind.

—But it sounds dangerous!

—Sure, said Bets. If you love somebody, you don't want them to get hurt, but you want them to be happy, to do what's best for them. That's one way you know you love somebody.

Bets had felt left out, sometimes, when it came to the mine. Raz spent so much time there, had so many friends there, yet it was such a mystery. She struggled to navigate the double vocabulary requirements of Raz's French, plus the unique jargon of the miners, which she called Minespeak. It was unfair, really, because if she asked him to tell her about the mine, if she pushed him beyond his usual ("We cycled a round. We always cycle a round"—and in the beginning, even *that* made no sense), then he launched into a story, which she loved, but every few moments, she'd need to interrupt, losing the thread—wait, what's the bit again? What's the stoper? What's the slusher? What's a blast pattern? It was annoying, she knew. She even started a Miner's Wife Vocabulary List, but ultimately Raz tired of explaining, and Bets tired of asking. Raz rarely seemed to think about work once he was home, and she envied him that, her head constantly full of women and babies, every minute of every day.

Let the babies sleep, Bets.

She liked his mining friends, especially Eddie, but had little in common with them. They came over to watch sports—especially to tease Raz if the Habs were losing—or to play cards or dice for money. The evenings with friends tended to be loud, late, and involve a lot of beer; Bets might watch the game with them, if there was one, but went to bed with her custom-made earplugs at her usual time. She couldn't understand how Raz could do shift work, stay up most of the night drinking, and still get up the next morning looking fresh and generally cheerful. She both disliked and admired this ability; usually he had fresh coffee ready when she got up, making ongoing resentment difficult.

Sometimes the mine seemed like a demanding colleague, or another woman, interfering in their relationship, and Raz, sensing her discontent, did what Bets called "pulling a Raz."

He liked to surprise Bets by cooking fancy meals for her at home, or making reservations at high-end restaurants, of which there were very few nearby. This dark, barrel-chested man who could swear like a truck driver, told her they were going on a date, opened and closed the car door for her as if automatic locks were never invented, offered his arm, pulled out her chair once the hostess figured out how to find Laframboise on the reservation list. He loved tasting menus, especially if they came with pre-selected wine pairings, this man who bought Bud Light by the case.

Bets found the restaurants pretentious, with their cucumber-infused water and their little silver pots for pouring sauces that were always "reductions" of this or that. The prices sometimes caused her to excuse herself briefly and go outside for a few deep breaths. Once, someone asked if she needed an ambulance; another time she was offered a cigarette. Both times, she gathered herself and went back into the restaurant because her husband was so excited about the scallops, about the lionfish, about the wine he had chosen that was a wonderful Rioja. He twinkled at these dinners, he was restless as a child waiting for each course, he made loud exclamations with each bite. He inhaled his wine glass, searching for the pear or the smoky nose, he swooshed it on his tongue, then took a bite of food, sighing in ecstasy, asking, how do they do that? How do they know? If it did not live up to his expectations, he rolled his eyes and said, I thought they would do so much more than this. It's so ordinary.

Bets, who enjoyed the food despite her difficulty justifying the price, did appreciate the show Raz provided, as well as the effort. She knew he was doing it mostly for her, to give her something novel, to make it a special evening. They didn't do it often.

—We work hard, Raz told her. We deserve something extra once in a while. What are you saving your money for?

Of course, it was not that simple. She saved her money for retirement, and disability, and emergencies, things not so easily dismissed.

—Ah, said Raz, but think of the people who save and save for retirement, they finally achieve it and then snap! (snapping his fingers for emphasis), *tout à coup*, they're diagnosed with cancer. We've both seen it happen!

It was true. The post-retirement malady was happening so often, at the periphery of their associates, that a dark humour was developing: "Well, Gerry Anderson retired this week." "And what type of cancer does he have?" (Or, "Did he have a heart attack yet?")

Bets was used to the dark humour of health care workers, but the dark humour of miners was new to her.

—You could use that logic for anything, she argued. That's the whole *carpe diem*, live for today thing. If everyone followed that strategy, then no one would have any savings, no one would do anything but indulge themselves.

—Ah, Raz said again, pointing his wineglass at her, but they usually don't, do they? Most people do the occasional indulgent thing, like we are, and the rest of the time live their responsible lives. Some don't, he admitted, but they are the ones who get themselves in trouble. It's all a balance.

He held his hands out to the sides and wobbled them up and down as if balancing himself on a curb or a tightrope.

—What about the people who have no balance? The ones who have no chance to do any of these things? How can we justify indulgence when there are people with nothing?

Raz swirled his wine in the glass.

—Remember, deep down we are all the same, said Raz. *Toi pis moi…* the difference between us and them is mostly luck and circumstance. We must help them, any way we can; you do, every day at work, you try to give them safe births, a good start with their babies, even in terrible situations. Then, you must appreciate your good fortune, which allows you to leave and go home to a safe, warm place. With a loving, handsome man.

He smiled, finished his glass.

—*Tu comprends?*

Asked for the scotch menu.

CHAPTER SEVENTEEN

Bets was old enough to be tactile, rather than digital. She grew up with books and newspapers, she loved the touch, the smell of the paper, she liked ink on her fingers. She couldn't get used to online reading, especially the news, which seemed to provide endless links without a clear start or end point, an inescapable labyrinth of words. The local newspaper was not great, tending towards pun-filled headlines, spelling errors, and photos of local children, but it was something tangible to occupy her during morning coffee, and keep her up to date on local affairs, if nothing else.

The main headline one day was "Opioid Crisis Needling Local Police." The article spoke about the rising number of overdoses, the powerful drugs that had infiltrated the community, the increasing assaults in the downtown. "We need funding," they quoted the police chief. "We need more detox beds."

—More detox beds, said Bets out loud, pushing the paper aside. What about the people who didn't want to go to detox, or rehab, or anywhere? How many times had she asked herself that question? Frequently, recently, her thoughts returned to her sister. Between Hannah's questions and the stream of news, it felt like Roxie was on her mind now more than ever, despite not seeing her for five years.

***

Bets remembered being so focused on work that day that she nearly missed the other nurses talking about Roxie. Conversations sometimes happened in the background as she did other tasks, and she didn't always pay attention. People complained about life, but were unwilling to change anything, and Bets had other things to do.

That day, five years ago, she remembered for two reasons. First, it was Hallowe'en, and the more enthusiastic staff members dressed up for the occasion, making Bets' focus even more impressive, working even as witches drifted up and down the hall, as the cleaner mopped in a sequined red devil suit. Second, the words "drug user" caught her ear and made her tune in. Two nurses (one dressed as Raggedy Ann, the other a pirate), spoke of a patient who required extra security due to violent behaviour. A patient waiting for cardiac surgery, because her valve was infected with bacteria after using a contaminated needle.

—Why do they even treat these people? Asked Raggedy Ann, exasperated. She'll just use again. She tried to inject the pills they gave her, crushed them up and stole a syringe. She keeps pulling out her IVs and trying to leave the hospital. She's on six weeks of antibiotics.

—Did you hear about the friend? The pirate asked. Smuggled in fentanyl patches, and the two of them were smoking them in her room! As if no one was going to notice!

—It's frustrating. Raggedy Ann shook her head. She's taking up space that could be used for someone we could actually help.

Bets moved out of earshot, heart pulsating. Shannon was charting at the desk, wearing flashing pumpkin earrings, and her eyes met Bets' briefly.

Could it be Roxie? What made her even think so? There were many drug users in the community, hundreds, and any of them could have prompted the words. Somehow, for reasons she couldn't explain, she felt they were talking about her sister.

The last contact had been a year and a half earlier. The phone rang, and Bets answered it while doing dishes, still wearing rubber gloves.

—Hello?

She heard an odd noise on the line.

—Hello?

She strained to hear, identified the sound of ragged breathing, like someone who had just been running.

—Who is this?

She saw Raz, drying, look over and make a questioning face. She shrugged.

—Okay, well, I'm hanging up now.

She went to turn off the phone and a hoarse voice said,

—No wait, Bets, I'm here.

—Who is this?

—It's Roxie.

—Roxie? What's going on? What's wrong with your voice?

—Bets, I need... I need money. I need money.

—Money? she repeated stupidly.

—Fuck, I'm in trouble, Bets, I need money. Can you give me some money? I'll pay you back.

Bets pulled a chair over, sat, and shook her head at Raz, who was trying to ask questions.

—Roxie, she said, tell me what is going on.

She held the phone against her shoulder, removed the gloves.

—I can't!

Roxie was crying on the other end now.

—I can't tell you, but I need money! Please, Bets! I can't stand here talking about it!

—Where are you? Bets asked, wishing that had been her first question, willing Roxie not to hang up and disappear again. Tell me where you are, and I'll come and get you. We'll figure it out.

Roxie's raspy breaths continued.

—Roxie? Where are you?

Finally, Roxie responded.

—I'm at the 7-11 on Northern Road. I'm using the cash guy's phone.

—Okay, said Bets with relief, don't leave. Don't leave, I'm coming to get you.

—You have to bring money, said Roxie. I need it tonight.

—How much money are we talking about? Bets was unsure why she suddenly felt like she was underwater.

Roxie's voice was barely audible.

—Two thousand.

—Two thousand DOLLARS? Bets couldn't help shouting. How do you owe someone two thousand dollars?

—Forget it, said Roxie, never mind. Goodbye.

—No, don't hang up!

The phone was dead.

Hands shaking, Bets turned to Raz, who was staring at her. *Stupid, stupid, stupid*, thought Bets, *how could I be so stupid?*

—I need help, it's Roxie.

It was raining, of course, it was dark, they couldn't find keys. Bets' shoe was wedged under a cupboard, Raz dropped his wallet as they raced out, there was no time. Visibility was poor, they got every red light. The third time it happened, Raz looked both ways and went through. Someone in front of them decided to turn left last minute and Bets screamed "Turning left!" and braced for impact, but Raz swerved in time, and eased up slightly after that. They raced through downtown, Raz pausing briefly as they passed the bank with its glowing ATM, but Bets shook her head.

—Keep going, we need to find her first!

Screeching around corners, pulling into the 7-11 parking lot and jerking into an empty spot, braking so hard Bets' head snapped on her neck.

—Stay here, stay here! Watch for her!

Bets ran into the variety store, squinting as the bright lights attacked her, scanning as she walked, ignoring the cashier's May I help you, Miss, in a slightly suspicious tone. Checking each aisle, checking corners, do you have a washroom? The cashier held up a key attached to an enormous piece of wood. The lone other customer, tall and lanky with his hood pulled up, eyed her blandly from the magazine rack. Bets approached the cash and saw the shadow of fear cross the cashier's face. Great, thought Bets, he thinks I'm about to hold up his store. She tried to smooth her hair a bit, forced a smile as she approached. The cashier eyed her as one might an approaching dog; possibly friendly, readying to run just in case.

—I think my sister was just here, said Bets. She may have used your phone to call me? About my height, blonde hair? Or actually, possibly black hair. I haven't seen her in a while.

—What do you want? He asked, and Bets appreciated his loyalty to Roxie.

—I just want to find her. I haven't seen her in months, and it seemed like she might be in trouble.

She saw, as she spoke, that the man at the magazines was listening. She saw the cashier's eyes flit to the man and back. The cashier was very tall and spoke with a slight accent. Probably, he didn't want to work in a variety store. Probably, he was qualified for some other, white-collar job, one that didn't involve late night shifts and desperate women using his phone, and strange hovering men, and slightly crazed sisters.

—Sorry, he said, it's been quiet this evening.

He held Bets' gaze for a moment, then looked down and rearranged the pepperoni sticks standing in a box beside the cash register. Bets was still standing there, unsure what to do, when a police officer opened the door and entered the store, nodding to the cashier.

—Hey Alexei, everything okay?

Alexei smiled, shoulders dropping in relief.

—Sure, need a coffee?

—Nah, said the cop, just stopping by, ticketed a guy in your parking lot, he was speeding. Really, really needed a Slurpee, I guess.

He chuckled at his own joke. Bets glanced out the door at Raz, pictured him with a ticket, cursing in French.

The magazine man skirted the outer aisles, not crossing the cash area, and left the store. Alexei closed his eyes and exhaled. The three of them were now alone in the store. The officer approached the counter, and Bets noticed that although he seemed to take up the entire entry when he arrived, he was not much taller than she was. Alexei towered over him. The cop spoke to Bets.

—Your husband—he jerked his head toward the parking lot—Mr. Speedy there, he said your sister was in trouble?

Bets looked at Alexei.

—She was here, said Alexei. I didn't want to say, that guy already asked about her and I told him no. I don't know what's going on, I don't want to be involved.

—I get it, said Bets. What can you tell us?

Roxie was gone. She'd been in occasionally, but often seemed high. Alexei watched Bets as he spoke, not wanting to offend her, it seemed. She tried to nod, tried to let him know—I'm aware of all this.

Tonight, Roxie had come in very distraught, begged to use his phone, but after she hung up, just gave it back and said, it's no use. She'd left immediately afterwards, and he wasn't sure which way she'd gone. He knew nothing else about her.

Bets turned to the cop, who shrugged.

—I'll keep my eyes open, he said, I'll take your number. I can't promise anything, she's not formally missing.

—But she's in danger! Said Bets.

—Maybe, but we don't know that. Maybe just needing a fix.

They didn't hear anything. Not from the police officer, not from Alexei, who had kindly agreed to call if he saw her again, not from Roxie herself. Bets, when she was home, couldn't sit still. She straightened pictures that were already straight; she organized books on the bookshelf; she wiped the kitchen counter endlessly. Raz let her carry on for a full day before he spoke.

—Bets, there's nothing you can do.

—That's not true! We could take her somewhere, to rehab. We have money. We could have given her the money.

Raz walked up to her, put his hands on her shoulders, waited for her to face him.

—Do you really think money would have made things better?

His eyes were so kind, Bets felt she might crumple to the floor. She shook her head and buried her face in her hands.

—Roxie is in charge of Roxie, whispered Raz finally.

How many times had he said those words to her? And yet. He had nearly killed them trying to get to her; he had received a speeding ticket for his troubles.

That Hallowe'en Day, more than a year later, all she could hear were the harsh words of her costumed colleagues, somehow applying them to her sister. Was she making it all up? She hadn't heard from Roxie since the night of the frantic phone call. Anything could have happened: Roxie could have left town, she could be in a crack house somewhere, she could be dead.

Could she be here, in the very hospital where Bets worked?

It was alarmingly easy to look people up if you wore your staff ID badge and moved with confidence. Unable to find Roxie's name on the database, she went to the medicine floors and asked boldly for the ward rosters, which were handed over with minimal scrutiny. So much for confidentiality.

She flipped through lists, searching until she found Roxanne Gray. Could that be her? Was it possible she had taken legal steps to change her name? Maybe she just lied. Maybe she didn't want to be Roxanne Malcolm anymore.

Room 2724.

Bets found the room and stood just out of view. She listened, and the voice she heard was Roxie's. She didn't look, although she meant to; another staff person came by, and Bets pretended she had dropped something and speed-walked back to maternity. She didn't sleep that night.

Once she knew it was Roxie, Bets tried to keep track of her. She was in hospital, transferred out of town for valve replacement surgery, transferred back, her room changed several times. Bets didn't visit her, but looked in on her occasionally, just stood at the door and watched her watching TV, or sleeping on the bed, with some improbable sunset lighting the window behind her, or snow gently falling, something that made her think of peace, and slumber, even though she had heard about the withdrawal symptoms, the screaming, the demands to leave, the medications, the restraints. She was surprised no one had called her to act as Roxie's substitute decision maker, but Roxie was, after all, a homeless drug user; they might have assumed there was no one to call. Perhaps Roxie was in no state to remember Bets. Their last names no longer matched.

Bets knew she should go in, but it bothered her to see Roxie this way: her hair lank and greasy, her eyes sunken with dark bruises beneath them, her body skeletal, all ridges and corners, protruding knobs of elbow and wrist. Her arms dotted with track marks and scabs, her smell harsh and acidic, filling the room, invading Bets' nostrils even as she stood outside the doorway, barely visible, fearful of discovery. One day, she walked past just as a nurse was talking to Roxie, and nearly cried out, covering her mouth with her hand to quiet herself.

Roxie's teeth were gone.

Bets knew tooth removal sometimes happened, the drugs caused decay, the decay could worsen the infections in the heart valves, but this was Roxie. Beautiful, beautiful Roxie.

Each day that she stood outside the room, or walked past, she told herself, *today I'll go in. I'll sit down and visit with her*. Each day, she stood, and she left, or walked by and kept on walking. Each day, she scolded herself for being selfish, and uncaring, and petty, even as the other, rational brain narrowed its eyes and sneered, *when was she selfless and caring for you?*

Roxie's course was complicated, and her hospitalization was lengthy. Bets began leaving little gifts outside Roxie's room, on the wall tray: hand cream (the hospital was always so dry), nice shampoo, lip balm, warm socks. She put little labels that said, "for Roxie." She was careful, and left the items when no one was watching, except, of course, someone was always watching.

—I was wondering who her little gift fairy was! Exclaimed a large, twinkly nurse Bets had never met, coming around the corner at just the wrong moment, her cornrows with their multiple beads settling around her shoulders. Bets raised her eyebrows, put a finger to her lips, and the twinkly nurse winked, zipped her lips with a finger, and threw away the imaginary key.

—You should make a hospital program! She whispered, coming closer to Bets. A Secret Santa sort of thing! Each patient could have one!

Bets smiled and nodded tightly, a wave of exhaustion overtaking her.

Most patients had family members to bring them everything they needed. Some families overflowed the rooms, spilling into hallways, with children running around, as if attending Thanksgiving dinner at Aunt Doreen's. The staff members had to take turns reminding families they were in a *hospital,* not a family home. They limited family members to two at a time. Bets felt that those patients, with those families, did not need a secret gift fairy.

She didn't visit Roxie for a couple of days after that, unable to explain why it was so important that no one connected them. Was it shame? Who was the shameful one? Was it fear? Fear of what? Of admitting she had failed to fix Roxie, who had never asked to be fixed? She did her work, and she tried to keep her mind clear, but every few minutes, there would be an image: Roxie's limp hair. Roxie's toothless mouth. Roxie's sunken eyes. She tried to focus on the plump, pretty babies coming into the world, their little dimpled hands, their soft fuzzy hair, their instinctive sucking as they turned hopefully toward her, as if she had something to offer them.

—Don't do drugs, she whispered. Not even once.

She knew exactly what Raz would tell her; hadn't he said it a thousand times over the years?

—She's your sister, he'd say. Not in an accusing way (emphasis on *your*), not in an imploring way (emphasis on *sister*), but as a statement of fact, to do what she would, with his implied support, saying so much within a single sentence, as he often did. *I should talk to him*, she thought. *I should tell him, talk it out so I know what to do.*

But she didn't.

After her next shift, Bets went back to the medical floor, and went to Roxie's room, ready to speak to her this time, no excuses. She entered and there was a large, bearded man in the bed hooked up to a BiPAP breathing machine.

At the nursing station, she found Tayo, a nurse who had previously worked maternity for a few years.

—Oh, hey Bets, what's up? What brings you to the dark side?

She smiled at Bets, smoothed her hair behind her ears.

—I'm just wondering, do you know where they moved the woman in 3231? Tayo frowned and flipped through some papers on the desk.

—She wasn't my patient… let's see… she ran her finger down a list on a clipboard.

—Oh, here she is. Roxanne? Do you know her?

Bets nodded. Tayo's smile faded, and she put down the clipboard.

—She's, um, she's been moved to hospice.

—Hospice, Bets repeated, looking at Tayo, whose face had completely rearranged.

KAREN LEA ARMSTRONG

—Yes, I remember this story now. She had valve replacement surgery, but it wasn't successful. She went into heart failure and then liver and kidney failure. So she's, you know. In hospice now.

—How did you know her? Asked Tayo, touching Bets' arm gently. She felt the heat of the touch.

—She's my sister, she said, more loudly than she intended. Roxie's my sister.

CHAPTER EIGHTEEN

I have a bad feeling, said Hannah.

Even with the blue spruce providing shade, it was hot in the yard. They had worked together, staining the deck for a couple of hours, when Hannah appeared pale and had to stop. Bets made her lie down, brought a cold cloth, some water. The bottle of water sat in a pool of its own sweat, and once rehydrated and cooled, Hannah said she felt better. They'd spoken little while they were working, although Bets managed to get an update on the still-strained relations between Hannah and her friends Kayla and Zoey.

—You have a bad feeling about what? Asked Bets. Your health?

—No. No. Not that. I want to know more about Roxie. I want the whole story. But I'm worried about it. You're leaving things out; I know you are.

—It's true. I have left things out.

—Why?

—I'm not sure. Sad stories.

Hannah, lying on the deck with her cold cloth, regained some vibrancy.

—I feel like she kept using drugs.

—Yes.

—And that usually means people are sick.

—Yes.

—Will you tell me? Or is it not a good day for that?

Was Hannah reading her thoughts? How did she know Bets had just been thinking about Roxie?

—Well. It's as good a day as any, I guess.

***

The hospice was like entering another world, despite being connected to the main hospital by a long hallway filled with windows and art. Entering the hospice, everything was quiet, in stark contrast to the general hospital floors. The hospice rooms were individual, and soundproof; families gathered in peace and privacy. There was a large communal kitchen at one end, and a couple of nooks with chairs and windows and tissues. There was a lot of light.

Bets scanned the admission note at the nursing station: intravenous drug use, blood infection, heart valve infection, kidney failure, liver failure. Surgery no longer an option, patient too ill to survive. Multisystem organ failure was the final diagnosis. Bets found Roxie's room and waited a few moments before pushing the door open.

There was a woman sitting on the sofa beside Roxie's bed. She was middle-aged, grey hair, kind eyes. Bets had never seen her before. Roxie lay on the bed, was it actually Roxie? She was bright yellow, emaciated, eyes closed. Someone had cut her hair, inexpertly, very short, and it stood up in all directions.

—Who are you? Bets asked the woman bluntly.

—I'm Maeve, the volunteer from Community Friends. I'm here to give Roxanne some company. And you?

Bets couldn't take her eyes off Roxie.

—I'm her sister.

Maeve jumped up.

—Oh, we didn't realize she had any family! I'm sure Roxanne will be very pleased to see you. I'll just step out and let you two visit.

Bets waited until Maeve was at the door before saying, It's Roxie.

—Pardon me? Asked Maeve.

—No one calls her Roxanne, said Bets. Her name is Roxie.

Bets sat down by the bed. Roxie's eyes remained closed.

—Hi Roxie.

No response. Bets took Roxie's hand, cool and smooth, but still no response. She called her name, and finally rubbed her knuckles on Roxie's prominent breastbone, a nursing trick to assess responsiveness. Roxie's eyes fluttered open with the sternal rub.

—Ow, she said in a whisper, eyes rolling upward, circling around, and locking on Bets.

–Hiya, Bets.

—Hi Roxie.

Roxie blinked, looked around her, eyeballs yellow with jaundice, lips crusted and dry.

—Am I dead? She asked.

—Not yet, said Bets.

—Soon?

Bets paused.

—Yes, she said finally. Soon.

Roxie exhaled, her eyelids fluttering back down. A moment later, they opened again.

—Thanks for the treats, she whispered.

—How did you know they were from me?

But Roxie had gone again, eyes closed, breathing deeply, occasionally giving a small muscle twitch.

—Roxie, said Bets, I need to know. What happened to you? Why did you do such harm to yourself? Did someone hurt you? When we were kids? Did something happen?

Roxie slept on, the only sounds her raspy breathing, the muted voices of people in the next room, and the soft whir of the air mattress when the pressure adjusted. The TV was off, the gas fireplace in the corner was off, there was only Bets, and Roxie, and breathing, and whirring.

After a while, Bets got up and left, and didn't go to look for Maeve, or the nurse. She walked home, fastening her collar in the wind, feeling all emotion squeezed from her like a sponge. She found Raz, who was vacuuming, with music blaring, who tried to grab her and spin her and when she resisted, he could see it in her face, and turned off the music.

There were so many questions, so many things Bets would never know. She didn't return to the hospice. Bets hadn't mentioned her name to Maeve, but a colleague contacted her, and she presented herself as next of kin. They had forms for her to sign, questions about payment for the funeral home.

—Who would do it if I wasn't here? Bets asked.

Well, there were charitable funds, but they didn't like to use them unless there was absolutely no family.

She had to attend the funeral home: would she like to have a service? Bets almost burst into inappropriate laughter at the thought of having a service for Roxie; who would she invite? She'd likely have a better turnout organizing a warehouse rave downtown. She asked them to cremate Roxie and declined when they offered to package up the remains for her.

They think I'm heartless and cold. The funeral home staff had the typical solemn expressions, the tissues, the soft voices, the palpable non-judgement, but she still felt wrong.

Bets wanted to feel sad about Roxie. She waited for grief and shock to hit, braced herself for the impact, but what she felt was the usual aching loss of her vibrant, charismatic sister, from way back when they were young, when the direction of Roxie's life went where Bets could not—would not—follow. The baby, perhaps, had sealed the deal—had taken a tiny last ember of hope, and doused it. Bets tried, as she had many times, to say "I forgive you," silently, out loud, but it didn't work. Likely, she reflected, because in her heart she didn't mean it, and in her heart, she knew Roxie didn't care one way or another. Or did she?

Bets felt oddly outside her body for the next few days. It was as if she was watching, seeing this thin middle-aged woman walking, speaking, working, and thinking, wait, that's me. I'm the one talking. I'm the one writing. The disconnect was jarring, and more than once she saw other nurses looking at her strangely and realized they'd asked her a question.

I shouldn't be working. She kept going, unable to imagine an alternative.

Raz, predictably, wanted her to rest, to take time to grieve and recover. She shook her head, shrugged away his embraces, met his suggestions with silence. He made her meals, and she ate them without really tasting.

Raz's soup—rich, homemade—made her think of her mother's suppers of canned soup. Made her think of Roxie crumbling more and more and more crackers into her bowl, until it was more crackers than liquid, her mother's voice saying Roxie, stop it. Eat properly. Roxie replying well, I'm just trying not to taste the soup. Flashing Bets a smile at her mother's exaggerated sigh.

Raz served pasta with his "Razalicious" tomato sauce, and Bets pictured Roxie spelling out words on the table with her canned alphabet pasta. When their mother or father told her to stop playing and eat her supper, she casually set aside letters for the word "MEAN," or "HELP," making Bets snort her milk, subsequently chastised, while Roxie looked on with wide, innocent eyes.

Bets went through old photographs, the few she possessed. She found the one taken at her graduation, had it enlarged, had it framed. Sometimes, she stopped to look at it, or touch it with her finger, waiting to feel something other than echoing nothingness.

It was common for medical staff to call people by their conditions rather than their names. The hysterectomy in room 2, the lady with twins, the D&C in recovery. Bets tried to avoid the habit, had certainly been instructed against it, but was very used to hearing it. In a way, the depersonalization helped with confidentiality, but of course there was no confidentiality among the staff, who all knew one another's business, or thought they did. Bets knew that although she hadn't discussed Roxie with anyone other than Shannon, likely the entire staff was aware of her loss, if not the details. Few approached her, and she didn't blame them. She, herself, felt the barrier she had unwittingly erected, which lacked a window, a door, an escape route.

She overheard a couple of nurses talking about another new admission, who was a drug user. One nurse referred to the patient as a "druggie," while the second made a joke about removing the IV as soon as possible before the patient could use it for "easy access." They both stood to get back to their tasks, and found Bets standing in front of them, barely aware of her own arrival.

—She's a person, said Bets.

The women looked at each other, then back at Bets.

—Pardon?

—She's a person, repeated Bets, more loudly. A person. Not a druggie. A person with an addiction. A person who used to be like you, who could be you, if things were different.

Bets' voice cracked on the last sentence. Two more nurses came in, all staring at Bets, who now had tears running down her face, whose voice was rising further with each sentence.

—These are people—gesturing around her—they are not diseases. They are people, with families, and lives, and we're supposed to care for them, not judge them! So what if they're injecting drugs, so what if they're on methadone! So what if their baby will be in withdrawal and need IV morphine! So what if they want to go out for a smoke! We're supposed to care for them all, without judgement! That's our job! *That's our job! That's our job!*

Bets cried and shouted, jabbing the air with her finger, and there was a terrible silence in the room other than her voice, and when she suddenly felt all the eyes on her, she bolted.

—Bets!

She didn't run, but she didn't stop. She wasn't even sure where she was going, until she found herself in the supply room, and sank to the floor, hands shaking.

Shannon arrived a few minutes later, settled onto the floor beside her. They shared the partial silence for a while, hearing in the distance muffled announcements, garbled voices, a cart rolling by.

—So, good times in this place, observed Shannon, picking up a urinary catheter, running it through her fingers.

Bets gave a small, choked laugh.

—I can never leave this room, now. I'll have to live in here. I don't know what happened.

—You don't? Asked Shannon. You lost it, is what happened. Because you lost your sister, and nobody gets it. Seems pretty easy to me.

She reached, squeezed Bets' hand.

—And you were about as approachable as a porcupine, so nobody could help, Shannon added. Bets felt the tight knot of her body slowly unwinding.

—I know. I know.

She sniffled loudly. Shannon reached for the stack of tiny facial tissue boxes and presented one to Bets.

—Use a lot of them. They're single ply.

—Budget cuts, said Bets, opening the box, removing a handful of tissues, blowing her nose.

—Bets, just go home, said Shannon.

—I'm charge.

—Who gives a shit?

—True.

—Listen, said Shannon, you won't like this, but you know I love you, right? Shannon shifted so she faced Bets directly.

—Uh-oh.

—You need counselling, Bets. You need help to work out everything with Roxie. Probably you needed it way before now.

Counselling was, of course, fine for other people. Weaker people.

—I guess, Bets said.

—I'm going back. You go home. Okay? I'll call you later?

—Okay.

Bets managed another small smile, barely lifting the corners of her mouth.

—Thanks, Shannon.

Shannon extended her hand, pulled Bets to her feet, kissed her cheek, and left.

Bets leaned against the metal utility rack for a moment, closing her eyes, rolling her shoulders, before pulling the door open and facing the harsh fluorescent lights of the hospital hallway.

***

Hannah wiped her cheeks and placed her hands behind her on the deck, arching her back.

—So, did you go? She asked.

—Go where?

—To counselling.

—Do you think I went?

—No, said Hannah, replacing her glasses.

—No, said Bets softly, you're right. I didn't, not then. I thought I could handle it. I did apologize to the girls at work, though. I told everyone what was going on, and I did some educational work about drug addiction with the staff.

—Did that help?

—Well, I didn't lose it again. So, I guess so. Sort of.

—I'm just like them. It could have been me.

Bets sat down next to Hannah on the step.

—What do you mean?

—There are kids at my school. We call them druggies, too. I always think of them as losers. I never think about their home life, or their past, or their families. I never even speak to them.

—Hannah, said Bets. It's not just you, it's everyone. It's like learning that you don't have to limit yourself because you're a woman. It's like learning about racism from Shannon. We aren't born knowing these things; we have to learn. I had to learn, too.

—I'm sorry about Roxie.

—Thank you, Hannah. I'm sorry, too. I wish I could have done something for her.

—You tried, said Hannah.

—Yes, said Bets. Sometimes that's all we can do. She smiled a tiny smile.

—Write that down.

CHAPTER NINETEEN

If asked to describe Hannah, Bets would have struggled. There was the hair, of course, the glasses, the small stature, but those details seemed completely inadequate. Hannah's true essence lay in her energy. Boundless, earnest energy poured from her, overflowing onto everything within her reach, transforming mundane events. It was like Hannah took her very heart and held it out in the palm of her hand, saying here, touch this, I want to share. And Bets was allowed to share it: Bets, who felt quite the opposite, who felt like her soft parts were all tucked away and protected, not only behind her ribcage, but within a shell, maybe a shell with thorns, who feared for Hannah, because the exposure came with such irrevocable risk.

It was easy to notice, then, when Hannah changed. She was quieter; there were longer silences, which would previously have made her uncomfortable. A stillness developed, which Bets appreciated in anyone else, but which seemed entirely wrong for Hannah.

Gradually, her hair was more unruly, an afterthought. Her face and eyes were different; puffier, with shadows. She looked, the day Bets really started worrying, like a piece of produce past its due date. She made Bets think of Roxie, a thought she immediately cast aside. Not Hannah.

Hannah sat at the table, lost in an oversized sweatshirt of unforgiving pale yellow, playing with a glass of lemonade, and she had taken out her notebook, but no question was forthcoming. Her colour was off, and finally she took a sip of her drink, and immediately pushed herself from the table.

—Oh my God, I have to... she stumbled from the room, knocking the notebook from the table, the glass tilting madly so Bets had to reach across and settle it. She heard Hannah retching in the powder room, and all became clear to her in a rush of insight. How had she missed it?

After a few moments, Hannah wobbled back into the kitchen. She lowered herself back into her chair, much as an eighty-year-old woman might, where normally she jumped and flopped and slid.

—I'm sorry, my stomach is upset today, she said.

She looked down, where Bets had set a plate of saltine crackers, a small pink tablet, and a fresh glass containing plain water with a slice of lemon.

—What's this?

—Some things that might settle your stomach, said Bets. Things that sometimes help with morning sickness. Even if it happens in the afternoons.

She met Hannah's red, puffy eyes, not looking away, until Hannah looked down at the table again.

—How did you know?

—I didn't until just now. But I've been very worried about you.

—Why didn't you ask anything before?

—Because, said Bets, I figured if you wanted me to know, you'd tell me. At some point.

Hannah picked up the tablet.

—What is this?

—It's just nausea medication.

—I thought that wasn't safe. I'm not taking anything because I'm so scared.

—It's okay, don't worry. You need to get nutrition, and fluids. There are prescriptions that can help, too. It goes away eventually.

Hannah rolled the tablet between her fingers, put it between her lips, took a sip of water, gagged, and ran to the sink to vomit.

—Hannah, you need to see a doctor. Have you seen anyone?

Hannah held onto the chair for a moment before sitting down. She started to speak, then instead burst into noisy sobs.

—I've screwed it all up, she managed. I've screwed. It all. Up. So much.

Bets reached across, touched Hannah's hand, let her cry for a while. There were no tissues available; Bets waited for the tears to slow and passed over a clean dish towel. Hannah mopped her face.

—Try the cracker, suggested Bets.

Hannah looked at it doubtfully, nibbled a corner, waited. She widened her eyes at Bets and nibbled again.

—There we go, said Bets. Tiny bites at a time. Good. Can you tell me more?

—I thought I had the flu. I was so tired, and so sick. But it usually only lasts a couple of days, and it kept going. So then—she took another nibble of cracker—you're going to think I'm so stupid, but I thought I had cancer. I mean, how could I not know what was happening? But stupid me, I thought, this is it, I'm dying. I couldn't sleep. I didn't know what to do. And then, my friend asked me for a tampon at school.

—A tampon, repeated Bets.

—Yeah, and I gave her one, and I thought, wow, it feels like I haven't needed a tampon in ages. I didn't think this could happen. I used protection, Bets! I was on the pill, I only missed a couple! Anyway, I went to the dollar store and got a pregnancy test. I was so scared that someone would see me, someone from school, or a friend of my mom's, so I went to a coffee shop to do the test. But the smell of coffee made me gag.

—Oh, boy.

—So I threw up, and then I peed, and then I threw up again, and then it was positive, and I just cried and cried, and then—Hannah reached for the dish towel again with both hands—they sent someone to check on me and asked if I was doing *drugs* in the washroom. In the coffee shop washroom! And I actually thought, maybe it's better if they think that than the truth! It's not fair! It's not fair!

Hannah was off again, although her crying was quieter, her face hidden in her tea towel. Bets said nothing, as Hannah sat blurry with misery. Bets' heart ached as she thought, why must this process of reproduction always be so damn complicated? Why does it never seem to be, I want a baby—I have a baby—all is well?

Of course, she was being ridiculous. She saw happy families and happy births all the time, although there was often more than met the eye. Bets forced her attention back to Hannah, whose crying had settled, whose eyes were puffier than ever, who looked unlike herself with her glasses sitting on the table, her intensity as faded as an old worn sofa. Hannah sniffled loudly.

—What am I going to do?

Bets looked at Hannah, at the slits of her eyes, her blotchy face.

—What do you want to do?

Hannah sniffled again.

—I don't want an abortion. I don't think I could ever get over it. Which is crazy, because I'm pro-choice.

—Okay, said Bets. Choice is the whole point, really, so not so crazy.

—And my mom wants me to give the baby up for adoption, but I don't know how anybody could go through a whole pregnancy, and a whole birth, and then give the baby away. It already feels like mine. It already feels real to me.

Robin. Riley. Mitch. Cory.

—Aren't you going to say anything? Aren't you supposed to tell me I'm making a horrible mistake?

—Am I? Asked Bets. Are you?

—I don't know.

They sat for a while, thoughts flying, landing, taking off again, chasing each other through the air.

—How much time do you have to decide? Asked Bets.

—I think I'm ten weeks. I have an app.

Not much time.

Bets opened her mouth, closed it. She felt their friendship, and Hannah's future, spread out before her like a quilt. Something that could be torn and ruined. Something that could end up beautiful and comforting, depending on her words.

—I can't tell you what to do, Hannah, this is your life. I can help talk you through it, but it sounds like you've made up your mind. I support whatever you choose, and I will help you.

—You will?

—Any way I can.

—I want to finish school, Bets. I still want to be a nurse.

Hannah grabbed Bets' hand. A flash of former Hannah appeared in her eyes.

—This has not all been for nothing.

—I didn't think so, said Bets, putting her other hand on top, stacking them. Finish your snack, we can meet in a couple of days and talk things over.

Hannah didn't speak much about her parents. Bets, from the little she knew, was surprised about the adoption idea. For that to work, Hannah would be visibly pregnant for months, and there would be no baby afterwards. It wasn't 1960; you didn't send your pregnant daughter away for six months. She could understand the desire to resolve the situation, however; even a visible pregnancy would eventually be forgotten. A baby, on the other hand: that was something else entirely.

Bets saw a lot of teen mothers at work. She divided them into two categories: the ones who got their shit together, and the ones who didn't. The first group grew up within months. They read, they listened, they breastfed, they got help, they got jobs, they kept their lives moving forward. Some of them—very few—stayed with their partners and made the relationship work. Most stayed with their parents. Some of them, Bets reflected, were very good teen parents, not getting wrapped up in the competition of older, educated parents, who seemed intent on molding their children into superstars. The competent teens called the maternity unit if they needed help, with reasonable questions about umbilical cords and bright yellow stools and newborns that constantly sneezed.

The young mothers in the second group bothered Bets. Still children themselves, they had no concept of parenting, or responsibility, or really anything other than their own adolescent needs and desires. They smoked, they drank, they watered down formula to make it last longer, they said the baby slept through the night when in fact they didn't get up to care for it. The babies sometimes came back severely dehydrated, or ill with infections, and Bets had seen a few with seizures, who had been shaken. It wasn't only the young mothers, of course, but she felt for them when it was. They weren't ready for the intense experience of a newborn. How could anyone expect otherwise? Should there be an age cut-off to take home a baby? An exam? An in- home assessment? The problem was, the older mothers did similar things, or were just as self- centred sometimes, and it was difficult to tell. Who should decide?

Shannon, perhaps influenced by the sixties scoop that took Indigenous babies away from their mothers by questionably well-meaning health professionals, had an easier time.

—Babies should be with their parents.

—But what if the parents just can't care for them? Argued Bets during their many discussions.

—Then we should help and support the parents.

—But what if it isn't enough? What if they are neglected, abused?

—Then we need to help. Maybe people who live in with them? Maybe not forever. The parents need a chance, unless they truly don't want a chance.

—But who is going to do that? Live with a family, help them, somehow not make them feel judged or irresponsible? How does that work?

—I don't know. But you could do it, Bets. You'd be great!

Bets wasn't so sure. It sounded perfect when Shannon said it with her simple confidence, but Bets didn't want any neglected, dehydrated, abused babies. She lay awake at night, sometimes, thinking about babies screaming in their cribs, diapers soaked, no one responding, their brains changing, adapting to never being held or loved. At the same time, she didn't want to be a foster parent; she and Raz had never wanted to adopt; she wanted babies to be with their own families.

Let the babies sleep, Bets.

What about Hannah? Would Hannah be a group one, or a group two? She was so young, so naïve, so clumsy. Even her tiny stature seemed wrong for parenthood. And yet, Hannah had been coming for months, researching a future career. She asked wonderful questions, she was interested, she was curious, she was caring and intuitive. She had such a bright future… other than being pregnant. How could something so unfair happen to a young couple who were being responsible? How could Hannah possibly be a nurse now, when she might have an infant at the end of high school? What impact would an abortion have on Hannah's mental health? Or giving up her baby? Horrified at her selfishness, she realized that one circling thought was, *what will I do without her?*

Bets considered these things, while Hannah took the tiniest bites of her saltines, sniffling intermittently.

—Bets, she said finally. Can you—would you—tell me a story to distract me? Hannah pushed up her glasses, and her eyes gazed out plaintively.

She's a child. Having a child.

—Please.

***

Sometimes, when they were having supper or a glass of wine together, or sitting on the couch with their legs entangled, Bets asked Raz for a story. She enjoyed hearing about his childhood in Québec, about his parents, his irritable sister. She liked hearing about the family going camping and fishing together, so different from her own family.

—Tell me about hunting with your dad, she'd say, tell me about your biggest fish. After many years, she knew the stories well, but still had favourites.

—Tell me about drownproofing.

—You've heard me tell that one so many times.

—I don't care, tell me again.

—Pay the fee, said Raz, and the fee was always a kiss.

When Raz was young, when they were at the lake, he and Josée had to wear life jackets nearly all the time. All the time in the boat, all the time in the lake, all the time when they were playing along the shore. Until they could swim alone to the rickety floating dock, that seemed to tilt and erode at the edges more each summer, as if being slowly reclaimed by the lake itself, they had to wear life jackets. The life jackets were bulky and hot, and Raz and Josée protested regularly, but the rules didn't change. *Vous pourrez les enlever quand vous pourrez nager tout seul jusqu'au quai.*

Point final.

Sometimes, when they played on shore, Raz removed his life jacket, partially out of discomfort, partially out of protest. He didn't go into the water past his knees, and he pretended to his wide-eyed sister that he wasn't nervous at all about their parents' reaction, or a sudden, inexplicable event that might result in swimming without it. A couple of times he was caught and reprimanded; I forgot, he said. We weren't going in the water. And, later: I can swim. You know I can! I can swim without it! But when he set out to show it could be done, he faltered. He became hyper-aware of weeds brushing his legs, threatening to pull him under. Looking into the dark water, his mind insisted on conjuring creatures of the deep, things that might lurk underneath, including the fish he himself sometimes caught, with sharp evil-looking teeth that could cut your fingers if you tried to remove a hook without using gloves. The jagged dock seemed to float further and further as he swam, taunting him, like older boys who swiped his hat at school, dangled it toward him, and snatched it away when he finally got close. Ultimately, he gave up each time, and swam back to a depth where he could stand, and when his father tossed him the life jacket, wordlessly, he put it back on.

He sat on shore, staring at the floating dock, hating it, willing it to disintegrate and sink into the depths of the lake, but it stubbornly remained, maddeningly close, impossibly far. He and Josée swam to it with the dog one day (the *dog* could do it, for God's sake) and with life jackets on, it was an easy distance, a short swim. How was that possible? The fish did not seem frightening, the weeds were benign, brushing his legs like soft gentle fingertips. The two siblings reached the dock and threw the ball into the water for the dog, and for each other; jumping off and catching the ball in the air, or spinning, before landing with a splash. It was a hot day, and after a while the dog got tired and returned to shore, and Raz and Josée lay on the dock in the sun, feeling the water prickle their skin as it dried, swatting errant horseflies that buzzed around their heads, listening to the lap of the water, and the white-throated sparrow who sang, according to their father, *Je t'aime* Canada! Canada! Canada!

Raz was hot, and his life jacket was wet and uncomfortable, so he took it off. After a while, he sat up and noticed the ball floating by. He stretched for it, but it bobbed out of reach, and he told Josée to get it, but she refused, not even opening her eyes. Raz tsked. Finally, he could stand it no longer and jumped in, pushing the ball further away in his wake. He came up sputtering from the cold water, spied the ball, swam to it, then headed back to the dock. He heard Josée's voice, but couldn't make out her words, with his ears full of water. She held up a yellow object, and he realized with horror he had jumped in without his life jacket. He was in deep water, without his life jacket! Instantly, he began to sink. He abandoned the ball, floundering with his arms, and a wave hit him in the face, just as he tried to inhale, filling his mouth, his throat, his nose, with muddy-tasting lake water, and he couldn't get air, and he tried to see the dock and couldn't, and he went under.

When he came up this time, he could see the dock again, and Josée shouting and waving her arms, and suddenly he kicked his legs, and his head stayed up, and he thought, what am I doing? I can swim. I was swimming two seconds ago. He found his stroke, and his head stayed up, and he turned away from the next wave, and he got to the dock, and pulled himself up onto it and lay on his side, gasping for air, just as his father also heaved himself onto the dock, his father who had been with his mother in the camp, who had heard the yelling and had charged into the water, fully clothed, to save his son.

—Well, Raz's father said finally, in French, that got my heart rate up. Why did you pretend to be drowning? Never do that. Never, ever do that.

—I wasn't pretending, said Raz. I thought I *was* drowning. For a minute. And then I realized I wasn't.

His father turned to Josée, who looked more panicky than Raz.

—How about you? Are you planning on drowning today, too?

He crinkled his eyes at her, poked her with a finger. Josée shook her head silently. They all swam to shore together, with Raz holding, but not wearing, his life jacket.

Later, when he found his father's soaked shoes sitting in the sun, he got some of the newspaper they used to start fires, and stuffed them into the shoes, to dry them more quickly.

That night around the fire, retelling the tale, his father told them about drownproofing. Conserving energy in cold water, or resting if you were tired, you just put your arms out in front of you to hold yourself up, and put your face into the water, and come up for air as needed.

—You can't panic. That's important! *Rester calme.* Think, figure out what just happened, do some drownproofing until you know where you are, and make a plan. Then, swim with purpose towards a goal.

Which, Raz told Bets during his tale, was brilliant advice, albeit somewhat late.

Which, Bets thought each time she heard it, applied to so many things in life other than swimming: be calm, stay safe, make a plan, move with purpose towards a goal.

—I think, said Hannah, Raz would say I need to do some drownproofing.

CHAPTER TWENTY

Bets spent a few days filled with indecision, questioning everything she and Hannah had ever spoken about together. So many sad stories about difficult births, or difficult people; stories of her own prowess, without enough stories of weakness; stories about nursing, mining, addiction, not enough, not nearly enough, about life itself. Not enough about the messiness and frustrations and sudden, veering path changes that made up life. Hannah needed to know there were choices; choices that only she could make. Beginning, of course, with the biggest choice of all: the choice that had, at either end of it, a life forever changed.

Bets paced, sat down, stood up again. Was she thinking clearly? Was she simply lonely? Was she planning a way to help, or to harm? What was her role? What about Hannah's parents? What about Nate? Bets was firm with herself. She knew she did not come first in the current scenario, not by a long shot.

She wandered, eventually, into Raz's study. An ironic name, since he was not a studious man. It was really the guest room, but they rarely had guests; Raz had an old rolltop desk that he loved, and a large executive-style chair, and bookcases along one wall that housed books for them both. She loved the room because Raz loved the room; she hated the still air, the silence, the lifelessness of it without him, like a skin he had shed and left behind.

She had opened and closed the drawers many times. Hoping, at some level, for an envelope addressed to her, some kind of communication in which they'd have a final moment, and know it was the final moment, in which he'd answer all her lingering questions and plot her path forward.

Going over and over their last morning, she's pretty sure her last words to Raz were, pick up milk if you have time.

Pick up milk if you have time.

Bets pulled aside the folding door of the small closet. She removed the plastic bag with Raz's work clothes. She set each item, one by one, on the double bed that took up one corner of the room. Yellow, black-streaked hard hat, stained blue coveralls, gloves permanently curled into grip shapes, as if hands still lived inside. She arranged the items in the shape of a person on the bed, gloves at the end of the arms, hard hat at the top, safety glasses. She placed his worn steel- toed boots on the floor, then after a moment turned them around and slid her feet into them, like a small child. Trying to calm her mind and stop the swirling thoughts of Hannah, Bets clomped a few steps and settled herself into the large leather desk chair, which gave a small creak. The sound of it conjured Raz, that creak she would hear from another room as he adjusted in his chair, doing the bills or his computer games or frowning at the tax returns. She sat and stared at the outline of Raz she had created on the bed, moved her feet inside his boots.

—I could use some advice, she said out loud.

***

Bets remembered hearing Eddie's boots in the hallway.

The nurses wore running shoes, for the most part: quiet, comfortable footwear. Bets was at the main desk reviewing shift schedules with Shannon when they both heard the slow, heavy tread of work boots. They looked up, expecting to see someone from maintenance: someone with a ladder, a toolbox, loops of electrical cord. Instead, they saw Eddie, the dark hulk of him, still in his coveralls, trying to speak, unable to start. His very presence, his blue eyes, drained of their usual mischief, and the streaks of tears smudging his dusty cheeks told Bets everything.

—Bets, he said.

Bets stood up, Shannon clutching her arm.

—Where is he, said Bets, what happened?

—Emergency, said Eddie.

Somehow, Bets walked. She followed Eddie back to the elevator, they rode together, Eddie again tried to speak but his voice caught. Bets couldn't think, it was as though her brain had jammed. She could feel her heart pumping out the rapid rhythm of the only word she could hear in her mind: No. No. No. No. No.

Later, Eddie told her about breaking his miner's lamp that day. It didn't matter, it changed nothing, but he told her about it over and over. I dropped my lamp, and it broke. We only had the one light between us, Raz teased me all the way to the raise, kept shining his light in my eyes to punish me. I should have gotten one from the guy running the cage, but I didn't.

When Raz shouted out and dropped to the ground, not even on the ladder, when Eddie turned to look, he could see the light moving as Raz rocked and cried out in pain. Eddie climbed down as fast as he could, trying to see what was wrong, trying to see an injury, but there was nothing visible. Raz went still, and Eddie took his head lamp and ran screaming for help.

—I left him in the dark, said Eddie. I left him lying alone in the dark.

Eddie called mine rescue and rode up to surface with Raz once they loaded him onto a stretcher, once they'd confirmed he was still alive.

—I threw up, said Eddie, I'm never sick in the cage, I felt like I suddenly had the flu. So many years together and I figured sometime, one of us will get hurt, really hurt, something bad will happen. But to see him there, and not know what was wrong... there was nothing I could do. There was nothing I could do, Bets, I'd have done anything.

One retelling, Eddie put his big hands up to his face and sobbed.

In the elevator, not knowing any of this yet, hearing the no-no-no in her heart and mind, Bets forced herself to breathe; she seemed to have forgotten how. She used her ID badge to take the back route into the ER, barely aware of people looking at her, speaking to her, stretchers rolling past, porters with wheelchairs. She stopped, the thrum of the ER moving around her, its shouts and beeps and clatters and cries, and looked up at Eddie, who pointed to the second trauma room, following her as she moved, as if in slow motion, or underwater, the sights and sounds distorted as she moved toward the room that contained Raz. Raz, and a lot of tubes, and a lot of monitors, and a lot of people. There were a lot of words. Words Bets had heard, but never pertaining to someone she knew personally.

Subarachnoid hemorrhage. Ruptured cerebral aneurysm.

Cardiac arrest, code blue, CPR, defibrillation. Asystole.

Raz had pointed out, when Bets talked about "minespeak," that her work jargon was just as bad as his, if not worse.

Raz was right, thought Bets, *we do speak a whole other language in the hospital. Raz was right.*

The doctors looked at her oddly, and she realized it was real, had she spoken out loud? She sat listening to words she didn't want to hear and could not process. She looked from one grave, kindly face to the other, unable to think, unable to restart her brain. She was supposed to weep, she knew, she was supposed to fall to the ground, keening, but it was as if she had left her body, and was looking down from above, thinking *why is that woman so calm? Doesn't she care?*

She watched the woman lift her head and look at the doctors, watched her open her mouth, heard her speak.

—Now what do we do?

CHAPTER TWENTY-ONE

After Raz was gone, Bets started thinking about the children again, after telling herself years ago, in no uncertain terms, that she had to stop.

In her grief, she had the eldest bringing her cups of tea (Bets hated tea, but that's what the child kept bringing), she had someone beside her on the couch (Cory?), she could hear someone keeping on top of the dirty dishes in the kitchen (Mitch?), could hear the clicking of plates, could smell the dish soap. One encouraged her to get outside for walks, another to answer sympathy cards.

—I don't want to, she said out loud. I don't want to do any of it!

And they all sighed, rolled their eyes, drifted, evaporated. Leaving her alone, wandering or staring out the window, trying to breathe, trying to keep her head above water, without clear direction, too fatigued to swim.

Shannon came, and she was firm, and calm, and steered Bets toward the bathroom with a towel, and vacuumed while Bets stood staring at the waffle-weave fabric of the shower curtain. Eventually, Bets did what she was guided to do, rewarded with Shannon's half smile, and a hot fresh cup of coffee, and a clean outfit laid out on the bed.

Shannon packed Bets into the car and went to pick up kids for her cousins, or bought groceries, and took Bets home and cooked while Bets sat on a kitchen chair distractedly peeling carrots, or tearing lettuce, or staring into space. Shannon didn't say, you need to get out; you need a schedule; you have to start living again; but sometimes when she arrived and Bets said, I don't want to, Shannon replied, I know, Bets, but it's the only way.

Bets knew she couldn't dwell on the lost children, or Raz, or Roxie. She knew she could not stop living, yet she lacked a compelling alternative.

People talked about gratitude.

Think about how fortunate you are, they said. Think of the time you had with your loved one, your privileged life. There are people with nothing. Sometimes it worked for a while.

Sometimes the general anger dissipated briefly, during a walk in the woods, or engaged with a small child at Shannon's, or during reflection in Raz's study. Bets reminded herself of people who were starving, abused, addicted, afraid. Wars, famine, tsunamis, fires. She thought, I don't have that. I'm safe, and warm, I have support people, I can pay the bills. It's not so bad.

It seemed like, at any moment of Zenlike acceptance, something interfered with it: the roof leaked, the toilet blocked, someone backed into the car and drove away. Food burned, she missed a call after waiting all day, she stood up too quickly and whacked her head underside a cupboard. Anything could start the cumulative tumble of inner grievance, starting with, *why are these things only happening to me*? And ending with, *why Raz? Why Raz? Why? He was one of the good ones.*

He was mine.

Three months after Raz, Shannon took Bets—protesting—to see a counsellor, a woman named Myrta, who was Bets' own age. Myrta, with her white hair, her pale eyes and piercing gaze, her relaxed posture, looked at Bets in her thorny shell, arms and legs crossed, chin raised, and said simply, in her soft-edged voice:

—Tell me, Bets.

She touched the arms of her chair lightly.

Shucked like an oyster, soft centre exposed in an instant, Bets found herself talking to a complete stranger. It was slow at first, her voice an old rusty wheel that needed some coaxing to turn, but gradually it became easier. Bets found herself, as weeks passed, talking more than she had ever talked in her life. Talking about Raz, and Roxie, and babies, and births.

—I don't know why I'm telling you this, she said frequently, I don't know why I'm telling you this.

Sometimes she cried, and Myrta simply waited.

—You don't have to carry the load alone, Bets, said Myrta over and over.

—You don't have to carry the load alone.

One day, Shannon brought a kitten to visit, borrowed from her neighbour for a couple of hours. She and Bets watched it explore the house: hiding, pouncing, playing with bits of yarn they dangled in front of it, racing around the hallways and suddenly, inexplicably, collapsing into sleep. Bets laughed when the kitten jumped and hung from her pants; laughed until tears came and turned her watery eyes to Shannon.

—You've saved my life. What would I do without you?

Shannon flipped her long hair behind her, plucked the kitten off her shirt.

—I'm your friend, Bets. It's my job to save you.

Even that moment, as she finally felt layers healing over the raw wound of her grief, swept her into Raz.

—What would I do without you? She had asked Raz, over the years, when he had fixed something in the house, or when he had calmed her mind, or once, memorably, when he had opened a jar of pickles in one twist, after her fifteen minutes of struggle.

—Shrivel, he'd answered immediately, waste away in the fetal position. Live a pickle- free life.

She'd whipped the dish towel at him but missed.

—What would I do without you?

Five years ago, after he had made a hummingbird feeder and hung it within view of the kitchen window, because she had mentioned her love of hummingbirds.

—Whatever you did for thirty-odd years before you met me, he had answered mildly, refilling his coffee cup.

Wearing a T-shirt and striped pyjama bottoms, his hair completely on end, he'd joined her at the window, where two hummingbirds were alternating feeding and hovering.

—Things were pointless before I met you. That's why I attacked you at the resort.

—Ah, but did you? Or did you fall into a trap I had cleverly created for you? Raz looked outside with her, blew on his coffee.

—Right, said Bets, what, you paid someone to lure away a small boy with their dog, just so you could return him and meet me?

—You have to admit it's a possibility.

—You're an idiot. You do not get the credit for that event. You were a sad-sack jilted lover.

—And you were a predator in a bikini, looking for vulnerable men.

—I did attack you on the beach, she admitted.

—It worked for me, he said, and you! You got all this—gesturing at himself—so really, we both did quite well in the end.

Bets snorted. Raz took eggs and milk out of the refrigerator, while Bets stayed at the window with her mug, in the slanting sunlight.

—I really love the feeder. Thank you.

—That, right there—Raz gestured with the egg carton—is why I put it up.

—What, so I'd thank you?

—No, he said. So you'd be happy.

***

Back in the study, still with her feet in Raz's boots, Bets frowned. *Ok Raz, you want me to be happy. Maybe you should have stayed around.* She rummaged in the desk, as she had frequently in the past. She found pens, and seven rulers (Who needed seven rulers?); paper clips, elastic bands. The side drawers held paper, printer ink, a comic book (for a sixty-two-year-old man?), a three- hole punch, a screwdriver, a bouncy rubber ball (why?), and a four-pack of chocolate bars, hidden like a high-schooler because Bets had told him he ate too much sugar.

The bottom drawer was large and deep, with multiple hanging files, which Bets had reviewed many times. She lifted a few folders onto the desktop. Being Raz, they were filed in French, but not in alphabetical order. Bets shook her head, and a small smile tugged her lips as she flipped. Banque, Voyages, Factures, Certificats. Bets pulled out a few more, planning to box them up, and saw the corner of a folder, never noticed before, lying at the very bottom of the drawer. She pulled out the hanging files, tugged at the folder until it came free, sat holding it in her hands. It was blue, with a white label that read Médical. Raz kept a medical folder? Raz?

She felt like everything around her stopped. As if the air was sucked out of the room, the overhead fan blades stopped their lazy whirring, the distant outside traffic came to a halt, the birds and dogs and children fell silent. Bets opened the folder and there, right on top, was an MRI brain angiogram report from two years earlier. Done locally, therefore reported in English. It was a long and detailed report, so she jumped to the summary: "There is an 11 mm berry aneurysm at the site of the posterior communicating artery, with no evidence of surrounding blood. This represents 2 mm growth from the prior study. Urgent neurosurgical referral is suggested."

He knew.

Bets read the report again, and then again. She turned on his computer, waited impatiently as it organized itself, searched "cerebral aneurysm risk," found that the growth, and the size, increased the risk of rupture. She turned to the report, turned back to the computer, typed "cerebral aneurysm treatment." Coils, clips, strokes, more risks. The nearest centre was Toronto.

Abandoning the papers, abandoning the boots, she lurched from the room, got to the back door, slid it open, gulped the air, sank slowly onto the steps. The sun, improbably, shone happily with full force onto the deck where she sat.

—No secrets, she said out loud, then shouted. No secrets!

But every couple had secrets. Raz had never talked about his previous relationships, and she certainly didn't want to know. She didn't tell him when she found a breast lump until it was confirmed to be a benign cyst. *Why didn't I tell him right away?* She hadn't told him about Roxie, at first, about the baby, or when she was in the hospice. *I didn't want to worry him.*

Of course, being Raz, he'd think, how can I tell Bets about this? She'll panic, she'll obsess about every headache, she'll research the treatments to death, she'll limit salt and check blood pressures and make him stop working underground. He was right, of course. He was always right, which made him incredibly irritating, even in death.

Drownproofing buys you time, Raz's father had said. *Rester calme.* Take a moment, breathe, figure out what just happened. Then swim with purpose towards a goal.

Bets put her arms on her knees, her head on her arms, and stayed that way for quite a long time, or maybe only a few minutes, the pressure cooker in her chest threatening to blow off the lid, explode all over the room.

I can't, she thought. *I can't I can't.*

Raz: *Si tu veux, tu peux.*

If you want to, you can.

Bets returned to the study and folded up Raz's coveralls, stacked his items, put them back in the bag, into the closet. She stood looking, imagining things in her mind, rearranging furniture, considering. She sat back down in the desk chair, facing the window, and the view of the blue spruce outside.

—*Oui, je veux,* she said out loud to no one.

CHAPTER TWENTY-TWO

With Hannah's pregnancy, Bets felt hope for the first time in a long time, but feared it. She saw a potential path, as if pencilled onto a map, faint and water-smudged.

Hannah sat at the table, three days after Bets found out she was pregnant, and looked like she had been crying nonstop; her eyes were so swollen they were barely visible. Her nose was red, her glasses smudged, her hair a wild tumbleweed. She sipped her ginger ale while Bets poured a finger of whiskey.

—I didn't know you drank.

—Well, said Bets, there's still a lot you don't know about me.

She poured another finger for good measure. She sat down, swirled her drink, and took a large swallow, feeling the burn as it went down. Liquid courage, it was called.

—So, I told Nate, said Hannah.

—Okay.

—He um, he told me to get rid of it. He said if I don't, then he's gone. He'll never speak to me again. He'll never acknowledge it. He says I'm screwing with his future.

His future, thought Bets.

—I thought he loved me, said Hannah. I was such an idiot. Why do men suck? She made a cup with her hands, hid her face in it.

Did teenagers ever make each other happy? Bets wondered. Adolescence felt, in retrospect, like a period of inevitable suffering. Every emotion heightened, every circumstance apparent in exquisite, unbearable focus; endless waxing and waning. *What is the point*, thought Bets. *Why such a struggle?*

—Nate sounds very afraid.

—*I'm* afraid!

—That's the unfair part. This situation is not yours alone. You shouldn't have to do it alone.

—I also talked to my mom again, and I tried, I tried to tell her I wanted to keep the baby, but she wouldn't listen. Not even a little bit. She said this was my mistake to fix, and I had to do the right thing, and that my parents won't support me.

Hannah pulled out a tissue, blew her nose, hiccupped.

—So, said Bets finally, what exactly does that mean?

—It means I don't have a choice. I have to end the pregnancy. Otherwise, I'll have to give it away.

Hannah sipped the ginger ale, pushed out her chair, ran to the sink to vomit, returned to the table slowly, gloom oozing from every pore.

Bets drank the rest of her whiskey in one go.

—All right, Hannah, I have a proposal. You can accept or refuse, it changes nothing. I will still meet with you, help you, support you in your decisions about nursing, everything.

Bets cleared her throat, rapped her whiskey glass on the table.

—As I see it, you have two options, since you don't want to adopt.

—Two?

—Yes, two, said Bets. One, you terminate the pregnancy. I will help you get through that. I'll go over your options with you and make sure you're treated well. We'll make sure you have all the support you need, psychologists and anyone else that can help. You'll continue to live at home and go to school and all of that.

—Okay, whispered Hannah. And option two?

Bets paused for a moment before starting, feeling the whiskey's hand on her back, prompting her forward. *You've got this.*

—Yes. Option two. I've been thinking. That you should be able to make this choice for yourself. You're in a terrible situation, that's a fact, and your life will never be the same.

—But, continued Bets, as you know, I'm alone, and I don't have children, and I wanted them very badly, at one point in my life. So, I was thinking,

if you're really sure that you want to keep your baby, then you could live…
here. With me. And the baby, when the time comes.

In her mind, the speech had gone more smoothly, sounded more
organized, like an offer no one could refuse. She had considered potential
reactions, from laughter to ridicule to refusal to happy—or horrified—
weeping. But Hannah just sat, and Bets hadn't prepared for that. She had
an unusual urge to continue talking, convincing, pleading even, but she
stopped and forced herself to wait.

—Bets, said Hannah finally, that's the most generous thing ever done by
anyone. Her tone was flat.

—But, said Bets, forcing her voice to remain steady.

—But I can't do it. I want to finish school, Bets. I want to be a nurse.
Even if you help me, we'd need money, I still have a year of high school!
University is expensive, my mother won't pay, my grades won't be high
enough for a scholarship. And babies need all kinds of stuff, I don't even
know what, but they need like, cribs and things, and you still work full
time. I want the baby to live, I really, really want my baby to live, with me.
But it's impossible.

Hannah removed her glasses, pressed the heels of her hands to her eyes.

—Hannah, said Bets. As I said, it's completely up to you. If you really
want this, then I can help you. I have a pension, a home, Raz's insurance.
My work options are flexible. There are student loans, I'm sure there are
scholarships for single parents. It's possible. *Si tu veux*. If you want this. But
you have to be the one to want this.

Bets washed her glass, turning her back to Hannah.

—It's a life-changing decision, Hannah. Please ask me anything. Think
about it for a bit.

—I don't have time. Twelve weeks for an abortion, I looked it up.

—No, Bets conceded, not much time.

She dried the glass, put it in the cupboard, as Hannah sat, head down so
that all Bets could see when she turned was the squirrel-nest hair.

—Bets.

—Yes?

—Will you cut my hair?

Bets gave a small laugh of surprise.

—What, like, now?

—Yes!

Hannah smacked the table with her hands.

—I can't stand it anymore; I can't even think! I haven't washed or combed it in days. It's completely wild, and I want it shorter. Please!

Bets saw the spark, the tiniest glimmer of past-Hannah. She got the kitchen scissors, washed them, held them up.

—This is all I have. And no experience whatsoever.

—It doesn't matter, said Hannah, coming to life. She shed the plaid shirt she was wearing, tossed it onto the floor, sat in her white tank top.

—Will we do it here? Is it too messy?

—Who cares about the mess? Said Bets. How short are we going?

—Not as short as yours. Hannah made a chopping motion above her shoulder. Maybe chin length? Shoulders?

—You got it.

Bets picked up the shirt and tied it around Hannah's neck to improvise a smock, then brandished her scissors. Here we go!

She grabbed a matted handful, chewed through the hair with the scissors, and threw the sizeable chunk on the floor. Hannah laughed, actually laughed, and bounced in her seat.

—Keep going! Keep going!

More chunks fell. Once the biggest, most matted pieces were gone, Bets wet a comb and began combing out Hannah's hair, trimming as she went.

—This is unbelievable, she said, working out a tangle. Were you sleeping in the forest?

—In a cave, agreed Hannah, with wolves.

—Were they living in your hair?

Bets continued combing, trimming, fluffing. It was by no means a professional result, but gradually it took some shape and by the time they were done, Hannah's crazed curls were tamed into a wavy bob just above her shoulders. Hannah, still wearing her plaid smock, followed Bets to the powder room in the hallway, keeping her glasses off until she got inside.

—Okay, I hope you're ready, said Bets, it's a bit of a hack job.

Hannah put her glasses on, turned to the mirror, gazed at her puffy eyes, her newly shorn hair, her plaid smock. She smiled widely.

—New Hannah, she said, with a deep breath.

—New Hannah, agreed Bets, placing a hand on her shoulder. Who knew you were in there under all that hair?

Hannah ate some crackers while Bets swept the kitchen. The hair was everywhere, on the chairs, the table, the countertop, stuck under the feet of the fridge, stuck to the kettle; they both felt like it was in their noses, their ears.

—Your hair, said Bets, was taking over the world.

Hannah ran her hand through her new cut.

—New Hannah has an announcement, she said.

—Oh? Bets swiped at the table leg with the broom, to dislodge a stubborn hair clump.

—New Hannah would like to accept your offer.

Throwing her arms in the air after her announcement, like a gymnast completing an Olympic games routine.

CHAPTER TWENTY-THREE

Bets had formulated a few images of Hannah's parents, based on nothing at all: a tall, domineering woman, shouting in the deli, making impossible demands of her clumsy daughter. Or the opposite: a tiny bulldog of a mother, like the one in Bets' neighbourhood growing up, with four enormous sons, all of whom were terrified of her. Or possibly a woman of immigrant background, someone who had worked incredibly hard to scrape together a life for herself, for her family, only to face collapse now that Hannah had become pregnant. In each scenario, somehow Bets' mental image of Hannah's father, before seeing him through the window, had been the same: a middle-aged man wearing a butcher's apron—despite not being a butcher— nothing like his actual appearance.

—I told her many times to stop bothering you, said Carol, Hannah's mother. I would have stopped her sooner had I known where things were leading.

They were sitting in the office at the back of the deli, each on a hard wooden chair, the desk a cluttered barrier between the two parents, Carol and Graham, and their daughter on the opposite side with Bets. In the end, Carol stood out by eluding all categorization: not tall, not short; not thin, not heavyset. Average. And angry.

—I'm not religious, said Bets, I want you to know that. I'm not trying to influence Hannah in any way. This is not about being anti-abortion, it's about being pro-choice.

Carol gave a snort.

—A seventeen-year-old cannot make this large of a choice.

—Maybe not, said Bets. Not all of them, anyway. But Hannah deserves to have a big say in this life-changing event.

Carol sat forward in her chair. Her husband put his hand on her arm.

— And how many children do you have, *Bets*, that you are so certain you know what is best for Hannah?

—Mom, protested Hannah.

—Carol, said Graham, but Carol's eyes never left Bets' face. Bets dug her fingernail into her thumb, focusing on the pain.

—It's okay, said Bets. Carol's right. I'm no expert in this area. I have no living children. I had only miscarriages.

—And now you want my daughter's baby to fill some kind of void in your life?

Hannah began to protest again, but Bets held an open hand to her. *Stop.*

—I don't think so. I've considered that motivation, it's a fair argument. But really, what I want is for Hannah to be able to continue with her plans. I want her to have the life she is dreaming about.

Carol tossed her husband's hand off her arm and stood.

—Dreams, everyone says live your dreams! Well, who dreams of a seventeen-year-old girl having a baby? Who dreams of that? If you think she should have the life she wants, she needs to get rid of this pregnancy— abortion, adoption—and then avoid being so stupid in the future!

Bets glanced at Graham, who had turned away from his wife to sit with his elbows on his knees, facing the floor.

—Carol, Graham, said Bets, I fully understand your position. I'm not here to ask your permission.

—You should ask our permission! You should! We don't even know you! We're her parents, we'll decide what's best for her, not some lonely widow. For God's sake, Graham, say something!

Graham looked like someone had produced a spotlight and told him to perform an aria. He cleared his throat twice, sat upright, smoothed his pants.

—We just want what's best for Hannah. We just want her to have the best possible life. And we know—glancing at his wife—that legally, this decision is up to her.

—Of course. Of course, you want what's best for Hannah, said Bets. That's what we all want. I'm here because I've offered Hannah a choice, and I want to be clear that if she chooses to continue the pregnancy, and keep her baby, I will take her in if needed, and I will support her. If that's her choice, you will always be welcome.

Carol edged past her husband's chair and left the room without a word.

CHAPTER TWENTY-FOUR

They only had two weeks before Hannah needed to start school again. Shannon came between shifts to help paint Hannah's room. Eddie loaded and unloaded Hannah's boxes and moved furniture, sometimes wandering in the hallway with a bookcase or filing cabinet on one shoulder, texting with the opposite hand. Bets moved boxes to the basement, and the bag of Raz's work clothes upstairs, into her own closet. She tried not to wince when she passed Raz's study, transformed into Hannah's room. Freshly painted, the only remaining pieces of Raz were the rolltop desk—now covered with Hannah's electronics—and the bed, hidden beneath discarded clothes and rumpled bedding. Soon, there would be baby furniture in there, too. It was a lot of change, expected and yet uncomfortable, like a scratchy tag in new clothing, and Bets looked in the mirror sometimes to remind herself, *oui, je veux.*

—You're crazy, Bets, you know that, right?

Shannon came for a glass of wine the night before Hannah's move-in date.

—Absolutely. One hundred percent. In way over my head. But did I tell you about the Raz baby?

Shannon choked on her wine, coughed a few times.

—At work, Bets said, spinning her wine glass, there was this newborn. He looked at me, and he crinkled up his eyes, just like Raz. I was holding the baby, showing the mother how to give him a bath, and he was looking at me and his eyes were just like Raz, and I had to give him back, and go and get myself together.

—Oh, Bets.

—The point being, I'm already crazy, however you want to define it. I've completely lost my marbles, and this situation with Hannah is the only thing that might possibly make any sense at all.

—Yes, said Shannon. I know you believe that.

—But?

—But I'm worried. We're talking *years,* potentially. Years! How can you look ahead years in the future?

—I can't, said Bets. That's the whole point. I look ahead, and this is all I can see right now. Which is better than the dark tunnel of nothingness I was seeing before.

One item transferred to Bets' home the next day was an instrument case that appeared nearly as big as Hannah.

—What is that, a cello?

—It's a guitar. I'm in a guitar course this year.

—A guitar course! Do you still take math? Chemistry?

Hannah rolled her eyes and laughed.

—Yes! This is an arts elective. You like balanced education, right?

—You never told me you played an instrument!

—Well, I don't, really. I just know a few chords. I bought the guitar last summer.

—Let's have a tune, suggested Bets.

The guitar appeared unwieldy and enormous on Hannah's knee, but somehow, she reached around it and strummed. She adjusted a couple of strings.

—Okay, said Hannah, I know three chords, and two songs, so this will be a short concert.

She ducked her head, arranged her fingers, and began to sing in a strong, clear voice. She paused to reposition her fingers periodically, and her notes were not all in tune, but the overall effect was enough to rouse something inside of Bets, something emerging from a cocoon after months of dormancy. She realized she hadn't listened to music for months, other than the radio, which barely penetrated her consciousness. She clapped.

—Hannah, that was great! You have a lovely voice!

Hannah cleared her throat.

—I messed up some of my chords.

—Here's a tip from an old lady, said Bets. When someone gives you a compliment, don't dismiss it. Just say "thanks" and enjoy it.

—Thanks.

—Write that down, Bets teased. What else have you got?

—My Bonnie Lies Over the Ocean.

—Great! Is it okay if I sing, too?

Hannah bent over the guitar again, placing her fingers. They sang together slowly, haltingly, stopping while Hannah switched chords. Bets applauded again when they finished.

—Well, it sounded better when you sang alone. I didn't realize how much I missed music.

—You can try it if you want. The strings really hurt my fingers after a while. Hannah held out the guitar, but Bets shook her head.

—That's okay. Old dog, new tricks. I'll just enjoy your playing.

—"Enjoy" might be a little strong, laughed Hannah, putting the guitar back in its case. But thanks. Maybe I'll practice more, here.

—Why?

—My parents don't really want me to spend time on an instrument. They want me taking courses that will prepare me for my future.

Hannah used her fingers to put air quotes around the word "future."

—Then again, I guess that's all up in the air, now.

She went to put her guitar in her new room, the jovial atmosphere flattening in her wake.

Bets came home from her shift exhausted one evening. A nurse had called in sick, no one could cover so, of course, there were women with labour pains and bleeding and ruptured membranes arriving in unprecedented numbers. Not to mention a forceps delivery, an emergency c-section, and a set of twins coming prematurely, who needed to be transferred out of town. High winds delayed the helicopter, and they were all preparing for the possibility of the babies arriving before the transfer could occur. Bets had never heard the pediatrician so stressed and abrupt. She stayed an extra hour, and the helicopter came, and the women and babies were all safe, but she felt that as a group, the staff had barely survived the shift.

Walking home, all she could think about was a bath and some supper. Maybe Hannah had cooked something for a change, since it was so late.

The house was quiet when Bets entered.

—Hello?

The entryway was a tumble of assorted footwear, which she moved to the side.

—Hannah?

In the kitchen, dishes overflowed the sink, beside which an open loaf of sliced bread sagged alongside a jar of peanut butter. The knife lay in a smear on the countertop.

Bets made an impatient noise in her throat. She found Hannah in her room, wearing headphones, looking at her phone. She jumped when Bets called her name.

—You scared me!

She pulled down her headphones.

—How was work?

The room was piled with laundry, plates, and mugs, and smelled of dirty socks. Hannah wore an oversized T-shirt and sweatpants, her hair pulled back.

—Work was exhausting, said Bets. It would have been great to come home to something other than a huge mess in the kitchen.

They looked at each other for a moment.

—You never asked me to clean the kitchen, said Hannah.

—I shouldn't need to! Should I? Who else is going to do it?

Hannah put her headphones back on and turned deliberately to the wall.

—Hannah?

No response. Bets closed the door, went back to the kitchen, cleared a path on the countertop, made a sandwich. *What have I done here,* she thought as she worked, *what have I done?*

During shifts, Bets spoke to Shannon about the difficulties of her new situation, but there wasn't much time to talk. Sometimes she'd break off in the middle of the discussion, but an hour or three or seven later, Shannon always remembered.

—You were saying about the long showers, she'd prompt, you were talking about the mess, and get Bets going again.

—I'm just complaining, said Bets after a while. I hate that! I want to say, here's the solution—I'm sure it's simple—but I can't find it. It's like we just irritate each other now, where before we had this wonderful connection, this easy conversation. You warned me; you told me this might happen.

—So, what happened to it? Asked Shannon. The wonderful connection, the easy conversation?

The lunchroom was strangely empty aside from the two of them. Bets put her feet up on the table while she thought.

—We've become, I don't know. Caught up in domestic squabbles, like an old married couple. I've become a nag, and everything she does is irritating me.

—Does she do anything? Does she cook? Laundry?

—Only if I ask, and tell her what to do. She's mostly on her phone, always the phone. She wasn't like that before. It's driving me crazy.

The comment struck them simultaneously; the words a perfect echo of the conversations that went on in the background of their day, when the other nursing and medical colleagues complained about their teenagers. Shannon met Bets' eyes, and they both burst out laughing.

—Oh my God, said Bets, eight weeks and I'm the annoyed mother of a teenager. I'm not even supposed to be her mother! I'm her friend! How did this happen?

—I think you're experiencing the universal frustration of dealing with adolescents, said Shannon. She wasn't your problem before.

—Okay. Okay. I need to fix this. This is fixable.

—You need to fix this together, suggested Shannon. Maybe give up a teensy little droplet of control.

—Yes. Yes. Get her input, let her choose responsibility, said Bets. Why didn't I see that?

She pointed her last bite of sandwich at Shannon before popping it into her mouth.

—I'm just going to ignore that bit about control issues. She reached across the table to touch her friend's hand.

—Thank you, Shannon. Maybe you should leave nursing and become a therapist. I could be your main client.

Shannon grinned.

—Just trying to prevent a supply room situation.

Bets wasn't sure what kind of response she'd get from Hannah. Although Hannah still bounced, slid across the hardwood floor in her socks, sang under her breath, she also wept easily, gave stony glares, shrugged. When Bets asked her to come into the living room to talk, Hannah avoided eye contact. She wore a baseball cap over her shortened hair, and a large sweatshirt that still hid her rounding abdomen, but less so each week. There was no notebook in sight; Bets hadn't seen the notebook in weeks.

—Can I get you anything? Asked Bets.

Hannah shook her head, crossed her arms. She placed her phone face down on the coffee table, and Bets caught one upward glance, a glimpse of Hannah's eyes, in which Bets saw no anger, only worry and fear. A look she had seen many, many times, on many other faces.

Bets sat down.

—Hannah, things are not going that well. I feel like there's a lot of tension.

Silence.

—I realized that I've been unfair to both of us. I've given you no expectations, I'm not even clear on my own role. But then I've been irritated about things, and nagging.

Hannah's eyes were now on Bets.

—I'm wondering if we can work together, develop some schedules, share some responsibilities, maybe be clearer about time together and time apart, that kind of thing. Do you think that would help?

Hannah remained quiet, but nodded. Bets waited.

—Hannah, she said, this is not going to work unless you are honest. You need to tell me what is going on. Please.

Hannah dropped her eyes again.

—You act like my mother, she said in a quiet voice. You sigh all the time.

—Yes, said Bets. And I'm not your mother, and that's why I want things to be more equal. I don't want us to be this way together.

—Okay.

—Do you cook? I'd love it if you cooked sometimes.

—Not like you. Not, you know, fancy.

—Fancy!

Bets sat back, nearly laughed, swallowed it. Images of Raz tenderly arranging scallops onto plates, with avocado topping and pea shoots, entered her mind.

—Hannah, I need nothing more than a grilled cheese sandwich or a plate of scrambled eggs. Can you handle that?

Hannah nodded, the tiniest smile lifting her mouth. She uncrossed her arms, adjusted her hat.

Okay, thought Bets. *Okay*.

They worked through plans for laundry, discussed which things went into the dryer. They developed a cleaning schedule. A shopping list posted on the fridge. A shared calendar. Hannah showed Bets how to enter the calendar into her phone, their heads bent together. As they progressed, Hannah participated more and more, waved her hands, gave suggestions. When they had completed quite a few items, Bets felt the last cracks of tension fusing together, felt her feet on solid ground again.

—I feel like we've got a good start here! She said. We should have done this right off the bat.

—I thought, said Hannah.

—You thought what?

—I thought you were calling me in here to kick me out.

—Kick you out! Just like that? No warning? You think I'd do that?

—I don't know. No. But I just felt like you were mad all the time, and that made me mad, and I guess I thought it wouldn't work.

—Hannah, said Bets, waiting for eye contact, I agreed to do this. I *suggested* we do this. I am not backing out at the first sign of conflict. We've got a long way to go here. But we need to be honest with each other, okay? We need to talk to each other. We won't agree all the time, but we need to talk.

Her fingers brushed Hannah's shoulder.

—Write that down, added Bets.

Both of them laughed: small, tentative, hopeful.

The following weeks were a blur. Bets invited Carol and Graham for supper, which they declined, but Hannah returned home to her parents each week for a meal on Sundays. There were late night sessions studying for Hannah's high school exams. There were confrontations when Hannah slammed cupboard doors as Bets tried to sleep after a night shift. There were questions and doubts and adjustments. There were more days when Bets thought, *what have we done here?*

There were tears as Hannah adjusted to her expanding midsection and the resulting stares and comments and judgements. Hannah tripped on carpets, and Bets removed them. Hannah broke dishes, dropped a full container of juice on the floor, used liquid dish soap in the dishwasher, which overflowed in a sudsy mess. Bets needed to go to bed at ten, then at nine thirty, still waking in the night. Hannah stayed up until one in the morning, then two.

I'm too old for this, thought Bets, after an argument with Hannah about breastfeeding.

—I'm too young, said Hannah, I can't do this.

Trying to understand her changing body, the options for prenatal care, the foods to avoid, the risks of medications, the concept of budgeting. She screeched in frustration, stomped to her room, she had surges of love and gratitude where she wrapped Bets into unexpected hugs, unable to say a word. Sometimes she let Bets touch the baby kicking away within her. Sometimes she jerked her body away abruptly, as if to say *my baby. Mine.*

After a while, Hannah returned from her Sunday suppers with food sent by her parents. One week, a jar of antipasto. The next, a ham. After her Christmas visit, Hannah returned with an entire wheel of cheese, which she placed on the table with a flourish.

—This is it, Bets, she said, this is the start of forgiveness. They never give cheese, it's too expensive. It's a Christmas miracle for you! A cheese of peace.

Bets laughed from the corner of the couch, where she sat by the fire with her legs tucked beneath her. Hannah displayed a big box of baby items, also from her parents: cardboard books, onesies, sleepers, a mobile to hang over a crib. Along with the adjustable playpen from Bets, a highchair from Shannon, and a refurbished dresser from Eddie, Hannah was well on her way. She sat down, flipping through the little books, running a finger along the edges of the thick pages. Bets was surprised when Hannah looked up and there were tears on her cheeks.

—What if I can't do this, Bets? What if I'm bad at it?

—You won't be bad at it.

—You don't know that!

—No. But I know you have great instincts. And you're curious. And smart. No one really knows what they're doing, Hannah. Don't let people fool you.

Hannah left the box behind and went to her room. Bets picked up her mug, watching the fire, the Christmas tree lights blinking on and off, on and off, giving glimpses of the baby items set up in the room, decorated with bows, waiting.

CHAPTER TWENTY-FIVE

Bets sat in a chair facing Raz's work clothes on the bed, her feet in his boots, when Hannah knocked and then burst through the door.

—Bets, I found a crib on sale online, I—oh.

Bets slid her feet from the boots, cleared her throat.

—Sometimes—gesturing toward the bed—sometimes I talk to Raz for a few minutes. Weird, I know.

Hannah sat on the bed, touched the coveralls.

—Anyway, that sale sounds like something we should definitely look at!

Bets was full of false cheer, but Hannah wasn't looking at her.

—You must really miss him.

Hannah touched the curled-up fingers of the glove, a whisper touch.

—I do. All the time. Please don't hug me.

—I don't think I'll ever find someone like that.

—You can't give up at seventeen. Lots of time yet.

Hannah placed her hand on her pregnant belly.

—Who's going to want to get involved with this? Anyway, I won't have time.

—Not for a while, agreed Bets, but it will get easier. You'll meet people. You'll find someone.

—You can't know that.

—No. Bets started folding and gathering Raz's things. But I think we'll find what we need, if we—I don't know—stay open to possibility. That's how you came tripping into my life, right?

Hannah didn't respond, silently passing the gloves, the hard hat, the ear protectors, as Bets put them all into the plastic bag, and into the closet.

—All right. Back to reality.

—Swimming toward the goal, said Hannah as she left the room, and Bets simply stopped and absorbed Raz's words through her skin.

The winter felt long, as it does when the snow arrives in October and doesn't leave until May. The deep freeze of January, with its bitter cold and short days, often affected the psyche of even the hardiest Northerners. Bets left for work in the dark, walked home in the dark, day shift and night shift. She'd never understood how the miners could also work all day in the dark raises, with nothing between them and the blackness but their headlamps.

After Christmas, after consultation with the principal, her teachers, and her parents, Hannah decided to complete her courses online. She was both listless and restless, alternating between lying on the couch watching TV and roaming around the house with no specific objective. She struggled to focus on her assignments. Relations between Bets and Hannah had improved, but when she got home, Bets wanted to be alone sometimes, and Hannah, alone much of the day, craved some human interaction.

—You should call a friend, said Bets, have someone come for dinner when I'm working.

—I don't want them to see me like this. Hannah indicated her volleyball-sized midsection, no longer hidden even with an oversized shirt. Besides, who would I ask? They'd just gawk at me, then go and tell everyone about it.

—I feel like they aren't thinking about you nearly as much as they're busy thinking about themselves.

—You haven't been in high school for a while, said Hannah.

Bets walked home one night listening to the squeak of her boots on the snow and admiring the full moon, so radiant it nearly felt like daytime. She slowed, savouring the quiet, then heard some shouts. They came from the schoolyard, and Bets turned toward the sound, despite being out of her way by a block. Was someone in trouble? She heard a slide, a crunch, more shouts, and as she came closer, Bets saw a person fly through the air. A snow-crunch when they landed, shouts from further in the darkness. She stopped to piece it together and realized it was a group of teenage boys. They wore skis, and had fashioned a large jump out of snow at the base of the hill in the schoolyard, launching themselves into the air in the moonlight. They landed on their skis, or crashed spectacularly, cartwheeling in explosions of snow, to the hoots and shouts of their friends.

They're going to kill themselves, thought Bets, pausing to watch, but even as she had the thought, she felt an idea forming. The boys finished their jumps, removed their skis, and started the hard slog back up the hill, jostling each other, pushing each other into the snow. Protests, laughter, profanity. Bets smiled to herself as she turned back toward home.

Hannah took some convincing. Her belly was too big, her coat too small, she was too tired, too short of breath.

—Isn't it dangerous? She asked, knowing Bets well.

—Being in here all winter is dangerous, said Bets. Didn't you read *The Shining?* We need to get out. You need to get out. And I need a little tiny adventure.

—Do you even have a sled? Asked Hannah, as Bets searched the closet. She emerged with a winter parka, which zipped up around Hannah with minimal straining, although the sleeves were long.

—Is this Raz's? Asked Hannah, rolling the sleeves.

—Yes. I'm glad I kept it. Here, put the snowmobile mitts overtop.

Bundled beyond recognition, armed with a plastic tray and a pizza box, they clomped toward the school in the cold, still air. The boys had left, as Bets hoped, and the hill glistened in the darkness.

—This is insane, said Hannah, as they began the steep climb, losing her balance, using her hands to push herself upright every few steps. Bets' heart pounded with exertion, her legs ached with the effort of climbing, but she also felt an inexplicable joy, lifting her, pulling her upwards, so that even as she reached a hand down to assist Hannah, she felt no fatigue.

At the hill's summit, they stood looking out at the houses below, mostly dark, some with white light spilling from windows, some with the blue tinge of televisions, some still decorated with coloured bulbs from Christmas.

—Ready? Asked Bets.

—This is insane, said Hannah again. Who gets the tray?

—You can use the tray; I'll take the box. Make sure you steer over here, away from the jump.

—Once I'm down, I'll never get up, warned Hannah, lowering herself awkwardly to the ground, sliding the plastic tray under her.

—I'll come and help you up. Want me to go first?

In response, Hannah pushed off with her feet, lifted her boots off the snow despite her bulk, and disappeared down the hill with surprising speed. A wake of snow swirled around her as her scream echoed down the hill. It was a straight run, and at the bottom she lay on her side, a shadow in the moonlight, her laughter spiralling up to Bets at the top, who centred herself on the pizza box, pushed off, and got halfway down before taking an awkward left turn that flipped her off into the snow. She dusted herself off, repositioned, aimed for Hannah, and finished her run nearby. They both lay in the snow, looking up at the stars and the moon, puffing clouds of wintry breath.

Bets turned to Hannah's outline a few metres away.

—So, she said. Nice run, how was it?

Hannah pushed herself into a sitting position.

—Again, she said.

The bleeding started the next morning.

Hannah pulled Bets by the arm, steered her to the toilet bowl, and they both looked down at the scarlet swirls within, strangely beautiful despite their ominous message.

—Any cramps?

—No.

—Do you feel the baby moving?

—Yes. What is it? What's wrong?

—We'd better go in and get you checked.

Bets kept her exterior matter-of-fact but dropped the car keys twice before getting them into the ignition.

—I'll be here if you need me, she told Hannah once they'd arrived at the maternity floor.

Hannah, who'd barely spoken since they left the house, followed the nurse without a word, leaving Bets in the empty waiting area, surrounded by posters of breastfeeding women, and culturally diverse groups at prenatal classes.

You should never have encouraged the sliding. That was reckless and stupid.

It wasn't! A new voice within her. *You both needed to get outside, to laugh, to let go.*

But what if I've caused a problem with the baby? What if something happens? I can't do this again.

Bets looked around as if someone could hear her thoughts. She heard voices in the hallway, an IV beeping, a fussing baby. The waiting room remained empty.

Bets, this is not about you.

I know.

If it is, you need to walk away. You need to walk away.

Bets stood, and Dr. Jenna came into the room with Hannah.

—All good here, said Dr. Jenna, one hand on Hannah's shoulder. The bleeding has stopped, there's no sign of labour, and the ultrasound looked fine. Baby's heartbeat is strong. We'll just keep an eye on it.

—Great news!

Bets held out Raz's enormous coat to Hannah, helped to zip around her belly, bulging so far in front of her it seemed miraculous she could stand upright.

—Were you scared? Asked Hannah once they were driving.

—A bit. Were you?

—I freaked out a bit, when I saw the blood. But then I thought, maybe I'm not having a baby after all. Which felt kind of like a relief, just for a second.

Hannah opened her window a crack, lifting her face to the cool air.

—But then, she continued, the baby gave a big kick, and she felt so strong, and I knew I had to see her, I had to know her. I know she might be a boy—in response to Bets' unasked question—but I just have a feeling.

Bets had parked, not at home, but at the nearby mini-mall, in front of the optician's office with its flashing neon glasses. Hannah tapped her frames into place, as she had multiple times during the drive.

—Why are we here?

—Hannah, we are getting those glasses fixed once and for all, said Bets.

Hannah opened her door, pulled at the doorframe to haul herself upright. She put her mittened hand on Bets' arm just as they reached the optician's storefront.

—Thanks, Bets. That's what I was trying to say.

CHAPTER TWENTY-SIX

The doorbell rang one day, unexpectedly.

—I'm not here, called Hannah, despite not having had visitors at all.

A tall young woman with a severe box-cut bob, black lipstick, and several facial piercings stood at the door.

—I'm Zoey, she said. I'm here for Hannah.

—Yes! said Bets. Zoey. I remember Hannah speaking about you. I'm Bets. Zoey held a large instrument case similar to Hannah's.

—Hannah can't come to the door just now. Maybe she could call you?

Zoey tsked.

—She won't call. That's why I'm here. She won't answer calls or texts. I don't know if I did something, or what.

She had a small round bead pierced through her lower lip and caught it under her teeth, releasing with a click.

—I'll definitely let her know you stopped by, said Bets. Maybe she'll change her mind.

Zoey reached into her pocket and pulled out a small, wrapped package.

—Will you give her this? She turned to leave.

—Zoey, wait. Come in for a moment.

Zoey glanced around and came inside, kicking snow off her boots. Bets went to Hannah's room and knocked softly.

—Hannah?

Hannah was on the bed, laptop open, wearing headphones, which she lowered.

—Zoey is here.

—I said to say I'm not here.

—I know. But she knows you're here. I think she wants to talk, Hannah. She brought you this.

Bets handed over the package, neatly wrapped in brown craft paper, tied with a red ribbon. Hannah looked at the gift for a moment, then opened it. She unfolded a baby's sleeper, white with *Spit Happens* written on the front. Hannah smiled, turning it to show Bets, who laughed.

—Say thanks, said Hannah, stroking the sleeper. I can't come down, I look terrible.

—I don't think she's here to judge. I really don't.

—I'll call her.

—She has her guitar, said Bets. I think she planned to stay for a bit.

Hannah's exaggerated breath sounded like she had just done a lap of the pool underwater.

—Fine.

Hannah picked up a pillow and held it across her front.

—She needed help with her B chord, Hannah told Bets, wandering into the living room after Zoey left. That one is really hard.

—I'm sure she really appreciated your help, said Bets, who was folding laundry and pairing socks. She tossed Hannah hers.

—We're going to go for a walk next week, said Hannah.

—About time, said Bets.

After weeks stuck in the house, Hannah suddenly went into a frenzy of cleaning, her old energy returning, applied to something upon which she and Bets could agree. Bets came home from her shifts in February to a newly sparkling front entryway, or bathroom, or kitchen countertop, or floor.

—You're nesting, she told Hannah. You're doing a great job.

—I'm bored out of my mind.

—Enjoy it while you can, said Bets, I certainly do!

Hannah rolled her eyes. Enjoy being bored? She managed a couple of walks with Zoey, but the winter was harsh, the temperatures bone-tingling. Bets didn't really like it when Hannah went off on her own, yet appreciated the need for alone time and exercise. She tried, she really tried, not to comment or nag or offer unsolicited advice. Hannah's time was coming soon, and Bets wasn't sure either of them were truly ready.

Then again, was anyone ever truly ready?

After some initial resistance, Hannah was attending teenage birth classes and admitted she liked the social interactions with people in no position to judge her.

—Did you know? She frequently asked Bets after the classes. Did you know the baby can poop inside you? Did you know you can push on your side? Did you know…

Sometimes she caught herself and said, of course you know. What am I talking about? Other times, she just forged ahead, and Bets let her chatter away, enjoying the renewed enthusiasm.

—In the classes, have you talked about having a support person? Asked Bets one night. It's really important to have someone with you, to help you through the labour pain.

Hannah chased some pasta around her plate with her fork.

—I just assumed you would be there with me, she said. Aren't you going to be there?

Bets felt warmth, like a smooth trickle of water on her skin.

—Well, I would love to be there, Hannah. I just wasn't sure.

—And Shannon should be my nurse. Can I ask her?

—You can ask. It depends if she's working when you go into labour.

Bets poked at her own supper.

—What about Carol?

—What about her?

—Do you want her there?

The question hung in the air for a moment. Hannah still saw her parents once a week, came home with baby items and food, sometimes happy, sometimes frustrated. They rarely discussed the visits.

—I don't think so, said Hannah finally. She didn't want this baby, and she's never asked to be there. She and Dad can see the baby afterwards; they're more positive about her now, at least.

—Okay, said Bets, relief washing over her. She had been worrying about Carol's presence in the delivery room, but it was her grandchild, after all.

—Are you afraid? She asked.

Hannah pushed away her plate.

—I'm so scared, she confessed.

—Everyone is, said Bets. I'm scared, too.

—You? Why?

—Because I don't want you to be in pain. Because I know it will be hard and I won't be able to fix it for you.

—But you do this every day.

—Yes, said Bets. But it's not usually you.

CHAPTER TWENTY-SEVEN

B ets dreamt she was tobogganing. She was with Raz, and they were sliding down an enormous hill, landing in soft snow, joyful and exhilarated. She could feel the cold of the melting snow down her neck, in the tops of her mittens. Her breath came in puffs as she dragged the toboggan back up to the top, her feet rubbing inside her winter boots, her socks falling down. It was a long, slow climb into consciousness when she became aware of her name.

—Bets.

—Bets.

She looked around the hill, and Raz was gone. She called, and her boots became heavier and heavier, so that she could no longer climb upward. She realized there was a blizzard, that she was going to be trapped halfway up the hill.

—Bets.

Groggily, Bets clawed her way awake. She blinked, and jumped, seeing Hannah's face looming in front of her.

—Hannah?

—You need to wake up. I'm having pain.

Bets was awake immediately, as if doused in cold water.

—What kind of pain?

In response, Hannah curled herself forward, began moaning, moved her feet in a marching rhythm.

—Ah. That kind of pain.

She rubbed Hannah's back, waited for the contraction to pass.

—How long have they been going on?

—A couple of hours. They're getting worse. They're getting worse, Bets! Hannah burst into tears. I can't do this. I don't want to do this.

Bets made soothing noises, pulled up the quilt.

—Come lie down here. I'll put some pressure on your back, and you can rock.

Hannah climbed into the bed, back towards Bets, who rubbed her lower back for a moment before Hannah jumped up again.

—I can't, said Hannah. I can't lie down. I have to move. I have to—Oh, God! She bent and marched again.

—That was only about five minutes. I need to check what's going on.

Bets got up, grabbed a robe off the chair, went to get some hospital gloves. She coaxed Hannah onto the bed, still crying.

—Okay, Hannah, we talked about this. Remember? Weird, but necessary. Checking the cervix. Remember?

Hannah nodded, knees tight together.

—Look at me, said Bets.

Hannah looked. Bets breathed in slowly, Hannah followed. Bets breathed out, Hannah followed. Bets pressed on Hannah's knees, which opened slightly. Three more breaths. Contraction, knees back together. Bets helped her through, kept the breathing going, waited it out. Finally, Hannah relaxed enough for Bets to check things out.

—Hannah, said Bets, this is it. Three centimetres, I can feel the membranes, things are happening. We're going to the hospital.

—I can't, said Hannah. I can't! I can't!

She sat on the bed, head in her hands. Bets squatted in front of Hannah, hands on her thighs.

—Hannah. You're ready. This is labour, it's supposed to be hard. It's hard for everyone, but I know you can do this.

Hannah removed her hands from her eyes, still looking down.

—I'll be there, every minute. Shannon will be there, Dr. Jenna will be there, we will all help you. You will not be alone in this. You can do this.

Hannah shook her head.

—You can.

—I can't.

Another contraction hit, and Hannah rocked back and forth, while Bets forced her to look, to breathe.

—Let me put this another way, said Bets when the pain passed. You don't have a choice, so let's get going before you break your water all over my bed.

It was a first baby, but things went quickly, as they often did with teenaged mothers. Bets guided Hannah through the labour, redirected her when she panicked, repeated over and over, look at me. Look at me. Breathe, follow my breath. Look at me. The baby's heartbeat was steady, the fluid, when the membranes ruptured, was clear. Shannon murmured words of encouragement, provided everything Hannah needed. Dr. Jenna came in once the pushing started and it was obvious things would not take long.

At one point, Hannah's contraction was so strong that she shouted for her mother. Bets had heard young girls before, but this time she felt it in her chest, like her heart was being twisted and wrung out. Hannah was a child. A child. What were they doing? How could this all possibly work? *Focus, Bets.* She worked hard to redirect Hannah's attention, to keep her centred, to take her mind off the pain. Hannah, who was so young, but doing so well, who refused an epidural, who said, after the initial panic passed, that she could do it.

Once she was pushing, Dr. Jenna was close by and ready, and all of them marvelled at the rapid descent of the baby. First babies, in older mothers, often took hours to push out.

Predictably, Hannah began to thrash, to climb backwards up the bed, not knowing what to do with the pain, the pressure, the sense of bursting. She screamed, she gripped Bets like a life preserver, with both of her arms, pushing her head into Bets' chest, refusing to let go even when pushing her baby, which she did remarkably well.

The top of the head appeared, slid back. More appeared, slid back. Then, one more push and the head stayed in place, visible to the temples, Hannah gasping for breath, eyes huge behind her glasses. Shannon smiling, from her spot beside the delivery table, as she picked up the baby blanket and spread it onto Hannah's chest, ready to receive. They had set up the portable mirror for Hannah, and Bets could see from her vantage point, could see they had reached the point of no return. She ignored the tears streaming down her face, as she panted with Hannah, as she pointed to the mirror, as she placed Hannah's hands in the doctor's, so that Dr. Jenna could guide Hannah to touch her baby's emerging head.

I'm coming, it felt like the infant was saying, *Get ready.*

I'm coming.

ACKNOWLEDGEMENTS

I had no idea it took so many people to create a book. I remember saying "I think I'm writing a novel," then looking into an abyss of the unknown. The past three years have been one of the most satisfying journeys of my life, and there are so many people who have helped me to get here. Thank you to:

-Author Ioanna Sahas Martin, my kindred spirit who also said, "I think I'm writing a novel," (I think she was first!) Writing that play together in grade school must have started something. I'm so grateful to have her wisdom in writing and life.

-Author Rhonda Douglas, whose information, support and developmental edits were critical, and whose Resilient Writers group provided accountability, resources and friendships.

-Author Zsuzsi Gartner, whose invaluable expertise during the editing stage (despite having COVID!) taught me, among many other things, the value of lopping off the last few sentences to make a paragraph so much better.

-Dr. Glenn and Paule Corneil, editors extraordinaire, who used valuable holiday time finding the medical, French language, and wording errors in my book. Merci! No more panting!

-Brian Millions, who spent hours helping me to understand raise mining (even when the Leafs were playing). All errors are entirely my own, and I apologize to raise miners everywhere if my fictionalized account misrepresents their dangerous work.

-Drs. Elaine Innes and Kevin Brousseau, for helping with Indigenous language and cultural queries. Mîkwec!

-Drs. Julie Samson, Yves and Jean Côté, Gérard Champion, and Christian Durepos, for assistance with French wording, insults and connotations. Merci encore, mille fois!

-Anna Armstrong and Dr. Elizabeth Paupst, who reviewed chapter drafts and gave important feedback early in the process.

-Author Matthew Trafford and my short story group at the Banff Centre for the Arts, back in 2014: you all helped to re-plant the seed.

-The nurses on maternity at Timmins and District Hospital, 1997-2012, especially Pat, Karen, Claire and Sue: none of the characters here are you, and yet you inspired their creation with your knowledge, humour, and deep caring.

-Paula Davalan, for being number one cheerleader despite her many questions ("What do you mean, you didn't know she'd do that? You WROTE it!")

-Dr. Trevor Harterre for his story about jumping into the water without a life jacket.

-My mom Chris Nanson, who was a nurse in the grocery store when a glass pop bottle exploded in the 1970's, and who has always been interested & involved.

-The editors and publishing assistants at Friesen Press.

And of course, Paul, Allison, and Robyn Armstrong, always in my corner, always there in everything I do. Love you so much.

ABOUT THE AUTHOR

KAREN LEA ARMSTRONG has had a lifelong passion for reading, writing, and languages. She has practised family medicine in Northern Ontario since 1997, including fifteen years of obstetrics, during which she delivered more than five hundred babies. She has been published in multiple genres including short fiction, poetry, and academic work. She's also on a mission to rid the world of misplaced apostrophes.

Armstrong lives in Timmins, Ontario, with her husband Paul. They have two grown daughters and a lovable but untrainable rescue dog.

Contact Karen at karenleaarmstrong.com